WINTER'S
LAW

STEPHEN PENNER

ISBN-13: 9780692822029
ISBN-10: 069282202X

Winter's Law

Joy A. Lorton and Lynette Melcher, Editor.
Cover by Nathan Wampler Book Covers.

WINTER'S
LAW

(1) Prosecutions for criminal offenses shall not be commenced after the periods prescribed in this section.

(a) The following offenses may be prosecuted at any time after their commission:

(i) Murder

—Revised Code of Washington 9A.04.080
Limitation of Actions

CHAPTER 1

'Talon Winter, Attorney at Law'

Talon put her fists on her hips and smiled at the words freshly added to her new office door.

But the smile faded slightly as she realized her name was the last of the five attorneys etched on the glass of the wood-framed door. Black adhesive letters stretched from eye level all the way down to the hem of her knee-length suit skirt.

Least among equals, she thought. Five independent attorneys, sharing office space and a receptionist to reduce overhead, but not combined into any type of firm. No sharing of profits and glory. And if she failed, she'd fail on her own.

It was a long drop from her previous job. Senior Associate Attorney at Gardelli, High & Steinmetz, the most prestigious corporate law firm in Tacoma, Washington. She'd been there seven years and was next up to make partner. Not only had she put in her years, she had littered those years with the bloodied corpses of her opponents. No one deserved the promotion more than her. No one.

But before the managing partners brought her fully into their fold, they wanted a showing of her loyalty. They asked her to sign an affidavit that she knew wasn't true. A senior partner had missed a filing deadline. Talon was supposed to swear she'd mailed the pleadings and they must have gotten lost in the mail. The case would be saved by 'the mailbox rule' and her declaration. The managing partners explained that it was the firm's biggest client. They explained that if they lost the case, they'd also lose half their expected revenue for the next year. They explained that no one would ask any questions and she could forget all about it.

She explained she couldn't sign something that wasn't true.

And they explained she was fired.

So the partnership went to Justin Gardelli, the boss' nephew. Three years out of law school and couldn't find the courthouse if you put him across the street and pointed.

Talon knew she had a cause of action. She also knew they'd fight her like hell and it could be years before she saw any money, if ever. And she knew she'd probably need to eat in those intervening years. So she had to figure out what to do.

Chaos equals opportunity.

Talon didn't have a clichéd Chinese character tattoo on her shoulder blade or anything, but she was aware of the concept that bad situations may be good opportunities in disguise. And she wasn't the type to go home and cry. She was the type to go home, get her sword, and make the other side cry. She'd been kicking opposing counsel around courtrooms for years. And enjoying it. So, as she contemplated her next career move, she tried to remember the time she enjoyed it the most.

That was easy.

It was the one time she wasn't doing what Gardelli, High & Steinmetz had told her to do. It was the time she defended a murder suspect against a hotshot Seattle D.A. There was always a rush when she stepped into a courtroom, but nothing before or after had compared to the feeling of defending a man accused of murder and locking horns with all the advantages and resources and arrogance of the government. Any Justin Gardelli could win a motion to compel discovery on an insurance subrogation claim. Yawn.

It took a Talon Winter to acquit a killer.

Talon glanced down again at her name emblazoned on the office door. Her residual smile descended to full frown. The tail of the R in 'Winter' was peeling up. She bent over to press the plastic back onto the glass. It took a moment to rub the adhesive letter sufficiently to keep it in place. Before Talon could stand up again, she heard a man behind her say, "Looking good."

She stood up, spun around, and tugged her skirt down—all in one fluid motion—to confront the dirty old pervert behind her. But when she did, she discovered the man was neither dirty nor old. And whether he was a pervert or not became a curiosity rather than a condemnation.

"Hi," the clean, young, possibly perverted man greeted her as he extended his hand. "I'm Curt. Curt Fairchild. I work across the hall."

Curt jerked a thumb in the general direction of the hallway behind him, but that only served to flex the muscles in his forearm and draw attention to the muscles under his shirt. He was either a few years younger than her 33 years or a few years older, with a boyish face but mature eyes. Thick black hair was cut stylishly and combed back from his face. He wore what passed for semi-formal business attire any more: khakis and a polo shirt, unbuttoned. The only people left in the Northwest who wore suits were the lawyers.

She remembered that she was irritated when she turned around to find Curt Fairchild standing there, but it took her a moment for her to remember why. When she did, though, she forgot all about his cute face and thick arms. She didn't shake his hand.

"What did you say to me?" she demanded.

But Curt just lowered his hand and smiled, either ignoring or oblivious to the edge in her voice. He pointed at the door behind her. "Your name on the door," he said. "That looks great. 'Talon Winter, Attorney at Law.' You just set up your own practice, right? Congratulations."

Talon turned back to the door. "Uh, right," she replied slowly. She wasn't convinced that's what Curt had really been talking about 'looking good.' But she admired his mental dexterity. "Thanks. I guess."

She was still having trouble convincing herself that going from a six-figure salary with gold-plated benefits to a glorified cubicle with no clients was something to celebrate.

"So what's your area of practice?" Curt asked, combing his hair back from his face with his fingers. He had really nice hair.

"Criminal defense," Talon answered, although there was the tinge of a question in her reply. It wasn't like she had any actual cases yet.

Curt just nodded. "Well, nice to meet you, Talon Winter, Criminal Defense Attorney at Law." He waved good-bye and took a small step backward toward his office. "I hope we'll see more of each other."

Talon offered a practiced smirk. "I'm sure you do."

Curt smiled back—a broad, honest grin—then turned and disappeared down the hall without any further conversation. Talon smiled more fully, at herself, then collected her thoughts and walked back into her new office.

"Hello, Ms. Winter," Hannah said from behind her elevated receptionist's desk. It sported small business card stands for each of the attorneys who office-shared there. Hannah worked for all of them, her salary divided equally among the attorneys. She answered the phones, greeted visitors, and generally made the place feel as if it were a unified office of a law firm, rather than a loose stable of solo practitioners.

"Call me Talon," Talon replied. Hannah seemed nice enough, although they really hadn't had much time to get to know each other. She was 20-something, with light brown hair and a round face. Talon hoped she'd be pleasant upon arrival and departure and competent in passing along messages. More interaction than that, Talon wasn't really interested in. Still, no reason to be formal. "Any messages?"

Hannah smiled. "Since you went outside to look at your name? No."

Talon smiled too. It had been a silly question. She was just trying to make conversation. Her mistake. "Right. Okay. Well, I guess I'll head back to my office then."

"I saw you talking with Curt," Hannah grinned. "He's really nice."

Talon tried to look casually over her shoulder at the hallway. "Yeah. He was admiring my name too."

Hannah raised an eyebrow. "Your name. Sure."

Talon decided to, if not change, at least deflect the conversation. "Is he a lawyer too? He said his office was down the hall."

Hannah shook her head. "No, he's an investigator. He does some work for some of the other attorneys here. Mostly personal injury stuff, I think. Maybe some criminal. I'm not sure."

Talon nodded. That was good information. If she needed an investigator maybe she could use her 'name' to get Curt to help her out for a discount. "Well, I really should get to my office," Talon said. "I have a lot to do."

Three hours later, Talon had arranged the stapler, tape dispenser, and two-holepunch on her desk, had selected the wallpaper pattern for her computer desktop, and was pretty sure where she was going to hang her diploma. Her phone hadn't rung once.

She leaned back in her chair and looked at the decorative clock atop her one bookshelf. 4:58. Quitting time. At least for Hannah. One of her office-mate attorneys was in a closed-door meeting with a client; another had left at 4:00. The other two had never even come into the office, as far as Talon could tell.

"Night, everyone," Talon heard Hannah shout out, the front door's electronic bell letting everyone know of her departure. Hannah didn't wait for any reply. Talon didn't offer one. She wasn't one to yell down the hall.

A half-hour later, the client meeting was done and Talon was alone in the office. She picked up her phone and dialed another attorney. But he'd gone home for the night too.

Hello. You've reached the desk of Samuel Sullivan. I'm sorry I missed your call. Please leave a message and I'll get back to you as soon as possible. Thanks. –Beep!

"Hello, Mr. Sullivan. This is Talon Winter. I was calling to see if there was any update on my lawsuit against Gardelli, High and Steinmetz. Just checking in, I guess. Please give me a call when you get a chance. Thanks."

Talon hung up and sighed. She did some quick calculations in her head. Without any clients, she'd run through her savings and have to shut down her practice in about five months. Six, if she started skipping lunch.

The front door chimed again and Talon heard Curt's voice call out, "Hello? Is anyone still here?"

Talon stood up and checked her appearance in the mirror she'd leaned against the wall by her office door.

"I'm here," she announced and walked toward the reception area. When she got there she was greeted not only by Curt, but also by a 40-something African-American man with a proud posture but worried eyes.

"Talon," Curt said. "I'm glad you're here." He gestured to his companion. "This good man needs a lawyer."

CHAPTER 2

"Murder?" Talon confirmed. "You're charged with murder?"

The man across her desk nodded. He had a name. Michael Jameson. Curt sat next to him in the other guest chair.

"Yes," Michael replied, somewhat formally. He was clearly nervous.

Good, Talon thought. *He should be. Shows he's paying attention.*

"Murder One or Murder Two?" she followed up. It was an important distinction. In Washington State, a first-time offender could serve as little as nine years on a second degree murder. First degree murder carried a mandatory minimum of twenty years.

"Murder in the first degree," Michael responded. "But not intentional or felony murder. It's charged as extreme indifference murder."

Talon took a beat to size up her potential client. Nervous or not, not a lot of murder defendants knew the difference between the two degrees of murder. Even fewer knew the three different ways a Murder One could be charged. Michael Jameson was already proving interesting. She'd get back to the crime. She wanted more information about the man.

"How are you even out of custody?" she questioned, leaning back and crossing her arms. "Bail for murder usually starts at a million."

Michael nodded. "So I've learned," he said. "But I have no criminal history. I've had the same job for sixteen years. I have a wife, two kids, and a mortgage. Plus, the case is twenty-five years old. The judge set bail at only five-hundred-thousand."

"That's still a lot," Curt observed.

Michael agreed. "Yes. But I've been paying that mortgage for eighteen years, and more than the minimum. Alicia and I were trying to get it paid off in twenty years instead of thirty so we could really start saving for retirement. Instead, I had enough equity to pull out fifty-thousand and pay a bonding company to post the full bail."

He shook his head. "I can't sit in jail. I have a family to support. I already sat in the jail for two weeks while we got that worked out. I'll never get those two week backs, but now that I'm out, I'll be damned if I'm going back to jail. Not without a fight."

Talon took another beat. She liked Michael Jameson. He was smart, informed, and a fighter. He reminded her of herself. She uncrossed her arms.

Michael had dumped a lot of information just then. People did that in conversations. But lawyers—good ones, anyway—stopped the conversation, backed up, and went through the information again, thoroughly and carefully.

"Murder in the first degree," she said. "By way of extreme indifference."

Michael nodded. "Yes. I had to look up the statute, but it says you can be charged with first degree murder three ways:

premeditated intent, an unintentional killing during the course of a serious felony, or doing something that shows an extreme indifference to human life and someone dies."

Talon nodded back. Revised Code of Washington, section 9A.32.020. She hadn't had time to pull her statute book out of its box, but she recalled the statute from her last—and only other—murder case. At the time, she'd wondered what 'extreme indifference to human life' even meant, until another lawyer explained it to her with the simplest way to commit it. "Firing into a crowd," she suggested. "Is that what happened?"

Michael's expression hardened ever so slightly. "Not exactly."

Talon leaned forward. "So what happened? Exactly."

But Michael wasn't about to let Talon run the meeting. Not all of it anyway. He'd obviously dealt with a lot in the last few weeks and his nerves didn't seem anywhere near shot. He had a tolerance for stress and knew how to protect himself. Or at least knew he should try to.

"I haven't hired you yet," he said. "I want the attorney-client privilege before I say anything."

The shade of a smile pressed into the corner of Talon's mouth. She liked his caution. She liked more that she could show off her knowledge too. There was no better way to impress a prospective client.

"The attorney-client privilege is already in effect," she assured. "It's automatic as soon as you start talking with an attorney about a legal issue, even if you don't end up hiring the attorney."

Michael considered the information for a few seconds, then pointed at Curt. "What about him?"

Talon hadn't expected that, but she was ready with a

response. "He's my investigator," she declared. "The privilege extends to the entire defense team."

Curt raised an eyebrow, but remained silent. Talon tried to ignore the grin he was suddenly wearing.

She focused intently on Michael Jameson. "Tell me what happened," she repeated.

Michael turned his attention back to Talon. He didn't cross his arms, or narrow his eyes, or anything else aggressive. He simply met Talon's gaze and calmly said, "No."

Talon's eyebrows raised. "No?"

Michael nodded. "No. I won't tell you what happened."

Although Talon knew she was irritated by Michael's response, her irritation was subsumed by a sort of admiration. The man was strong-willed.

But so was she.

"I can't represent you if I don't know what happened," she insisted.

Michael disagreed. "Of course you can. It doesn't matter what happened. It only matters what they can prove."

Talon surrendered a small nod. He had a point. But only to a point. "If you don't tell me what really happened, how will I know if they got something wrong? How will I know the truth?"

Michael smiled darkly and leaned forward. "The truth? You want to know the truth? Fine, I'll tell you truth." He locked eyes with Talon once more. "The truth is, I'm a forty-three-year-old Black man with a good job, a great family, and a house in the suburbs. And the truth is, I'm not supposed to have all that.

"I grew up on the Hilltop when the gangs ran everything and there were drive-by shootings every night. If there were only three murders, it was a slow weekend. I grew up in that shit and I did what I had to do to survive. I'm not proud of what I did, but I did it, and now it's over.

"I got out of there and turned my life around. I went to college. I got a good job and make good money. I've been married to the same woman for almost twenty years. We have two great kids. And I did all that despite the fact that I'm a Black man from the Hilltop.

"Do you have any idea how many roadblocks there are between where I was and where I am now? And now the cops are gonna reach back to something that happened when I was eighteen and try to take away everything I have, everything I've built since then?"

He leaned back again and crossed his arms. "No." He shook his head. "No fucking way. You want to know the truth? The truth is, it doesn't matter what I did back then. It doesn't matter at all. What matters is what I've done since then. And I'll be damned if I'm gonna let them show up twenty-five years later and take it all away from me."

Talon raised her fingers to her lips in contemplation. She kept her expression controlled as she considered his soliloquy.

"The real question," Michael leaned forward again and challenged her, "is whether you're going to help me fight this battle."

Talon allowed her expression to slip. "A battle, huh?" She grinned. "I like battles."

CHAPTER 3

Unlike its cousin to the north in Seattle, the Pierce County Superior Court didn't reside in its own 'county courthouse.' Instead, it was spread throughout the 11-story 'County-City Building,' sharing space with the sheriff, the county council, and local government departments. The building was five blocks uphill from the waterfront, and three blocks down from MLK Jr. Blvd., the edge of the Hilltop neighborhood where Michael Jameson grew up.

Talon had been smart enough to rent space a few blocks over on Tacoma Avenue, thereby avoiding a daily climb up the hill. That morning, she also avoided the nine flights of stairs from the lobby to the Pierce County Prosecutor's Office. Instead, she stepped off the elevator and turned left into the prosecutor's waiting room.

The belly of the beast.

"Hello," she greeted the receptionist with her sharpest smile. "My name is Talon Winter. I'm a defense attorney and I represent Michael Jameson." She extracted a sheet of paper from her briefcase and slid it to the middle-aged woman behind the safety glass. "Here's my Notice of Appearance. I'd like to speak with the assigned prosecutor if he or she is available right now."

The receptionist glanced down at Talon's N.O.A. then back up at the lawyer who'd signed it. "You're new," she observed. "I know most of the defense attorneys, but I've never seen you before." She looked Talon up and down again, from her dark tailored suit to hair that fell to her shoulders like black rain. Her Native features completed the look she liked to think of as exotic and deadly. Like a cobra. Cobras knew when, and whom, to strike. Not yet; and not the receptionist.

"Is the prosecutor available?" she repeated.

The receptionist smiled away Talon's brush-off and turned to her computer. "Let me see who's assigned to this one." A few key-strokes and mouse-clicks later, she looked back up to Talon. "It's Eric Quinlan." She picked up her phone. "I'll see if he's in yet."

Talon raised an eyebrow at the 'yet.' She glanced at the lobby clock. It was already 8:42. These government types were supposed to start at 8:30. She hoped her tax dollars weren't being wasted.

The receptionist hung up the phone. "Mr. Quinlan is in. He said he'll be right out. Please have a seat."

Talon thanked the receptionist and sat down in one of the cushy faux-leather chairs her tax dollars had also paid for. The lobby was nice, but not extravagant. About what she'd hope for from a government agency. She wondered if Eric Quinlan would also meet her expectations of a government lawyer.

If punctuality had been one of her expectations, she realized after fifteen minutes of sitting in the lobby that Quinlan wasn't going to meet that one. When he finally showed up three minutes after that, he also failed any expectation of making a good first impression.

He opened the door from the lobby to the interior of the

prosecutor's office and offered a low whistle upon seeing her. "Wow. Look at you. All shiny and new, ready to take on a murder case. I'm Eric Quinlan." He extended a hand. "Nice to meet you."

He was late thirties, maybe forty, with thinning black hair and beady eyes. He was short for a man, although not exceptionally so. He was on the thin side, but with a gut pushing against the end of his tie. His suit coat was off and his sleeves were turned up at the cuff, apparently ready to dig into whatever the day had to offer him.

Talon shook his hand. It was small, and a little too warm. She extracted hers quickly. "Talon Winter," she identified herself. "I represent Michael Jameson."

She followed Quinlan back into the bowels of the office. He led her down several twisting corridors, like a rat in a maze.

"I know," Quinlan replied as they walked. "Becky told me your name. I looked you up while you were waiting."

Talon nodded. "Ah." That explained the delay.

"You don't have any other cases," Quinlan went on. "He must be paying you a hell of a lot to only have one client."

They'd reached Quinlan's office. He stepped inside and gestured toward the two guest chairs jammed into the small space. Quinlan himself shimmied between the wall and his desk and sat down. The cramped room made Talon's office look palatial in comparison.

"I don't really discuss fees with the prosecutor, Mr. Quinlan," Talon replied, her disapproval not at all hidden.

"Oh no, of course not," Quinlan replied with a chuckle. "You have no problem taking the money, you just don't want to be reminded you're doing it."

Talon didn't force a smile. Not her style. She also didn't take the bait. Instead, she sat down and got to business.

"I represent Mr. Jameson and I wanted to introduce myself. And see if I could find out a little more about the case. My client indicated he was charged with first degree murder by way of extreme indifference. That's fairly unusual, isn't it?"

Quinlan shrugged. "I don't know, maybe. But it matches what your guy did."

"And what exactly did my guy do?" Talon asked, adding the all-important, "allegedly."

Quinlan scoffed at the 'allegedly.' "He shot into a crowd of rival gang members. Hit and killed one Jordan McCabe."

Talon considered the information. She could hardly claim the victim wasn't shot. That left claiming her guy wasn't the shooter. "Did the witnesses say my client was the shooter?"

Quinlan shook his head. "No. The only description was Black male, eighteen to twenty-two. That's why the case went cold."

"What made it go hot again?"

Quinlan smiled. "That's the best part. Your guy did it to himself."

Talon raised an eyebrow. "He confessed?" Why wouldn't he tell Talon what had happened if he'd already told the cops?

"No," Quinlan replied. "Better. Well, nothing's better than a confession. But this is hilarious."

Talon doubted that very much. But she let him continue.

"Your guy's house was burglarized a couple months back. He reported it and soon enough they found the guys who did it. But here's the great part: the burglars stole some guns and when we recovered them we test-fired them to make sure they were operable." He paused, then added, "We need to make sure they're operable to charge possession of stolen firearms and up the burglary from residential burglary to burglary one."

"Of course," Talon said. She didn't give a crap about the

burglars. She just wanted him to keep talking.

"So anyway," he continued, "we uploaded the test-fires to IBIS, the nationwide ballistics database."

"I've heard of it," Talon said. She knew what was next.

"Right. And when they do: Bam! It matches the shooting. Your guy was stupid enough to keep the gun all these years." Quinlan shook his head. "The jury should find him guilty just for being so stupid."

Talon acknowledged the joke with a frown. "No one should be found guilty of anything unless the State can prove it beyond a reasonable doubt."

Quinlan frowned too, but a less serious, more condescending expression. "Come on, Talon. Your guy's guilty. Do the right thing and plead him out."

"The right thing," Talon explained, "is to represent my client to the best of my ability." She'd obtained the information she wanted. No need to humor him any more. "I expect to receive the police reports by the end of the week, or I'll be filing a motion to compel. My investigator and I will need to view the property as soon as possible, so please contact the property room to schedule that. As for witness interviews..."

"Whoa, whoa, whoa." Quinlan put his hands up. "Hold on there, honey. That's not how these things go."

Talon's eyebrow raised again. *'Honey'?* That was almost entertaining.

"Is that right, Eric?" She leaned back and crossed her legs. "And how do these things go?"

Quinlan leaned back too, and put his hands behind his head. "The way these things go, Talon, is I make an offer to settle the case. You make a counter-offer. I reject your counter-offer, then you plead your guy to my offer. Then we both move on to our next case and forget about this one. Any questions?"

Talon just stared at Quinlan for several seconds. She narrowed her eyes and focused in on his smarmy smile. She was going to enjoy smacking it off his pasty face. Metaphorically, of course.

"Now, let me explain how these really go," she said. "I represent Mr. Jameson. Just him. Not you and not the victim's family or the citizens or justice or whatever. I'm not about to plead him out just so I can get on to the next case. My guy has no criminal history and your evidence is twenty-five years old. So you dump it or we go to trial and I win. Any questions?"

Eric Quinlan wasn't smiling any more. He lowered his hands and puffed up what there was of his chest. "I win almost all of my trials."

Talon didn't need to puff out her chest. She knew it was perfect as it was. And she'd let her lawyering do its own talking.

"That's because," she responded, "you deal away the hard cases and only go to trial on the ones you know you can win. But you can't win this one and he's not taking any deals."

She stood up. "I'll see myself out. And don't forget to get me those reports by Friday. I'd hate to have to start kicking your ass so early in the case."

Quinlan didn't have a response ready.

Good. She filed that away. Easy to rattle. She decided to have a little fun. Instead of stepping into the hallway, she leaned onto Quinlan's desk, highlighting that perfect chest. "Actually, I hope the case goes to trial. I'd like to spend more time with you. Intense time."

Quinlan couldn't quite find his breath. *Even better.* She was going to have fun with this one.

She turned and headed into the corridor.

After another moment, Quinlan managed to call out, "Nice to meet you, Talon."

Talon would have returned the sentiment, but lying wasn't her style either.

CHAPTER 4

Talon threw open the door to her office. "What a douche bag!"

Hannah looked up with a start. "Who? Curt?"

That surprised Talon. "Wha—? Curt? No, not Curt." Her brow wrinkled. "Why would I mean Curt?"

"Oh, well, he was just in here talking about you," Hannah explained. "He just left. I guess I figured you ran into him in the hallway or something."

"No," Talon answered. "I— Wait. You were talking about me?"

"Who's a douche bag?" Greg Olsen, one of the other attorneys who shared space there, popped his bald head out of his office.

"Uh, the prosecutor," Talon answered him, still distracted by Hannah's comments. "On my murder case."

"Oh yeah," Olsen agreed. "They're all douche bags."

Talon shrugged. She wasn't sure that was necessarily true. On the other hand, she was still learning. Quinlan hadn't helped their cause.

"What'd he do?" Olsen came all the way out of his office and joined the women in the lobby. He had a bit of hair still over his ears and around the back of his head; classic male baldness. His face was pasty and his waist was round. His sleeves were rolled up and his tie loosened.

"It's more like what he didn't do," Talon explained. "He didn't listen to me. He didn't respect me. And," she considered for a moment, "he didn't impress me."

Hannah giggled at that. Olsen seemed to appreciate it too. "Who was it?" he asked.

Olsen didn't do a lot of criminal defense. He handled more of a grab-bag of divorces, wills, and car accidents. Typical small-time lawyer hustling to make ends meet. But he'd been hustling for a long time and knew most of the lawyers in town.

"Quinlan," Talon answered. "Eric Quinlan. Eric Quinlan, Douche Bag."

Olsen smiled and thought for a moment. "Yeah, I've heard of him, but I don't really know him."

Talon shrugged. That wasn't terribly helpful.

Then Olsen offered some advice, "But don't trust him."

Talon cocked her head. "Oh yeah? Why not?"

"Because," Olsen replied, as if the answer were as obvious as the stain on his tie, "he's a prosecutor."

Talon liked that answer, but before she could pile on, Curt walked into the office.

"Oh," Talon said, a bit too loudly. "Curt. Uh, hey." She grasped for something to say. "I heard you were just in here looking for me."

Curt glanced at Hannah. She looked away. "Not exactly," Curt answered. "But I was wondering how your meeting with the prosecutor went."

Olsen cleared his throat and excused himself. "I'm gonna get back to work, Talon. Remember my advice."

Talon acknowledged Olsen's departure with a nominal, "Mm-hmm," but kept her attention on Curt. "So how did you know I was meeting with the prosecutor?"

Curt smiled, and flashed another quick glance at Hannah. Hannah suddenly became very interested in something on her computer screen. "I'm an investigator," Curt answered. "It's my job to know things."

"Oh yeah?" Talon crossed her arms. "Then why don't you tell me how my meeting went? You know, since you're an investigator and all."

Curt crossed his arms too, but more in thought. "Hm. The prosecutor was a douche bag."

Talon laughed. "How did you know that?'

"They're all douche bags," Curt said with his own laugh. "Plus I heard you yell it before your front door closed."

Talon smiled at that. "I suppose I should be more careful about that kind of thing."

But Curt shook his head. "Not at all. I'm going to need to know about the prosecutor if I'm going to work this case with you."

Hannah looked up at that comment. Talon noticed, but decided not to engage her just yet. Instead, she engaged Curt. "Work the case? I don't know about that. I mean, why would you be working the case with me?"

Curt cocked his head. "You told Mr. Jameson I was your investigator."

Hannah definitely looked at Talon that time. Talon couldn't help but meet her gaze before turning back to Curt and shrugging. "I, I was just saying that so you could stay in the meeting."

Curt tried on a few expressions in under a second then settled on a smirk. "You wanted me to stay?"

Talon wasn't fond of smirks on men. Usually. She stood up a bit taller. "I didn't want to be alone with a stranger after hours." She crossed her arms. "Thank you for that, but I wasn't recruiting you for the case."

Curt's smile faded. "Oh. Okay. Well, that's too bad. I was kind of hoping to help out on that one. Especially if the prosecutor is a douche bag."

Suddenly, Talon felt bad for Curt. "I'm sorry," she said. "I mean, it's not like I wouldn't welcome some help. It's just that, uh, well, Jameson doesn't have money for an investigator. Hell, he can barely pay me. I probably won't see anything after that initial retainer." Talon uncrossed her arms. "I couldn't pay you."

Curt's smile returned. "No worries. You can take me out to dinner sometime."

Before Talon could respond, Curt punched her lightly on the shoulder and headed back to his office across the hall.

Talon watched Curt leave. When the office door closed, she finally turned and looked fully at Hannah.

"Did he just ask me out?"

CHAPTER 5

Talon found the conversation with Curt troubling. It just underscored her tenuous financial position as she started up her practice. She didn't like that she couldn't pay him. Not for his sake—if he was dumb enough to work for free, that was his problem—but she was used to having a large firm backing her up and being able to front the costs of an investigator for a client. It just reminded her of how empty her business account was.

But what bothered her even more was her first thought when he offered to buy her dinner: it wasn't butterflies at being asked out, it was relief at the thought of one free meal.

It was time for Talon to check in with her own lawyer.

By the looks of his office lobby, Samuel Sullivan was doing just fine, thank you. First of all, his office was in Seattle, not Tacoma, so rent was much higher. Second, it was on the top floor of a ten-story building with a deck overlooking Elliott Bay. But then again, that had been part of why Talon had hired him. Everyone wants a successful lawyer—it shows they win a lot.

With a frown, she wondered what her new office showed

about her.

Before she could get too melancholy, the receptionist hung up the phone and announced, "Mr. Sullivan will see you now."

Talon's frown turned into a practiced smile. She stood up and straightened her skirt. "Thank you." She really hoped Sullivan had good news.

She followed the young receptionist back to Sullivan's office, passing several smaller associate attorney offices along the way. Talon couldn't help but wonder if he might be hiring. But they reached the office door and she returned her thoughts to her role as the client.

"Good morning, Mr. Sullivan," she said, extending her hand. "Thank you for finding the time to meet with me."

Sullivan stood up from his large, ornate desk, and stuck a meaty hand in hers. He was a large man, well over six feet and at least 250 pounds, with thick white hair and stubbly jowls. "Of course, of course," he answered. "I always have time for you. Sit down, sit down. Can we get you anything to drink? Coffee? Water?"

Talon took a seat across Sullivan's desk. "No, thank you. I'm fine."

Sullivan nodded and dismissed his receptionist with a quick gesture. She slipped out and closed the door behind her. Then Sullivan lumbered back to his desk and dropped into his leather chair.

"How the hell are you, Talon?" he asked. "How's the new practice going? Taken over the world yet?"

Talon smiled. She appreciated his confidence in her. Or at least the flattery.

"Not yet," she admitted with a light laugh, "but I'm working on it. I just got a client charged with murder. My first big case."

Sullivan raised a questioning eyebrow.

"Well, my only case," Talon admitted. "But a good one to start with."

Sullivan pushed out an approving lip and nodded. "Yes, ma'am. That should get your name in the papers. Free advertising never hurts. Can he pay you?"

Talon shrugged. "Barely, but yes."

Sullivan smiled again. "Did you charge enough?'

Talon shrugged again. "Probably not, but it's all he can afford. And I want the case."

"For the publicity?" Sullivan confirmed.

But Talon shook her head. "No, because he's innocent."

Sullivan's eyebrow shot back up. "Innocent? Really?"

Talon had to pause before replying. "Well, maybe not completely innocent. But he shouldn't be convicted either. It's a twenty-year-old cold case. Even if he did do it, he's moved on. He's got a wife and couple of kids, a good job."

Sullivan took a moment to size her up, his thoughts masked behind appraising eyes. "Sounds like he hired the right attorney."

Talon surrendered a half-smile. "Thanks. But I didn't come to talk about his attorney. I came to talk with *my* attorney. How's the case going?"

Sullivan provided his own half-smile. "Oh, you know how these civil cases are. They take forever. Not like criminal cases."

Talon shrugged. "I guess so. I'm still getting used to the criminal practice. Negotiations are a little different. Lives instead of money."

Sullivan nodded. "That's why I stay the hell away from criminal cases." He looked around his opulent office. "I like money."

Talon wasn't allergic to it either. Especially lately. "Speaking of which," she broached, "have they made any settlement offers?"

She hoped her voice didn't betray her financial concerns.

Sullivan frowned. "No, not yet. That's not how these go. You know that. We have a lot of discovery ahead of us. Interrogatories, requests for production, depositions. The only offer now would be a nuisance value offer. Five thousand and go away. But I didn't take this case to get thirty-three percent of five-k. That won't pay a week's rent here."

It would pay Talon's rent for the month. But she knew Sullivan was right. The case would be worth a lot more if she could be patient and get it all the way to a jury.

"Should we suggest a settlement amount?" she asked anyway.

Sullivan frowned slightly. He shook his head. "No, not yet. It's too soon. We need to do some discovery. Get their documents. Depose the partners. Make them sweat. Make it hurt. Then, maybe, we can talk settlement."

He leaned forward onto his desk. "Are you getting cold feet, Talon?"

Talon shook her head. "No. No, definitely not. It's just—" She hesitated, unsure for a moment whether she should share her thoughts. Then she recalled the nature of their relationship, and how much she hated it when clients wouldn't tell her the whole story. They always did eventually, but in the meantime it could really skew her strategy and waste her time if the client wasn't honest about their true goals. "It's just that it's hard setting up a practice. Harder than I expected, I guess. If there was a lot of money on the table, I'd be tempted to take it."

Sullivan leaned back in his chair again. "That's what I thought. Sorry, Talon. There's no money on the table at all. We're going to have to earn that. Pry it out of their good-for-nothing hands."

Talon nodded. "Right. We can do that."

"Let me do some work on this," Sullivan offered. "Take a look at where we're at. Maybe we can accelerate things a bit, put some pressure on them. Who knows? If they see how strong our case is, maybe they'll blink first and we can get that settlement for you after all."

"Okay." Talon was glad to hear it.

"But let me ask you this," Sullivan went on. "What would you tell your murder client if the prosecutor made a crappy offer?"

Talon thought for a moment. "I'd advise him to reject it."

"Why?" Sullivan pressed.

Talon considered for a moment. "Because he shouldn't be convicted. Any offer is a crappy offer. Better to go to trial and win."

"You go to trial," Sullivan countered, "you could lose."

Talon nodded. "I know that."

"Then know it here too," Sullivan answered. "We could lose. But I'm going to do everything I can to win."

Talon thought about it for a moment. Then she met Sullivan's gaze and smiled. "Me too."

CHAPTER 6

As with her own civil case, there was no offer in Michael Jameson's criminal case yet either. That was fine with Talon, though. She knew not to be the first one to make an offer. That was Negotiating 101. And if it applied to salary negotiations or buying a new car, it sure as hell applied to plea negotiations on a murder case. Besides, Jameson hadn't given her authority to make any offers. So, Talon would wait for the offer from Quinlan and then she and Michael could talk about it. In the meantime, there was a barbeque to attend.

Michael's son was graduating from high school. Michael had invited Talon to the party. She knew not to say no. They didn't need to be friends, but they needed to trust each other. Something less than friends, but more than attorney-client.

Plus, it would give her insight into her client. Never a bad thing.

The first thing Talon noticed when she arrived at the Jameson residence was that Michael—or his son—was very popular. She had to park two blocks away. The next thing she noticed was that Michael—or his wife—was highly competent. There were probably over a hundred people there, and every one of them looked like they had all the drinks, food, or whatever they could possibly want. Michael was at the grill, slinging burgers and dogs into waiting buns. He nodded at Talon when she stepped through the gate into the backyard. Before she could nod back, Mrs. Jameson appeared out of nowhere and took her gently by the arm.

"You must be Ms. Winter," the forty-something African-American woman said. She was average height, with toned arms and an enviously flat stomach. Probably a runner, Talon thought with that mixture of admiration and disdain non-runners had for runners and their lean runners' bodies. "I'm Alicia, Michael's wife. Nice to meet you finally. Michael's told me all about you."

Talon relaxed into Alicia's grip as she guided her into the backyard, surrounded by a mixture of high schoolers and their parents. "Good things, I hope," Talon said.

"Yes, definitely," Alicia confirmed. "I'm glad you came. Michael wasn't sure about inviting you. Mixing business with pleasure, and all that. But I wanted to meet you, and not at your office. Anyone can look good in an office. I wanted to meet you on my turf."

Talon couldn't help but smile at Alicia. She liked her already. And she told her as much.

Alicia laughed, but it was a polite laugh with a confident strength supporting it. "This is the most important thing that's ever happened to our family. I trust Michael. But I trust myself more. I want to make sure our family can rely on you."

Talon felt the weight of the comment, and thought back on her conversation with Sullivan. He liked money. Good for him. She liked it too, back when she worked for Gardelli, High & Steinmetz. Now she was working for more than money. A man's life was at stake. That much she understood from the get go. Alicia was now reminding her it was even more important than that. She had an entire family in her hands.

Alicia nodded toward a gaggle of twelve-year-old girls talking and laughing on the deck. "The girl in the white dress is our daughter, Kaylee. She's very social."

Then Alicia pointed to the back corner of the yard. "And that young man there is Marcus," she said, the pride in her voice betraying the impending identification. "Our son."

Talon craned her neck slightly to get a good look at him, seated atop a picnic table, his status as guest of honor confirmed by the semicircle of friends attending him.

"Nice looking young man," Talon remarked. He had the build of an athlete, but the face of a scholar, with bright eyes and a staid expression. Almost too staid. "How's he doing?"

Alicia's own expression slipped at the question. Or rather at the answer she had to admit. "Not well."

Talon nodded. She could hardly expect differently.

"Come on." Alicia took Talon's arm again. "Let me introduce you."

The backyard was ample but not enormous, and a short walk through the maze of guests brought them quickly enough to Marcus' location. His courtiers gave way to Ms. Jameson and she stepped into the circle with Talon. "Marcus, this is Talon Winter. Dad's lawyer."

Marcus regarded Talon. Maybe critically, but Talon wasn't quite sure. His eyes were bright, but also guarded. Like light through cracks in armor. After a moment, he nodded in acknowledgement, and offered a barely audible grunt of greeting. It was then that Talon realized the entire time she'd been watching him, it was his friends who had been doing the talking. Marcus's mouth had held a tight line the entire time.

No matter. Lawyers can always fill silence. "Nice to meet you, Marcus. Congratulations."

Marcus offered a small, pained grin, somehow more frown than smile. "Yeah."

A couple of the friends decided to take their leave, offering an 'I'm gonna get another soda' and 'I gotta pee' as excuses. Talon knew they weren't abandoning their friend; they were giving him privacy. A small-statured Asian girl climbed up onto the table and sat next to Marcus, taking his hand in hers. The girlfriend. Maybe she'd be more talkative.

"Hi," Talon tried. "I'm Talon."

The girl nodded. "Christie," she practically conceded, with no words to follow. *Guess not.*

Not only were lawyers usually adept at filling silences, they also knew that not filling a silence could prompt the other party to talk. So Talon waited a moment to see if Marcus might open up a bit. It might have worked too, except his mom was there.

"Marcus," Alicia admonished. "Be polite. Ms. Winter is our guest. And she's helping your father, so show some respect."

Marcus frowned at his mother. Then he looked over at his father. Talon followed his gaze. Michael Jameson was at the grill, sliding a hamburger patty onto some other parent's plate and generally pretending like he wasn't facing the rest of his life in prison. Marcus looked back at Talon, then at his mom.

"You had to hire a White lawyer?" he asked. "Are all the Black ones in jail?"

Talon felt the force of the question. Race was never far from the surface for her, but it was nowhere but on the surface for Marcus.

"Marcus!" Alicia responded. "That was uncalled for. You

apologize right now."

Marcus frowned at Talon. "I'm sorry you're White."

Alicia released an audible gasp, but this time Talon placed her hand on Alicia's arm. "It's okay, Alicia. I understand. He's got a point." Then, looking back to Marcus, she added, "And anyway, I'm not White."

Marcus' frown gave way to a confused expression. He sat up slightly and looked to his girlfriend who only offered her own shrug in reply.

"I'm Native American," Talon explained. "While your ancestors were being enslaved, mine were being exterminated."

Even Alicia seemed surprised. Talon was used to it. Absent traditional garb, there wasn't anything about her that screamed 'Native!' She just looked exotic. Hispanic maybe, or Italian. She could blend in as White. But not Marcus. And not Michael. Talon understood that, but she wasn't going to wallow in it either.

"Let's try to move past what you and I are," she said, "and worry about what your dad is. Not guilty."

It was a nice sound bite, but Marcus hadn't become bitter without cause. "That's just it. It doesn't matter if my dad's not guilty. He's Black. So he's going to prison. That's how it works, right?"

Talon wished she could just say no. But instead, she fell back reflexively on the law. "He's presumed innocent."

"Yeah, right," Marcus laughed. He shook his head. "You know, growing up, Dad always told me I could be anything I wanted to be. A doctor, a lawyer, even President. But my friends, they told me no way. I'm Black and everything's gonna be twice as hard for half the reward, if I'm lucky. And that's only if I don't get shot walking home from school, or arrested 'cause I was driving through a White neighborhood. And they knew. They knew because they went home to shitty houses, with cop cars slowing to look at them, and their own dads in prison. But me," Marcus paused and gestured to his home: the large backyard, the yellow two-story house, the deck with the grill. "I came home to this. All this. And Mom, and Dad, and Kaylee. And even though everyone else said Dad was wrong, I believed him. Because of all of this. I believed him."

Marcus lowered his head for a moment, then punched the picnic table and looked up again. "But it was a lie. Because no matter how much good he did, no matter how hard he worked for his family, no matter how much he succeeded, he's still a Black man. And they'll go back twenty-five years if they have to, but they'll take it all away. They can take it all away."

Talon looked over again at Michael Jameson. He was still manning the grill, but he turned his head and caught her gaze. He was acting the part of strong father, but she could see the fear in his eyes, even across the crowded yard. She turned back to Marcus and leaned into his space, grabbing him by the back of the neck and staring into his equally frightened eyes. "Not if I can help it."

CHAPTER 7

It was easy enough to tell Marcus Jameson that she'd keep his dad out of prison. It was another thing to actually do it.

Facts, it's said, are stubborn things. And words are empty things. Full of meaning but devoid of anything tangible. The currency of politicians and cheating lovers, of con men and cult leaders. And lawyers.

So when the offer from Quinlan finally came, Talon knew it was only so many words. But still, words she had to share with her client. Even the worst offer had to be communicated to the client; it was the client's decision to accept or reject it, after appropriate advice from the lawyer. A lawyer who failed to communicate an offer was just asking for a bar complaint later—especially if the client got convicted as charged at trial.

And the offer from Quinlan wasn't the worst offer. Unfortunately, it was a pretty good offer. Unfortunate for three reasons. One, because she knew Jameson wouldn't take it; two, because she would have to counsel him to at least consider it; and three, because her advice to at least consider it could threaten the trust they needed between them if they were possibly going to win the case at trial.

It was best to do that kind of conversation in person. With a witness. So a few emails later, she'd scheduled a client meeting with both Michael Jameson and Curt Fairchild, to discuss the offer, then start preparing for the inevitable trial. Curt arrived a few minutes early, which was nice since it gave them a chance to prepare for the preparation. Hannah waved him through reception and he settled into one of Talon's office guest chairs almost before she knew he was in her office.

"Hey, boss," he started with a boyish grin. "What's the plan?"

Talon felt a combination of irritation that Hannah hadn't given her a moment to compose herself before Curt stepped into her office and pleasure at seeing him again even if she wasn't fully ready for the meeting. And anyway, she was mostly ready. She knew he was coming after all.

"Here," she said, pulling a print-out of Quinlan's email from her file and sliding it across the desk.

Curt leaned forward and took the document. He read in silence for a moment, then looked up. "Murder Two? That's not a terrible offer."

Talon nodded. "I know. But it's not good enough. Even with no criminal history, he'll still do ten years."

Curt shrugged. "So counter with a manslaughter. That's, what, three years?"

"Two-and-a-half for Manslaughter Two," Talon corrected. "But seven for Manslaughter One. And that's exactly what Quinlan wants me to do. A Murder Two offer means he'll accept a Man One counter. Seven years for Michael and case closed for you and me."

"Are you gonna do it?" Curt asked.

"No. She isn't."

Talon and Curt jerked their heads up to see Michael Jameson in the office doorway, Hannah peeking out from behind him.

"No deals," Michael reaffirmed. "I already told you that."

Talon stood up to greet her guest. "Michael. Good to see you again. Great barbeque. Thanks again for the invitation." She looked past him to Hannah, who was doing a terrible job receptionist-ing that day. "That'll be all for now, Hannah."

Hannah offered a contrite nod and headed back toward the front desk.

Talon gestured Michael into her office and the three of them sat down again.

"I know what you told me," Talon assured. "In fact, that's what I was just telling Curt when you walked in. That you wouldn't take any deals. But I still have to communicate it to you."

"Why?" Michael demanded. There was more of an edge to him than at their initial meeting. The stress of the case, Talon supposed.

"Because it's your case," Talon answered, "not mine. You make the decisions, even the decision to reject something. But you can't make the decision if I don't tell you the information."

Michael crossed his arms. "Fine. But I'm not taking any deals. I can't go to prison. I can't lose my job. I can't take anything but an acquittal."

"Or a dismissal," Curt offered. Not all that helpfully, Talon thought. But at least it reflected a positive attitude.

Michael must have thought so too. He offered a half-smile. "Or a dismissal," he confirmed. "So how do we get there?"

"Hard work," Talon answered. "And preparation."

"And a little bit of luck," Curt added.

Michael looked at him, a bit shocked. Talon glared at him

too, annoyed. She didn't need that.

"What?" Curt protested. "I thought we were being honest."

Talon remained tense for a moment longer, then sighed. "Fine. A little bit of luck never hurts." She looked at the clock. They'd set the meeting at 5:30 so Michael wouldn't miss any work. "How late can you guys stay tonight?"

"As late as it takes," was Michael's answer.

Curt nodded and offered Talon another boyish smile. "Ditto."

Talon sighed again. Between Michael's life in her hands and Curt's beautiful face in her office, it was going to be a long night.

* * *

It was even longer than she expected. It was after eight o'clock and they'd gotten almost nowhere.

"Michael," Talon practically gasped, "this isn't going to work if you won't tell us what happened."

But Michael just crossed his arms. "It doesn't matter what happened. It matters what the prosecution can prove."

Talon ran a hand through her thick, black hair. He was right, technically, but he was missing the bigger picture. "Look, if this were law school, I'd agree with you. But it's not. It's real life. Those twelve jurors, whoever they are, are going to be real people, with real lives and real life experience. They don't go through their lives holding accusers to pre-set burdens of proof. They listen to both sides, then make a decision. They can't listen to both sides if our side doesn't give them anything."

"The judge is going to tell them we don't have to prove anything," Michael insisted.

"Right," Talon agreed. "The judge is going to tell them that a dozen different times, from the beginning of jury selection to the end of closing arguments. And do you know why? Because nobody does that in real life!"

Michael was taken aback by Talon's sudden shout. He uncrossed his arms and looked to Curt for support, but found none. Curt was equally surprised, but he knew which side he was on. Talon's. And she knew too. She pressed her advantage.

"This is real life, Michael. You are really facing a murder charge. And you are really looking at twenty-five years in prison. The prosecutor is really going to call witnesses against you. And the jury is really, truly, honestly, whether they should or not, think you're probably guilty if you're sitting in the defendant's chair. Jurors don't want to live in a country where innocent people are charged with crimes. We all know it happens because it's on the news. But it's on the news because it's not supposed to happen."

"And it won't happen here," Michael asserted, but his voice wavered.

"It will if you don't wise up," Talon retorted. "Look, I admire your bravado. And I admire that you're willing to go to the mat on this. But sometimes people go to the mat and get pinned. They lose. And if you lose, it's more than some stupid wrestling match. It's your life. It's twenty-five years. You're already, what, forty-five? You think you'll make it to seventy in prison? No way. Life expectancy in prison is way lower than on the outside. You'll die in there. And while that's happening, your family will lose everything. Everything. That beautiful house of yours, college funds, everything. And Marcus will know once and for all that there is no justice for a Black man in this country. And his dad lied to him all those years."

Michael stood up abruptly. "You leave Marcus out of this!"

"No!" Talon stood up just as forcefully. "I can't leave Marcus out of this! I can't leave Kaylee out of this and I can't leave Alicia out of this. They're all in this because you're in it. And if you refuse to help yourself, then you're refusing to help them. Maybe that means you deserve whatever happens to you, but damn it, Michael, they don't deserve it!"

Michael ran a hand over his head and looked to the ceiling. "What do you need?"

"I need you to tell me who pulled the trigger," Talon answered. "Somebody shot him. I can't tell the jury he was faking it. The medical examiner will call bullshit on that. That means somebody shot him. I know it wasn't you, but I need to tell the jury who it was."

Michael hesitated for a moment, but only a moment. "No."

"Damn it, Michael!" Talon slapped her desk. "If I don't tell them who really shot the victim, the jury is going to think it was you. The prosecutor is going to tell them it was you. I need to be able to tell them who it really was."

"No," Michael repeated. "I'm not throwing him under the bus."

"Who, Michael?" Curt tried, in a calmer tone. "Who can't you throw under the bus?"

"There is no fucking bus!" Talon interjected. "There's a prison! A big, dark, scary fucking prison. And that's where you're going to die if you don't let me help you!"

"No," Michael insisted, but he avoided eye contact.

Talon let out an exasperated sigh and pulled at her hair. "Whoever this person is, he better be pretty fucking important. Because you know who else is going to prison? Not just you, Michael. You know who else? How about a young Black man named Marcus who's about to learn there's no reason to go to college, no reason to get a good job, no reason to find a good woman and settle down in a nice four-bedroom house in the suburbs? How about someone so angry at the system it won't be long before he's dealing drugs, robbing liquor stores, pimping girls—and sharing a cell block with his old man? If you don't care about yourself, then care about your son, God damn it! Who could be more important than your son? Who could be that fucking important?!"

Michael absorbed Talon's verbal onslaught like so much Kevlar. But it still hurts when the bullets hit the vest. He looked up again and met Talon's gaze with narrowed eyes. "My brother."

CHAPTER 8

"Your brother?" Curt repeated. Talon would have asked it, but her jaw was still hanging open.

But Michael just slumped back into his chair. "Never mind. I shouldn't have said anything."

Talon hesitated then sat down again herself. Curt followed suit. "No," she assured. "It's good that you did. I need to know the truth."

But Michael was unmoved. "I told you, the truth doesn't matter."

"Of course it matters," Talon insisted. "It's *all* that matters."

Michael shrugged, but didn't reply.

"Michael, tell me what happened," Talon nearly pleaded.

"I didn't shoot anyone," Michael answered. "That's the truth."

"And your brother did?" Talon tried to confirm.

"I didn't say that," Michael pointed out.

"You didn't *not* say it," Curt tried. Both Talon and Michael looked at him disapprovingly.

"Look," Michael ran a hand over his head. We've been here a long time. I'm exhausted. I don't want to talk any more. I've said too much already."

"Maybe you have," Talon agreed, "so you might as well keep talking."

But Michael just crossed his arms and looked away.

"Look, Michael," Talon softened her tone, trying a different tack. "I really respect your desire to protect your brother. I totally understand it and I admire it. And I'll respect it. If you ultimately decide we can't use the information in your case, well then, that's your call. You're the client and I have to do what you say. But let's have a full discussion about it. You hired me to give you the best legal advice I can. Don't hamstring me by withholding information. Tell me everything and I'll tell you what's important and why. There may be ways of doing this that help you without implicating your brother at all. But I can't know if you won't tell me anything."

Michael continued to stare at the wall for several seconds. Curt raised a hopeful eyebrow to Talon but didn't say anything. Finally, Michael looked up again. "If I tell you not to use something, then you don't use it, right?"

Talon was quick to nod. "Right. You're the client. I advise, but you decide."

Michael nodded lightly too. "Okay." He took a deep breath. Talon and Curt leaned forward.

"It was twenty-five years ago," Michael began. "I was living up on the Hilltop with my mom and my brother. My dad lived nearby but was never around. He was always off hustling, doing something he didn't want us around for. Just as well. He was a good role model for me later—exactly the kind of father I was never gonna be. But back then, I was just a kid, fresh out of high school with no prospects and no plans. Our mom was working two jobs to pay the rent, so she wasn't around much either. It was just me and Ricky, hanging out with too much time and too little money.

"Ricky was two years older than me. He'd had a couple of jobs, but never for very long and they never paid much. Back then, if you wanted to make real money, you ran drugs. Crack and crystal meth—the good stuff, from Mexico. Not that crap you make at home from Sudafed and battery acid.

"Mom raised us right, and I never saw my dad do drugs, but you hear stuff. And you see stuff. Like guys younger than us with new cars and tons of girls. You wanna get an 18-year-old boy's attention? Flash money and girls at him. Throw in some weed and a bad-ass looking .45, and it's too much for anyone to resist."

Michael stopped for a moment, then admitted, "Well, it was too much for *me* to resist. Especially when Ricky told me he had a plan for us to score an easy two-grand. A thousand bucks each. That seemed like a fortune back then. Now, it doesn't even cover a month's mortgage payment, but back then, it seemed like all the money in the world. Especially with the promise of more.

"Now, Ricky and I weren't in a gang. Mom at least succeeded in that. She told us our dad had been in the Hilltop Crips, the biggest gang up there, and we both hated the old man enough that we both wanted to stay out of it. But there were plenty of gangs to choose from. Mostly the Hilltops, but the Bloods were around too, plus a couple of smaller Crip gangs. They had all of the drug distribution worked out among them. As long as the Bloods didn't try to sell on Hilltop territory, nobody got shot. Well, not for that anyway.

"So when Ricky came to me with this plan, it seemed crazy at first. Some O.G. from Compton had come up and wanted to break into the game. He thought the Tacoma gangs were weak, and I guess they were by Compton standards. He figured as long as he was willing to shoot first, he'd be able to carve out some action. But in case the Hilltops shot quicker than he thought, he wanted someone else to be the first target. That was Ricky. And Ricky brought me in."

Michael paused again as he remembered the details from so long ago. Talon supposed he probably hadn't talked about it much since then—maybe never, if he was as smart as he seemed. The emotion of reliving it caught up with him for a moment. But only a moment.

"The guy fronted Ricky ten-grand worth of ecstasy. Something a little different than what the Hilltops were running. Maybe that was on purpose, so they wouldn't feel threatened. But it didn't matter. Anyone making money was a threat, or a target. Ricky started selling it, and it sold. Man, did it sell. You ever use that stuff? Of course it sold. It's called ecstasy for a reason, and there were plenty of unemployed teenagers and twenty-somethings looking for something new for their parties.

"The Hilltops came looking for Ricky. Not to hurt him. To rob him. They wanted the ecstasy. But Ricky had to sell the stuff and get the money to the O.G. from Compton. If he stiffed that guy, well, there wouldn't be any doubt about who shot who.

"So one night, me and Ricky were making a delivery. He'd sold about half the stuff by that point. He mostly kept me out of it. Just had me come with him in the car, act as a lookout, keep him company mostly. But that night, he was really agitated. He was usually clean when he ran the stuff, but it seemed like he was on something. Not the ecstasy; that would've made him relaxed and happy. It was some kind of stimulant. Crack, probably. He'd never done crack—that was our old man's drug of choice, so, yeah. But that's how he was acting. All jumpy and wide-eyed. He seemed cracked out. And scared."

Michael paused, his eyes open but fixed twenty-five years earlier. "Yeah, he was really scared. Most of the sales had been to people we knew. Hell, everyone knew everyone. We'd even sold to some of the Hilltops and Bloods—guys Ricky knew since grade school, before anybody was wearing colors. Looking back, that's probably how they found out about it. And why they decided to take Ricky's supply for themselves.

"It was a set-up. Ricky was scared because he didn't know the buyers. It was supposed to be some guys down from Seattle to party. But they wanted a lot. Basically everything Ricky had left, and they were willing to pay extra. If it was a legit sale, we'd be done in two weeks instead of four, and we'd have sold it all for fourteen grand instead of twelve. After paying the O.G. back, we would've cleared two-grand each. It was too good to be true, but too good to pass up.

"But yeah, it was a set-up. Ricky walked up to the door, but he left the stuff in the car just in case. Sure enough, when the door opened up, there were three Hilltops, all with guns drawn. Ricky ran back to the car and they chased after him. I was driving, so Ricky ran to the passenger side and I started pulling away as soon as he opened the door. He jumped in and I floored it. They fired at us, but nothing hit. I was scared shitless, but when we turned the corner, I thought we were safe.

"I was wrong.

"They came peeling around after us, two leaning out of their car firing at us. I drove like crazy, weaving side to side and taking turns at the last second. I just wanted to get us the hell out of there, but then I turned into a dead end. They had us. I pulled to a stop and tried to turn around, but they came whipping around the corner. They stopped and got out of the car. It seemed like everything was in slow motion. There were three of them, all armed. They started walking toward us, slow and cocky, guns pointing down. They still thought it was a robbery.

"But Ricky... Ricky came prepared. He opened the glove box, and in it was one of those bad-ass .45s. Silver and shiny and big as fuck."

Michael closed his eyes and leaned back, exhaling deeply. Talon waited for him to continue. Curt, too, sat silently, waiting for the story to end. But Michael just sat there, eyes closed, face tipped toward the ceiling. He didn't say anything, he just sat there, breathing deeply and evenly.

Finally, Talon couldn't stand it any more. "Then what happened?"

Michael opened his eyes and leaned forward. He smiled and shrugged. "I don't remember."

"You don't remember?" Talon parroted. "What do you mean you don't remember?"

"I mean," Michael repeated, "I don't remember."

"Of course you remember," Talon replied.

"Yeah, come on, Michael," Curt added. "There's no way you forget something like that. You had a perfect memory of it until that point. We know you don't just not remember."

Michael shrugged. "I must have blacked out. Somebody got shot. Somebody deserved it. Next thing I know, it's twenty-five years later and I'm charged with murder."

"Are you kidding me?" Curt was beside himself. "You didn't black out. You're just lying to us."

"I told you everything you need to know," Michael said. He turned to Talon for confirmation. "Right?"

Talon wasn't about to let him off the hook completely, but it was a lot more than she'd expected. She finally had something to work with. She decided to ignore the question. She wanted the flexibility to revisit the narrative later, if necessary. And she was pretty sure it was going to be necessary.

"I'll email the prosecutor and tell him we're rejecting his offer," she said. "And I won't make any counter-offer. I don't want to waste time on negotiating. We have too much to do."

CHAPTER 9

The following Saturday found Talon at work. Being a solo practitioner meant being not just a lawyer but also a small business owner. And while there were no days off, being her own boss meant she could set her own hours, and where those hours were spent. If she was going to work on a Saturday, she could at least change the scenery. So rather than another day in her cramped office, she decided to spend the day sprawled across a table at the back of 'Maestro's,' the coffee shop around the corner.

She dropped her stuff on a back table and then headed to the front counter to order the first of several caffeine-infused drinks. If her work took longer than she hoped, she was already considering moving to another location for alcohol-infused drinks after 5:00.

The barista was a tall man she'd seen before. He flashed a wide smile when she stepped up.

"Good morning," he chimed. "What can I get for you?"

Talon squinted at the drink menu for a moment, then ordered what she always ordered anyway. "Raspberry mocha, grande, triple shot, non-fat milk, no whip."

The tall barista dutifully transferred her order onto the side of her paper coffee cup with his Sharpie. "And can I get a name for the order?"

"Talon," she replied as she eyed the pastries under the glass next to the register.

"Talon?" the barista confirmed. "Cool name."

Talon offered the same half-cringe, half-smile she'd been offering ever since people started asking her name. She was used to getting the reaction, but never really welcomed it. Still, she was glad for a name with personality. "Thanks."

The barista thought for a moment as he added the name to her cup. "Is it Native?"

The smile part of her expression started to fade. "No, it's English," she deadpanned. "It means bird's claw."

The barista laughed. "Right, right. No, I knew that. I just meant, is it like a Native American thing. You look Native."

Talon took some pleasure in that. "I do?"

"Oh yeah," he replied. "I mean, everybody looks different, you know. But Talon. Yeah, that fits you really well. It wouldn't fit me. I'm Swedish." He gestured at his own body, which Talon noticed was wrapped in a tight polo shirt that showed off his biceps and flat stomach.

"Uh, okay." Talon probably wouldn't have been able to tell Swedish from German from English. She noticed he had sandy brown hair and blue eyes, and the previously noticed biceps. She wasn't sure what else to say.

"Okay," the barista looked back at the cup still in his hand and raised the Sharpie again. "And can I get a phone number?"

Talon almost started to recite her number, but caught herself. The barista smiled. "I get off at six. I thought maybe we could grab a drink and compare names. I'm Kyle."

Talon was flattered, and not completely uninterested. But she didn't really see herself dating the barista long-term, and she wasn't sure she had the energy to start something she knew she'd have to break off well before Kyle wanted it to end. Also, she had a lot of work to do and if she was going to be drinking that night, it would be by herself while she reviewed the case.

"Uh, hi, Kyle," she answered. "Maybe just the coffee. Thanks though."

Kyle shrugged and offered a grin, half-embarrassed but still confident somehow. It suited him. "Okay, Talon. One grande triple-shot raspberry mocha, non-fat, no whip, coming up." He glanced back to her stuff in the back. "I'll bring it your table."

Talon nodded and thanked him. She paid for the drink and returned to her table, happy to focus on her work. She sat with her back to the register, but couldn't help but wonder if Kyle was still checking her out. It was nice to be noticed.

Kyle delivered the drink with a smile but no further flirting and Talon dove into her case. One good thing about having only one case was that she could devote all of her attention to it. The bad thing was, it didn't pay the bills and so her attention was nevertheless distracted by practical worries like paying her overhead the next month. Several hours later, she was on her third coffee and still hadn't done half of what she'd planned for the day. She checked the time on her phone. 4:41. Time to pack it in.

But before she mustered the strength to close her laptop and begin stuffing her files into her briefcase, she heard a familiar voice behind her.

"Talon? Is that you?"

Talon turned to see Curt standing at the cash register, handing the barista his credit card but looking her way. "What are you doing here?"

Talon took a moment to look at the work files strewn across the table next to her open laptop. She nodded to herself. It was completely obvious what she was doing there. When she turned back around, Curt was already stepping up to her table.

"Working on a Saturday, huh?" he asked with that lopsided, boyish grin of his.

Talon shrugged. "A lawyer's work is never done," she offered with her own smile.

Curt sat down next to her, not waiting for an invitation, comfortable in his own skin. She liked that about him. He craned his neck to view her screen. "Which case?"

Talon shrugged. "I only have one case. The Jameson case."

Curt nodded. "Right." He leaned back, his tall frame draped pleasingly across his chair. "I should have known. So what are you doing exactly?"

Talon's attention snapped back from Curt's frame to Michael Jameson's case. "Uh, I'm going through the police reports line-by-line and identifying potential—"

"Your drinks are ready," Kyle interrupted from behind his espresso machine. Talon and Curt both looked over at the interruption. There were two drinks on the bar.

That was nice of Curt, Talon thought. She decided she could stick around for another cup of coffee with her investigator. Then maybe he could join her for that drink she had planned. And they'd need to eat dinner...

Curt came back to her table, a to-go cup in each hand. "Sorry. What were you saying?"

Talon again had to force her thoughts back to the job. "Oh, just that I'm reading the police reports, looking for potential witnesses. Anyone who might have seen something."

"Those reports are twenty-five years old," Curt observed.

He hadn't sat down again. He just stood next to her, coffees still in hand, and glanced at her laptop screen. "It's gonna be tough to track down witnesses after all this time."

"Oh yeah," Talon agreed. "These addresses are all bad, I'm sure. But we've got full names and dates of birth. We should be able to track them down."

"You mean," Curt corrected her again, "I should be able to."

Talon offered another shrug and smile. "You are the investigator."

Curt responded with a deep bow. "Whatever your heart desires, milady."

Talon took a moment to assess her desires, but she wasn't sure they were coming solely from her heart. Maybe they could drink the coffee on the way to the bar.

She closed out of the program on her computer and stood up. "You know," she said as she reached down to close the laptop and gather her things, "maybe we could—?"

"Hey, there you are!" Curt said, completely not in reply to her budding suggestion. He wasn't even looking at her. He was looking at the woman who had just walked into the coffee shop. A young blonde woman, with tight pants and high heels. Talon immediately hated her. She stepped across the store and took one of the coffees from Curt.

"Talon," Curt gestured toward the young, hateful blonde. "This is Laurie. We're going to the Mollycrank show tonight."

"Oh," was all Talon could manage to reply. Then she pulled on a smile and offered her hand. "Nice to meet you, Laurie."

Laurie, took a sip of her coffee—not Talon's coffee, *hers*— and ignored the extended hand. "You too, uh—Talon?"

Talon nodded. "Yes, Talon," she confirmed. "It's Native."

"Yeeahhh," Laurie sneered. "I didn't ask." She grabbed

Curt's hand. "You ready, Curty?"

Curty? Talon raised a disgusted eyebrow at her investigator.

He just shrugged back with an embarrassed smile. Then he raised his own eyebrows at Laurie's taut figure, as if that explained everything. Unfortunately, it kind of did. Sometimes you just need a lay.

"Enjoy your evening, Curty," Talon said. She was glad the coffee wasn't for her. More room for another drink. A real drink. "I'll see you Monday."

Laurie made some further whiny entreaty and Curt acquiesced in as sickening a manner as possible. But Talon focused on packing her things as Curt and Laurie giggled their way out of the coffee shop. She slung the strap of her briefcase over her shoulder, and grabbed her empty coffee paper cup.

She walked up to the register. "Kyle," she barked.

The barista stood up suddenly from whatever task required him to look through the cupboards under the espresso machine. "Huh? What? Oh, hi. Did you want another drink?"

She ignored the question. Instead she picked up his Sharpie and an empty cup.

'Castle Pub,' she wrote the name of the bar she was going to. '6th Ave. 7:00.'

"It's your lucky day." She handed him the cup. "Don't be late."

His wide eyes and even wider grin told her he wouldn't be. And she had almost two hours to get buzzed before he arrived, far too eager but adequate enough for her own needs that night.

CHAPTER 10

When Monday finally rolled around, Talon was glad to get back to the office. Sunday morning had been filled with extracting herself from Kyle. Sunday afternoon and evening had been spent ignoring his texts. It was good to have something else to focus on.

"How was your weekend?" Hannah chimed, far too cheerily, as soon as Talon broke the plane of the doorway.

Talon managed a noncommittal shrug. "Good enough." She considered for a moment. "I worked a lot."

Hannah cocked her head and appraised Talon. "Yeah, you look like you got rode hard and put away wet."

Talon's jaw dropped. How did she respond to that?

But Hannah kept on smiling. "Don't worry about it though. You just need a fresh week and some strong coffee."

Coffee. Ugh. That was Talon's only regret. Not that she hooked up with Kyle. He was nice enough. He tried a little too hard and stayed a little too long, but she'd had worse dates. The only problem was that she could never, ever go back to that coffee shop.

Which really sucked because it was right around the corner and had really good coffee. Now, she'd have to go twice as far for coffee half as good.

Or maybe Hannah would.

"Can you run to Maestro's and get me a double tall mocha?" Talon asked. "Nonfat. No whip. Peppermint syrup. No, wait, raspberry."

Hannah raised an eyebrow. "Coffee? You want me to get you coffee?"

Talon thought for a moment. On the one hand, great coffee. On the other hand, Kyle.

"Yes," she confirmed. "Please. Coffee."

Hannah took a moment, then popped up from her seat, smile blazing. "Alrighty then! Two coffees coming up!"

Talon's own eyebrow raised. "Two?"

Hannah nodded. "Curt's in your office. He's been here since eight."

Talon felt a rush of different emotions. She decided to ignore them all and smash them beneath the march to her office. When she got there, Hannah and her errand forgotten behind her, Talon stormed in to find Curt sitting in her chair, feet on her desk, and a file open across his lap. He had a pen in his mouth as he examined the contents of the file.

"What do you think you're doing?" she demanded, dropping her briefcase loudly on the floor. Her floor.

But Curt disregarded her tone and looked up pleasantly. "I had a thought about the Jameson case."

Talon crossed her arms. She really hated that she liked his face so much. Especially that stupid smile of his. "Oh, really?" She tried to still sound annoyed.

"Yeah," Curt answered. He finally put his feet back on the floor, then pointed to her computer monitor and raised the paper file in his hand. "But I couldn't figure out your password, so I had to go old school."

She knew that was Curt's own Jameson file; it was thinner than hers, which was still in her briefcase anyway. "Wait, you tried to log on to my computer?"

Curt nodded. "Yeah, but I couldn't figure out your password." He moved the mouse so the screen lit up again. "It's not any variation on my name. I have to admit, I'm a little hurt."

Talon narrowed her eyes. She wasn't that smitten with him, He was just cute. And nice. And maybe a little too cocky. Which was also cute. She decided to change the subject. Turn the tables a bit and regain control of the conversation.

"By the way, how was Laurie-skank?"

Curt jerked his gaze from the computer screen. "What?"

"Your date?" she reminded him.

Curt gave a disappointed frown. "The band was called 'Mollycrank.'"

Talon smiled. "Who said I was talking about the band?"

"Me-ow," Curt replied. He spun in her chair to face her again. "It was fine, thanks. Maybe you should try going on a date. Take the edge off a little. I think that barista may have been into you."

Talon looked away, ostensibly to pick up her briefcase. "Not really my type," she insisted. Before Curt could counter with a 'What *is* your type?' she stepped toward her desk. "Get out of my chair, then tell me your idea."

Curt only hesitated for a moment. Another moment later, Talon had regained her desk and Curt was sitting across it in one of the guest chairs.

"We need to interview Michael's brother," he said.

Talon frowned. "That's your great idea? We've already talked about that. I have to do what my client says, even if it's stupid."

"It's suicidal," Curt replied.

Talon shrugged. "Not technically, no. It won't kill him."

"It'll end his life as he knows it," Curt pointed out.

"Still not technically suicide," she maintained. "And irrelevant. I have to follow his instructions."

"I know," Curt admitted.

"So your brilliant idea is to do something you know we can't do?" Talon didn't try to disguise the incredulity in her voice.

"No," Curt responded with a flash of a grin. "But since we can't do that, we need to interview someone else."

Talon waited for more, but that seemed to be it. "Okay," she answered. "That seems kind of obvious."

"Someone Michael won't object to," Curt continued.

Talon nodded. "Again, obvious."

"So we don't tell him," Curt said. "At least not until afterward."

Talon bristled at the suggestion. But it had its appeal. They didn't need to get Jameson's approval on every step they took. That's why he'd hired them: to take up the defense and do the things that needed to be done. Except blame his brother, apparently—the one strategy that might actually work.

"So if we're not going to interview his brother," Talon questioned, "then who do we interview?"

Curt smiled that smile of his. "Ask it again, but say 'accomplice' instead of 'brother,'" he instructed.

Talon wanted to say no, but she enjoyed Curt's combination of drama and intelligence. She wasn't sure what he was driving at, but she trusted him enough to say, "If we're not going to interview his accomplice, who do we interview?"

And saying it that way, she knew the answer. "His victim's

accomplices," she realized.

They could hardly interview the murder victim. He was, by definition, dead. But just as Michael had been with Ricky, the late Jordan McCabe had been with two friends of his own. They were alive, and they could be interviewed. If they could be found.

Curt anticipated the question. "Their names are Reggie Oliphant and Earl Daggett. Oliphant is finishing up an eight-year sentence for armed robbery. He's already at Shelton, getting ready to process out. Daggett got out of prison two years ago after a stint for manslaughter. His last known address is all the way over in Spokane. His last reported job was working at a scrapyard outside of town, but that data is six months old."

Talon frowned. The Washington Correctional Facility in Shelton, Washington, was the main processing center for incarcerated felons in Washington State. It was where they all went first, before getting assigned out to one of Washington's eleven other prisons, and it was the place they all came to last, to get ready to re-acclimate to life on the outside. It was also a one-hour drive from downtown Tacoma.

Spokane was on the other side of the state, on the other side of the Cascade Mountains, and at least four hours by car. The choice was easy: drive an hour to talk with someone who would be exactly where they could find him, or drive four hours to hope they might find someone who could be anywhere now.

"Spokane it is," Talon announced.

Curt's eyes flew wide. "Spokane? Are you kidding? We could be in Shelton before lunch." He looked at the clock on Talon's wall. "Hell, we could be there before McDonald's stops serving breakfast."

"They serve breakfast all day now," Talon pointed out. "And no. We're going to Spokane."

Curt's expression betrayed his confusion. Then it softened into a sly smile. "Oh, I get it. You want to spend four hours in a car with me. That's it, isn't it?"

Talon smiled back, but coldly. "We'll drive separately. Give me his last known address and I'll meet you there. We can work out the details later."

Curt's smile dropped into a frown. "I don't understand," he started.

"You don't have to," Talon interrupted. "I'm the lawyer and I call the shots. We're not going to Shelton. We're going to Spokane. If you have any further objections, keep them to yourself because I don't care."

Curt's frown shifted from confused to hurt. "Okay. Right. You're the lawyer. Whatever you say." He stood up. "I guess I should be going now. I'll go check my schedule and let you know my availability for a trip to Spokane."

He turned to go, but Talon stopped him.

"Curt."

He looked back at her. "Yeah?"

She nodded toward her monitor. "If you found out all that stuff on your own, why did you need to get on my computer?"

Curt shrugged, his smile returning. "I didn't. I was just curious what your password was."

He stepped into the hallway and Talon let him go without further conversation. She lost herself in thought for several moments, then shook her head and returned to her surroundings. She turned to her computer and pulled out the keyboard to type in her password:

W-I-L-L-I-A-M-1-2-3.

CHAPTER 11

The drive to Spokane always seemed to take both longer and shorter than Talon expected. Longer, because four-and-a-half hours is just a long time to be sitting behind the wheel of a car. Shorter, because there really wasn't much between Tacoma and Spokane, so the milestones were few and far between. She took the State Route 18 bypass to Interstate 90 to avoid the perpetual Seattle traffic. It was a drive through yet-to-be-developed exurbs then up the side of the Cascade Mountains. There was a ski resort at the pass, but it was closed that time of year, and then it was downhill from there, literally and figuratively. She drove past small Eastern Washington towns with names like Cle Elum and Vantage, but mostly it was farm after farm, broken halfway by the Columbia River.

She'd left early enough that when she arrived in Spokane it was only a little after 1:00. That gave her time to grab lunch before meeting Curt at 2:00 at the fountain in Spokane's Riverfront Park.

Talon knew it would have made more sense to drive over with Curt, but she didn't want to spend four-plus hours trying to come up with small talk. Laurieskank would undoubtedly come up, and that would lead to Kyle the Barista, and her love life generally. Even if they talked about the case, that would just have led to questioning about why they'd come all the way to Spokane rather than just down the road to Shelton. And anyway, there wasn't four hours' worth of material about the case. Not yet.

But hopefully that was about to change. Lunch was soup and sandwich at a small restaurant near the park, then she walked across the street and found a bench in front of the fountain. She was five minutes early. Curt was six minutes late.

"Did I ever mention," he asked as he walked up to her, rubbing the back of his neck and looking more haggard than she was used to seeing him, "that I hate driving?"

Talon smiled at that. It was always good to acquire information on other people. Plus, she kind of liked the idea of him having to do something he didn't really like. Payback for her night with Kyle.

"No," she answered sweetly. "But then again, I never asked."

Curt took a moment, then laughed. "Okay then. You're still vaguely angry at me about something. Good to know. That should make this whole thing go quicker, but seem longer." He rubbed his neck again. "Kind of like the drive over here."

Talon looked up at him, but he had turned away to gaze at the fountain. This time her smile was smaller, but more genuine, at their shared sentiment about the drive. She wasn't going to be able to stay mad at him for long.

"So what's the plan of attack?" she asked him.

Curt nodded and pulled his Jameson file out of his shoulder bag. "I did some more research after we talked. It's hard to verify where someone works when they're a laborer getting paid under the table, but I was able to find a recent apartment application for a place here in Spokane. Under employment he wrote 'meat packer' and listed a business east of town."

"Meat packing?" Talon replied. "So he works at a slaughterhouse?"

Curt shrugged. "I guess so. Why? Is that going to be a problem for you?"

"Hardly," Talon answered as she stood up. "It'll remind me of being a kid."

Curt cocked his head at her. But before he could ask, she said. "This time we can carpool. But you're driving."

"Why?" Curt responded as she walked past him.

"Because," she smiled over her shoulder, "you hate driving."

* * *

The Inland Empire Meat Company was about fifteen minutes outside of Spokane, east on I-90 toward Idaho. There weren't any signs, but there also weren't really any other buildings around. The curse of the slaughterhouse, Talon supposed. She vaguely recalled learning about the pivotal role slaughterhouses played in the development of western zoning laws. But she'd forgotten most of it after the final exam. She wanted to be in a courtroom, not a municipal zoning department.

And there she was, in the dusty parking lot of a meat packing plant. Not as far from the courtroom as one might think. No one likes to see the sausage made, literally or figuratively. People just want to know the bacon is on the grocery store shelf and the criminals are in jail.

They stepped out of the car and were immediately hit by the smell that led to all those zoning law decisions. Talon knew modern ventilation technology had undoubtedly made the situation more tolerable than in days past, but it was still bracing. But there was no way she was going to let Curt know it bothered her.

He wasn't nearly as concerned about appearances. "Yuck. Glad I don't work here every day."

"If you worked here every day," Talon supposed, "it wouldn't bother you."

Curt admitted as much with a loose nod. Then he started for the building. "Come on. Let's go ask for Daggett at the main office."

It smelled better inside; again, the ventilation. The business office was right off the main entrance. There was a young woman working at the reception desk. Talon and Curt introduced themselves by name only and asked if the manager was in. He was, and a few minutes later the young woman took them back to the office of a Mr. Derrick Reynolds.

"Call me Derrick," he insisted as he sat down again behind his paper-covered desk and motioned toward the guest chairs. He was a heavy-set man in his fifties, with thinning hair and a thick moustache. The office sported several bookshelves of binders, family photos, and a large stuffed-and-mounted bass. "How can I help you?"

Talon took the lead. Curt had gotten them there, but it was her case. "As I said, my name is Talon Winter. I'm a criminal defense attorney from Tacoma. This is my investigator, Curt Fairchild. I represent a man named Michael Jameson who is charged with murder. We're looking for a man named Earl Daggett who may work here."

"Earl?" Reynolds replied. "Sure. He works here. Good worker. Hope he's not in any trouble."

Talon shook her head. "No. It happened a long time ago and he was just a witness."

Reynolds nodded. "Good to hear. Earl's a good guy. Works hard. Never causes trouble."

"Is he working right now?" Talon asked. She was glad to hear they'd found him. She was hoping they wouldn't have to wait three days until his next shift.

"Oh yeah," Reynolds confirmed. "Been here since six. His shift's just about over. I'll have Cindy go get him. You can use my office."

Talon considered protesting the offer of Reynolds' office, out of politeness, but decided to accept it after all. It was useful, so why stand on ceremony? She doubted they had a conference room. "Thanks, Derrick."

Reynolds took his leave and a few minutes later, Cindy the Receptionist escorted Earl the Witness into the office.

Daggett was pretty much what Talon expected, maybe even a little tougher looking. Not rougher; he was sharp even in his Inland Empire Meats uniform, with a shaved head, neatly trimmed goatee and athletic build beneath the one-piece jumpsuit. But he was tall, with hard eyes, and dark brown skin. Intimidating. Perfect for a wingman on a shooting. But then again, he may have been a lot less tough-looking twenty years ago, before he'd spent a dozen years in and out of prison.

"Mr. Reynolds said you folks wanted to speak with me?" Daggett started. He had a smooth voice, deep and confident. There was no trace of the trepidation Talon thought their visit might generate.

Talon stood up and extended her hand. "Yes, Mr. Daggett. My name is Talon Winter. I'm a criminal defense attorney from Tacoma. This is Curt Fairchild, my investigator."

Daggett nodded and shook Talon's hand. "Okay. Am I in some sort of trouble? I been checking in with my probation officer every week."

"No, no," Talon assured. "This isn't about you."

They all sat down.

"It's about Michael Jameson," she explained.

Daggett didn't give the reaction Talon expected. He just shrugged. "I don't know that name."

Curt finally spoke up. "How about the name Jordan McCabe?"

The dead man. It was funny how, after a murder, the one name everyone forgets was the victim's. The case was named after the defendant: State of Washington v. Michael Jameson. The witnesses all said their own names to the jury. But the victim, his name hardly mattered any more. Except to his friends.

"Jordy?" Daggett confirmed. "Shit. Yeah, I know that name."

"I represent the man charged with killing him," Talon admitted. "We'd like to talk to you about what happened."

Talon had expected some sort of negative reaction. Either an explosive, 'No!' or a crossed-armed 'Sorry, I can't help you.' Instead she got another shrug.

"I can tell you what happened," Daggett said. "I don't know how much it's gonna help your guy, though." He paused. "Huh, they finally solved it, huh? How'd they do that?"

"They found the gun that fired the shot," Curt answered. "But that doesn't mean our guy did it."

"Well, he was the only one there," Daggett replied. "So if it was his gun, he fired it."

"Wait," Talon interrupted. "The only one? Are you sure?"

Daggett frowned in thought. "Well, there were four people there. Jordy, Reggie, me, and whoever shot Jordy. I never seen the guy before. Anyway it was dark and I was pretty fucked up. I probably wouldn't recognize him after all this time anyway. So that's good for your guy."

Talon had to admit as much. But she wanted more

information. "What happened? Was it a drug rip gone bad?"

Daggett smiled at the vernacular. "Drug rip?" he repeated. "Nice, Mrs. Lawyer. Yeah, it was a drug rip. Well, it was supposed to be. Jordy had it all set up. Said there was some kid trying to step on our territory. But he didn't tell us who it was. He just wanted us with him. Figured the kid would drop the drugs as soon as he saw our guns."

"But he didn't?" Talon encouraged.

"Nope, he turned and ran back to his car. We took off after him, but he got to his car first. Jumped in and pulled away. Jordy and Reggie shot at the car. Dude shot back and hit Jordy right in the throat. He never had a chance."

Daggett retold the story with almost no emotion. Just a distant nostalgia.

"So it was just the one guy?" Curt tried to confirm.

Daggett shrugged. "That's all I ever saw." Daggett shrugged. "But shit, it was dark and once Jordy got hit, I wasn't too concerned about how many of them there were."

"Do you remember chasing after them in your car?" Talon asked. "Anything like that?"

"A car chase?" Daggett's face twisted up in thought. "Naw, I don't remember that. But like I said, I was pretty fucked up."

"And you never shot at anyone?" Curt asked.

Daggett smiled slightly. "I didn't even have a gun. I was just there for moral support."

Talon nodded dubiously. "Sure."

"Anyway, it don't matter if I shot. Your guy's the one who killed Jordy."

"Maybe," Talon replied.

Curt reached into his pocket and handed Daggett a business card. "It took a little bit for us to find you. I don't know if the prosecutor will go to that much trouble. They should, but they get lazy working for the government. Do us a favor, call us if they contact you."

Daggett took the card and stared at it for a moment. Then he looked up. "Why should I?"

"Because our guy is innocent," Talon asserted.

But Daggett was unimpressed. "Prison's full of innocent men."

CHAPTER 12

Daggett went back to work and Talon and Curt stepped out into the parking lot. The smell was there again, so instead of lingering in the sun to debrief, they both climbed into Curt's car and headed back toward Spokane.

"So, what do you think?" Talon started. She was interested in Curt's thoughts, but also still processing her own.

"He seemed credible," Curt responded. "I don't know. Probably not our best witness."

"Friends of the victim probably aren't going to be the murderer's best witnesses," Talon opined.

Curt looked at her out of the corner of his eye. "So you think he's guilty?"

"I didn't say that," Talon insisted. "I didn't mean Michael is a murderer. I just meant..."

"I know, I know," Curt interrupted as he pulled onto the roadway. "I was just giving you crap. If anything, maybe he does help us. He said there was only one shooter. So that's Ricky, right? Maybe Michael wasn't there at all."

"Well, that would be difficult to conclude," Talon replied, "since Michael himself told us he was there, and gave us a pretty detailed account. If there was only one person there, it was probably him and not Ricky."

Curt nodded. "Maybe, but again, that's based on Michael's version. Maybe Ricky went alone and Michael just added himself into the story so Ricky wouldn't get charged."

"Hell of a way for him not to get charged." Talon shook her head. "Michael said Ricky is the one who pulled the gun out of the glove box and shot."

"No, Michael said he blacked out and didn't remember who shot what," Curt pointed out. "He put Ricky there, but he didn't have Ricky pulling the trigger."

Talon appreciated the accuracy. "Okay, you're right. He didn't say it. He just strongly suggested it. But Daggett never saw Michael."

"Or he never saw Ricky. Maybe Michael was the one running the drugs and got jumped by Daggett and his crew."

Talon considered. "Maybe. It seems more likely that Michael never left the car and Daggett just didn't see him. Didn't Michael say he stayed in the car?"

Curt nodded. "I think so. But we better figure it out. The prosecutor's going to find Daggett once they actually start looking. He wasn't that hard to find. And when he tells the jury there was only one shooter, the jury's going to think it was our guy. Especially if our guy won't take the stand and say it was his brother."

They were on the freeway, heading back toward Spokane. They'd be there in a few minutes and could split up or stay together for more strategizing. Talon considered their options.

"Dinner," she announced.

Curt turned to look at her. "What?"

"Dinner," she repeated. "We're going to have dinner here and figure this out. Either we can do this without bringing Ricky into it or we can't. If we can, then we do it. If we can't, then we tell Michael and give him a choice: do it our way or find another lawyer. I'm not going to lose my first case because my client ties my hands behind my back."

Curt looked back at the freeway and nodded. After a moment, he said, "I knew it."

Talon looked over at him. "You knew I wasn't going to let Michael ruin his own case?"

"Oh, I knew that too," Curt smiled. "But no. I knew you wanted to have dinner with me."

CHAPTER 13

The road from I-90 into town was five lanes wide and flanked on either side by an army of fast food signs and casual dining establishments. Talon turned the car into the parking lot of one of the sit-down restaurants. It was a local place, not a franchise. That wasn't why she'd chosen it—she knew their pre-prepared food had come off the same truck as every other restaurant on the strip—it was just easier than trying to make a left-hand turn and traffic was backing up from the stoplight ahead.

"Here we are," she announced. Then, craning her neck to read the sign through the windshield, "Uh, Andy's American Diner."

"Good as any," Curt agreed with a nod.

Talon guided the car into an annoyingly narrow parking spot and they made their way inside. There was no line yet so the hostess took them directly to a booth by a window. They had a lovely view of the road they'd just been driving on.

They were there to talk about the case, but Talon suddenly

realized how hungry she was. The smell of fried food permeating the diner prompted an audible stomach growl. Talon slid into the booth and practically snatched her menu out of the hostess' hands. Curt slipped into the seat opposite her, but Talon barely noticed as she buried her nose in the menu. Her eyes were immediately drawn to an unpleasantly tinted photograph of the bacon cheeseburger and fries. The description next to the photo listed the dietary information as well: '930 calories as prepared. 1105 calories as served.'

Talon scowled at the menu. *What the hell does that mean?*

"What looks good?" Curt asked cheerily.

Talon shrugged. "I'm not sure," she replied without looking up.

Opposite the cheeseburger was a Caesar salad. '625 calories.' *Damn it.* If she ordered that, she'd just be hungry again in an hour or two. She considered her stomach, then her thighs, then the man sitting across from her, blissfully ignorant of her internal dialogue. Talon frowned. Why should she care what Curt thought? So what if she ordered something that would likely go straight to her ass? He should be so lucky to get to worry about the size of her ass.

Curt set his menu down and looked around the restaurant. "There sure are a lot of couples here tonight," he observed. "Friday night in Spokane, I guess."

That took Talon's attention off her stomach for a moment. She surveyed the nearby tables. Sure enough, the place was filling up with young couples, and groups of young couples. Without knowing for sure, Talon could guess there was a multiplex theater somewhere nearby. She had the urge to make some sort of snarky comment, either about the double-daters surrounding them, or about Curt's lack of taste in women. The term 'Laurieskank' definitely came to mind. But she caught herself.

"Yeah," she agreed, in a consciously pleasant tone. "Sure looks like it. Speaking of which, how's Laurie?"

Curt wasn't really a 'poker face' kind of guy, but he made no effort to conceal his surprise at Talon's question.

"Uh, well, wow," he sputtered. "Uh, yeah, well, that didn't really work out so well. It went downhill pretty fast after the coffee shop. I didn't see her again after that night."

"Oh." Talon tried to sound disappointed, but not too disappointed—not too interested. "That's too bad."

Curt shrugged and flashed that boyish grin of his. "Yeah, well, live and learn, I guess. Apparently, you're not supposed to agree when your date says another woman is attractive."

Talon had to try even harder not to react to that statement. Luckily, the waitress arrived just then to take their orders.

"Hi, I'm Kelly," the young woman announced cheerily, her energy not yet drained from a long night of patrons having more fun than her. "I'll be your waitress tonight. Have you folks decided on anything yet?"

Curt nodded. "I'll take the chicken sandwich, no mayo, with fries and a Coke."

Kelly dutifully recorded the order on her notepad. "And for you, ma'am?"

Talon decided to ignore the age implications of being called 'ma'am.' She forced a smile and handed her menu to Kelly. "I'll take the Caesar salad, please. And a water."

Kelly took down Talon's order as well and disappeared with the menus.

"So," Talon jumped in, eager to avoid the topic they'd stumbled into, "what did you think of Daggett?"

Curt thought for a moment, apparently also willing to talk shop. "He seemed pretty credible. He didn't seem like he had an axe to grind. It happened a long time ago. I think the jury will believe him."

Talon agreed with that assessment. "Yeah, but is that a good thing or not?"

"Depends on whether it hurts us or helps us," Curt replied.

"He only saw one person," Talon recalled.

"So that's good," Curt said. "It corroborates Michael's story that he stayed in the car."

"Of course, it could have been Ricky who stayed in the car," Talon considered. "And anyway, the jury only gets to hear Michael's version if I put him on the stand."

"Why wouldn't you?" Curt asked.

Before Talon could respond, Kelly returned with their drinks and a wide smile. A moment later, she was gone again and Talon took a sip of water.

"If I put him on the stand," Talon explained, "then that puts him at the scene of the murder. Right now, all they have is the ballistics match."

"And Daggett," Curt pointed out.

"Maybe," Talon replied. "He saw a young Black male. So what? That could have been anyone. I only put Michael on the stand if Quinlan's able to put Michael there and I have to explain why."

"And that he didn't do anything," Curt added.

"Right."

Curt took a drink from his own glass, then frowned. "Did Daggett say he saw a gun?"

Talon tried to remember. "I, I'm not sure."

Curt slapped the table. "Damn it. I forgot to ask him that. I got so caught up on how many people he saw, I forgot to ask if he ever saw a gun."

"Crap," Talon agreed. "We should know that."

"Maybe it doesn't matter?" Curt tried. "I mean we know the victim was shot, so there had to be a gun."

But Talon shook her head. "Yeah, but even if there was only one person outside of the car, the shot could have come from inside the car. If Daggett testifies there was one guy outside the car, but he didn't have a gun, then I can't put Michael on the stand to say he stayed in the car. That makes him the shooter."

"Shit." Curt punched the table again. "We have to go back and ask him."

Talon wasn't so sure. "Maybe, maybe not. It would signal to him that we made a mistake, that we're sloppy. He seemed to like us. I don't want to undercut our credibility with him. I want him to think we're confident in our case."

Curt didn't immediately reply as he considered Talon's argument.

"Besides," Talon added, "we might not like the answer. It might be better to leave it alone, rather than get him to thinking about it. The logical assumption is that the guy outside the car had the gun. Quinlan isn't too sharp. He might forget to ask about that. No need to draw Daggett's attention to it."

"But we need to know," Curt countered. "Regardless of whether Quinlan remembers to ask, we still should know. We can't go into a trial and not have every fact tied down."

"It was over two decades ago," Talon countered. "We're not going to get every fact tied down. But we don't have to. That's the prosecutor's job. It's good if the facts are in doubt."

Curt wasn't convinced. "It's better if we know. We don't have to tell Quinlan, but we should know what happened. If we don't go back to Daggett, then we better remember to ask Oliphant."

Talon had forgotten about Oliphant. "Well, yeah. Uh, I guess we can cross that bridge when we come to it."

"Well, if Oliphant says the guy outside had the gun," Curt reasoned, "then we can stop there. Even if Daggett disagrees, we can explain it away because it was dark and he probably just didn't see it. He won't say there was no gun, just that he didn't see it."

Talon couldn't disagree. Nevertheless, she said, "Well, maybe we should go back and talk to Daggett…"

Curt looked at her for a beat, then hung his head. "Shit, Talon. I'm sorry. I really screwed that up. I can't believe I forgot to ask him about the gun. It's a fucking shooting and I didn't ask about the gun."

"Well, I didn't ask either," Talon pointed out. She didn't like seeing Curt beating himself up. "It's my case after all."

"Yeah, but I'm the investigator," Curt argued. "You're the courtroom person. I'm supposed to get you the information you need to shine in front of the jury."

Talon liked the idea of shining. "No, it's on both of us. We're a team."

Curt shrugged. "Yeah, but if we're going to stay a team, I can't mess up stuff like this. I mean, you're going to have other cases, other investigators. If you can't rely on me to do a good job, you'll start using a different investigator. You'll have to, for your clients' sake."

It hadn't occurred to Talon that she'd have other cases with other investigators. This was her only case. And she was getting quite used to working with Curt.

"I think you're doing fine," she assured him.

Another shrug. "Yeah, but there are some damn good investigators out there. People with lots of experience, on both sides. Former cops who really know how to work up a case."

Talon tried to bolster Curt's confidence. "Yeah, well, cops suck, right? That's why we're doing defense work."

But Curt raised a hand. "Careful," he said. "Cops are like anybody else. There are good ones and bad ones. In fact..." He hesitated, then admitted, "In fact, I was almost a cop."

Talon was picking up her glass for another drink, but she set it right back down again. "What? You were? You never told me that."

Curt shrugged again and offered a faint grin. "I don't talk much about it."

"Too late," Talon declared. She rolled her hand at him. "Spill."

Curt sighed, then leaned back and pushed his hair out of his eyes. "Okay. I was a criminal justice major in college. I knew I wanted to do something in that area. In fact, I thought I wanted to be a cop, so I applied to every department in the county. Eventually I got hired on as a cadet with Fircrest P.D."

"Fircrest? Nice," Talon interjected. "Quiet suburb. Country club. Good place to start."

"Right." Curt nodded. "That's what I thought too. But even with the job lined up, you can't be a cop in Washington unless you graduate from the Basic Law Enforcement Academy up in Burien. So I did classes during the day in Burien, and ride-alongs at night in Fircrest. I wasn't the top of my class, but I did well enough and everything was on track."

"So what happened?" Talon asked as she reached for her glass again.

Curt laughed a little. "Life happened. My mom got sick. Really sick. Leukemia. Late stage."

"Oh, no," Talon offered. "I'm sorry." And she was. That was terrible news.

But Curt just shrugged. "It happens. She was old. In fact, she was retired and living in Arizona. The doctors gave her about two months to live. It just so happened, those were the last two months of the academy. I had to choose between finishing out my classes or taking care of my dying mother. Not much of a choice really, when you think about it."

"So you quit the academy?"

"And my job at Fircrest," Curt confirmed. "They couldn't hold it open for me. And then I moved down to Arizona to take care of my mom."

"Couldn't anyone else do it?" Talon asked. "Do you have any brothers or sisters?"

Curt offered a pained grin. "I have a brother. He lives in San Diego. But there was no way he was going to do it."

"Why not?" Talon inquired. "Job or family or something?"

"Or something," Curt answered. He took a drink of his Coke. "I mean he has a job and a family, but that wasn't it. He could have gotten the time off. And his wife and kids would have been fine with a couple trips to Phoenix to see grandma. No, it was just, well, he wasn't going to be there for my mom because she wasn't there for us. He was still pretty angry, pretty bitter." Curt stared into his glass for a few seconds, then added, "He still is."

Talon hesitated for just a moment—that split second assessment of whether a follow-up question shows concern, or is just prying. But Curt brought it up, and Talon wasn't one to favor politeness over directness. "What do you mean?" she asked.

Curt smiled weakly and looked down at the table. "Uh, yeah... So, my dad wasn't exactly the warm and fuzzy type. He was more the angry and yelling type. He never hit us. Well, not really. Not regularly. But he had a temper, and it was never far from the surface. My brother, he was two years older than me, so he got the worst of it. He left home as soon as he turned eighteen, and never looked back."

Talon nodded, but didn't interrupt.

"I thought maybe when our dad died," Curt continued, "Jake would soften up, a least a little. But that didn't happen. See, our dad was the angry one. The abusive one. The one who yelled, and broke things, and always seemed an inch away from exploding physically. But it was our mom who let it all happen. She never tried to stop him. She just let it happen. Then afterward, she'd blame us. Tell us how hard our dad worked for us, how much stress he was under. And tell us whatever *we* had done to *make* him get angry."

Curt shrugged again and took another sip of soda. "So when my mom got sick, Jake didn't want to hear about it. 'She was never there for us,' he said, 'so why should we be there for her?'"

Talon thought for moment. "That's actually a fair question. Why should you?"

Curt looked up and then smiled weakly. "I'm not my brother. He dealt with it his way, but that's his way, not mine. But like I said, Dad was scary and angry and we were always afraid he was going to beat us. But he didn't. Not like *his* dad. His dad beat the shit out of him on a regular basis. So, say what you want about him, he broke that cycle. Jake doesn't hit his kids and if I ever have kids, they won't have to be afraid of me either."

Talon's expression softened. She could imagine Curt as a father: a baby in his arms, playing catch in the backyard, running alongside a teetering bicycle. And one thing she couldn't imagine was him being abusive.

"I can't blame my mother for being as afraid of him as we were," Curt continued. "And I don't blame my brother for staying angry. But I wasn't going to let my mother die alone. Like I said, easy decision."

"Wow." Talon shook her head. "You must hate your brother now."

Curt's eyebrows shot up. "Hate? No. Of course not. I love him."

"But he ruined your dream."

"Dream?" Curt laughed. "No. Being a cop wasn't a dream. It was a plan. But you can make new plans."

He picked up his drink and leaned back. "I'm not one of those people who thinks things happen for a reason. It's pretty hard to think that after you work a couple of child sex cases. When I first went to Arizona, I figured I'd just re-enroll in the academy when I got back to Tacoma, but when it was all over, I decided to take a break and think about what I wanted to do with my life. Ultimately, I decided I wanted to do something to help people, so I gave up on the cop thing and decided to become a private investigator."

Talon cocked her head. "But cops help people."

Curt shrugged. "Kinda. Cops enforce rules. Sometimes that helps people. Maybe even most of the time. But putting a drug addict in jail doesn't help anyone. That's a real person. You're just enforcing a rule because somebody else thinks it should be the rule. We used to put people in jail for smoking pot. Now you can buy it on every street corner in Washington. Rules change, there are always people who need help."

Curt leaned forward and shook his head slightly. "No, my brother did me a favor. I'd much rather sit next to a real person and help them get out of trouble, than pretend that person is just a nameless criminal. There are too many people who pretend they're something they're not. I don't want to do that to other people. I just want everyone to be what they really are."

Just then Kelly arrived with their meals. "Chicken sandwich

for the gentleman." She set one plate in front of Curt. The other landed in front of Talon. "And a salad for the lady."

Talon looked down at her lettuce-and-crouton-covered plate, then up at the man across the table from her. After a moment, she handed the salad back to Kelly. "I've changed my mind," she said. "I'll take the bacon cheeseburger, please. Extra bacon."

CHAPTER 14

Part of getting back to the office was going through the mail. There was the usual stuff, mostly junk mail headed straight to the recycling bin. But there was one she couldn't ignore. The envelope was two inches thick, at least. It wasn't even really an envelope. It was more like a paper box. The return address was Gardelli, High & Steinmetz. She knew what was inside.

"I got the interrogatories," she told Sullivan when he picked up. "There must be a hundred pages of questions here."

"A hundred and seven," Sullivan corrected. "I've already looked through my copies. They arrived this morning."

"I don't have time to answer all of these," Talon protested. "What about the limit? The court rules cap the number of interrogatories at forty. This is way over that."

"Well, technically, there are only forty questions," Sullivan responded. "There are just a lot of sub-questions."

"That's bull," Talon shot back. "I say we answer the first forty and let them cry about it."

"That's one approach," Sullivan agreed. "We could also ask

the court to strike them completely for exceeding the limit."

Talon shook her head. "The judge won't do that."

"No, he won't," Sullivan agreed.

"He'll just give them leave to exceed the forty-question limit," Talon knew.

"Yes, he will," Sullivan confirmed.

"Shit," Talon breathed. "I really don't have time for this, Stan."

"I thought you only had one case," Sullivan replied. "That should leave you enough time to answer a few questions."

"A hundred and seven questions," Talon corrected, looking at the stack of papers. "And I suppose they're as personally invasive as possible, right? Every last bit of information about my finances, everything?"

"You used to do this for a living, right?" Sullivan asked.

"Yeah," Talon admitted.

"Then you know the answer. Every question you ever put to a plaintiff to embarrass and burden them, it's in there. Hell, they probably took them from your old directory."

Talon shook her head at that. "Using my own methods against me. Ugh. And what happens if I just refuse to answer them?"

"Hm, well, there are probably a few where you can legitimately claim privilege," Sullivan considered, "but you have to answer the rest. You know that. And if you don't, they'll make a motion to dismiss your case for want of prosecution. You can't risk that. The judge will grant it if you don't have a good reason not to answer."

"Is them being complete dickheads a good reason?"

Sullivan laughed. "Lawyers suing lawyers. Even the judge is a lawyer. We're all dickheads."

Talon ran a hand through her hair. She was questioning whether the lawsuit was really worth her time any more. She also knew it was normal for plaintiffs to get tired and have second thoughts, and that 107-question interrogatories were designed to increase that fatigue to the breaking point. Still, knowing it didn't make it any less true.

"Any new offers on the table?" she asked.

Sullivan laughed again. "There aren't even any old offers on the table. We talked about this already. It's too soon to talk settlement. Unless you want to give up."

Talon frowned. She wasn't a quitter. She was just having a bad run of things. Secret brothers, credible victims, confusing investigators. "No, I don't want to give up. I just want to win without having to work so hard for it."

"That doesn't sound like you."

Talon nodded to herself. "It's not."

"Good," Sullivan answered. "You've got thirty days to answer those interrogatories. Don't take a minute less. We'll schedule a meeting to go over them before we submit them, along with a hundred and eight of our own. Sound good?"

"Sounds great," Talon said. "Thanks, Stan."

"Now go win your other case," he said.

Talon smiled. "Deal."

She hung up the phone and looked again at the interrogatories. She'd gotten pretty good over the years at estimating how many hours of work any given task might take her. You can't budget your time if you don't know the currency. But this time was different. The hours it would take to answer those 107 questions—and it would be a lot of hours—weren't just hours of her life wasted; they were hours not spent on Michael Jameson's case.

Suddenly that seemed very important to her.

The bills piling up on her desk were growing increasingly urgent as well.

She picked up the phone again. After a few moments, Sullivan's secretary put her through to him.

"Samuel Sullivan," he answered.

"Stan, it's Talon again. I want you to make them an offer. Fifty thousand to settle everything."

"Fifty thousand?" Sullivan practically choked on the number. "This case is worth a hell of a lot more than that. My time is worth a lot more than that. You didn't hire me to settle this case for fifty thousand."

"I hired you to represent me," Talon answered. "And this is how I want to proceed."

"They're going to reject it, Talon. It's too soon. We just started discovery. They're going to know you're losing your nerve and they're going to reject it."

"Fine," she said. "Let them reject it. Then we get attorneys' fees if the jury gives me one dollar more. Remind them of that when they say I've lost my nerve."

She could hear Sullivan shaking his head over the phone. "'Talon, Talon, Talon. This is a mistake. Answer the interrogatories. I can ask for more time. I can make a motion to limit it to forty real questions, not the hundred and seven bullshit they're pulling. I thought you'd have time, with just the one case, but we can handle it differently."

"That's just it, Stan," Talon replied. "I don't have time. And it's because I just have one case. Make the offer, and let me know what they say."

"You know what they're going to say," Sullivan complained.

"Then make them say it and we'll go from there."

"This is a mistake, Talon."

Talon thought for a moment. She'd spent her entire career trying to do everything perfectly. Then one small 'mistake'—trying to do the right thing—and she lost everything. She understood Michael Jameson's attitude better than she thought she would. It should be okay to make a mistake. Life goes on.

"Maybe," she answered. "But it's my mistake to make."

CHAPTER 15

The next time Talon saw Michael Jameson was in court, at the omnibus hearing. Like every criminal defendant, Jameson had asked her what an 'omnibus hearing' was. Lawyers seemed to take particular pleasure in giving normal things obscure names so they could look smarter than everyone else in the room.

"Omnibus is Latin for 'everything,'" Talon explained. "This is the hearing where the judge makes sure everything is ready for trial."

"Is it?" Jameson asked.

Talon thought for a moment. Not really, she knew. They had more witnesses to interview. They hadn't even settled on their defense yet. Self-defense? Alibi? Or the dreaded 'general denial,' which basically meant, 'Yes, I did it, but I'm going to make you prove it.' The problem with that defense was the prosecution usually did prove it.

"No," Talon admitted. "But we'll get it done before the trial date. We have to. I mean, we could ask the judge to delay the trial date, but delaying the trial just gives the prosecutor more time to build his case. We're better off moving forward today, advising the judge what's left to be done, and promising we'll get it done." She paused. "Unless you want to talk about settling the case. Judges always give more time if it means a case might settle. One less trial to jam into the already overcrowded courtrooms."

But Jameson shook his head. "No. No deals. I've told you that from the beginning."

"I know." Talon nodded. "But people change their minds. I wouldn't be doing my job if I didn't at least check in with you every now and again."

"How noble," came a voice over Talon's shoulder. It was Quinlan. "Your job is very important. Not as important as mine, but it has its role."

Talon forced a tight smile to her opponent. "Good morning, Eric."

"Good morning, Talon," Quinlan replied, then added, "Mr. Jameson," even though he wasn't supposed to speak with a represented defendant. "The judge will be out in a few minutes. Shall we go through the form?"

The omnibus hearing consisted of the judge reviewing the omnibus form on the record, confirming what the parties had reduced to writing regarding what preparation had been completed, and what remained to be done.

Talon had obtained a blank form from the judge's clerk prior to Quinlan's arrival and written in the case name and case number. "I've already started one."

But Quinlan waved it away. "Oh no, I've already completed it." He pulled a three-page omnibus order from his briefcase and handed it to Talon. The blanks were filled in with type-written answers. She wondered who even had a typewriter any more.

"You filled in my sections too," she observed.

"Yes," Quinlan replied. "I thought it would save time."

"You do know you don't represent both sides, right?" she replied.

Quinlan rolled his eyes. "Look," he started. "We both have a job to do here, but that doesn't mean we can't work together. My job is to prove your guy committed the crime. Your job is to protect his rights while I do that."

Talon raised an eyebrow but let him continue. She was aware Jameson was also listening—he was sitting right there—but Quinlan was acting like he wasn't there, or didn't matter.

"So," Quinlan continued, "I went through the form and filled in the parts where you protect his rights, but don't assert anything stupid. For example, I put the defense as general denial, since he obviously can't claim alibi."

Talon finally interrupted. "Why is that obvious?"

Quinlan sighed again. He appeared to enjoy being exasperated. "Because the gun was found in his house. He kept it for twenty-five years. He can hardly claim he wasn't there if he's the one who fired the gun."

Talon knew two things right then: that was faulty logic, and not to correct it. Not until the trial. There was no reason to warn her opponent of his errors in advance. "Okay. What else did you fill in?"

"I put in that we won't need a suppression hearing regarding your client's statements."

"Because he didn't make any statements?" Talon tried to confirm.

"Not exactly," Quinlan responded. "He did ask for a lawyer. If he takes the stand and tells some b.s. story, then we get to tell the jury he didn't tell the cops that story when he was arrested."

"No, you don't," Talon countered. "He has the right to

remain silent and the right to a lawyer. You can't use any of that against him at trial."

"I can if he tells a different story on the stand," Quinlan insisted.

Talon knew he was wrong, which meant he was also stupid. Or at least ignorant. That was good. Overconfident, ignorant prosecutor. Very good.

"Look, Eric," she interrupted. "I appreciate you trying to do my job for me and everything, but maybe we should just each do our own job. Mr. Jameson didn't hire you to represent him. I think he might prefer if I made the decisions about what our defense will be and how we'll try the case."

Quinlan paused and looked at his neatly typed form. After a few moments, he sighed through his nose. "It took a long time to type this out."

"I know," Talon soothed. "And we appreciate the effort."

Quinlan looked up at the clock on the wall. "And the judge will be out any minute. He won't be happy if we don't have our form ready. Can't we just use mine? We could always amend it later."

But Talon shook her head. "No, Eric. I'm sorry. We can't do that. I really do have to represent my client's best interests, not what you think those interests should be."

Quinlan's countenance hardened. "You're just being obstructionist."

Talon nodded. "If you want to send my client to prison for a crime he didn't commit, then yes, I will try to obstruct that."

Just then, the judge entered the courtroom from his chambers.

"All rise!" ordered the clerk. "The Pierce County Superior Court is now in session, The Honorable Patrick Gallagher presiding."

Gallagher ascended the few stairs to the bench and took his seat above the attorneys. "Please be seated," he instructed. Gallagher had a reputation for being reasonably affable. Not friendly exactly—that wouldn't be judicial—but not standoffish either. Just an old lawyer finishing out his career on the bench. One disadvantage Talon had as a civil litigator was that civil cases went to trial a lot less often than criminal cases. The judges tended to get to know the public defenders and the prosecutors the best because they were the attorneys who tried the most cases. That meant she knew Gallagher by reputation only, but Gallagher already knew Quinlan by experience.

On the other hand, familiarity can breed contempt.

"Are the parties ready in the matter of The State of Washington versus Michael Jameson?" Gallagher asked. He looked first to the prosecutor.

"Uh, well, Your Honor," Quinlan started. "I think we're not quite ready actually. I filled out the omnibus form, but, uh, the defense attorney is refusing to sign it."

Gallagher frowned. "The defense attorney has a name, I presume?"

"Uh, yes, Your Honor," Quinlan practically admitted. "Ms. Winter refused to sign the form."

Talon stood up, the protocol for addressing a judge in open court. "Talon Winter for Mr. Jameson, Your Honor. And I didn't refuse to sign the form. I simply declined to endorse Mr. Quinlan's theory of how I should defend the case."

Gallagher smiled. "Nice to meet you, Ms. Winter. I'm sure I've seen you in the courthouse, but I don't believe I've had the pleasure of having you appear before me. Welcome."

Talon nodded. "Thank you, Your Honor."

Gallagher looked at the clock and sighed. Criminal practice was all about the volume—high volume. Charge 'em, plead 'em, try' em, next. "Would the attorneys like me to step off the bench for a few minutes so you can work out your differences?"

It would be a lot quicker for the judge if he could just sign off whatever the attorneys agreed on. In the meantime, he could be in chambers reading the briefs for his next hearing.

Talon was willing to give it a try, if only to please the judge, but Quinlan answered for them, "I don't believe that will be productive, Your Honor. Ms. Winter doesn't seem to appreciate the situation the defendant finds himself in."

Gallagher's eyebrows raised at the assertion. He looked back to the defense table. "Ms. Winter?"

Talon resisted the urge to verbally attack Quinlan—and the smaller, but extant, urge to attack him physically. "I fully appreciate the position Mr. Jameson is in. Certainly, I appreciate it more than Mr. Quinlan whose advice to me has been to do nothing more than protect my client's rights while he convicts him of murder and sends him off to prison. I'd be willing to save Your Honor some time, but I fear it will be fruitless to try to work with Mr. Quinlan."

Gallagher sighed and allowed an almost imperceptible nod. "All right then. Why don't we go through the form and see whether the case is ready to proceed to trial?"

Talon assented. "Yes, Your Honor. Thank you."

Quinlan just nodded.

"Mr. Quinlan," the judge started, "has the State provided the defense all of the discovery in the case?"

The answer to that should be easy: *Yes.* It should always be yes. The prosecution can't hold anything back. The defense gets to see everything, no interrogatories required.

"Yes, Your Honor," Quinlan confirmed.

"Has the State provided the defense with a list of its expected witnesses?"

Quinlan nodded. "Yes, Your Honor."

"Are there any outstanding forensic tests which will need to be disclosed before trial?"

Quinlan shook his head. "No, Your Honor."

Talon began to understand why Quinlan wanted to fill out her part of the omnibus order. It was boring to be a prosecutor. Turn everything over, do it on time, wait for the defense to pull a fast one.

"Will we need any interpreters?"

"No, Your Honor."

"Will we need a hearing regarding competency of child witnesses?"

"No, Your Honor."

"Any out-of-state witnesses with scheduling difficulties?"

"No, Your Honor."

Quinlan sounded like a glorified secretary. Or a waiter. *'Do you want fries with your indictment?'*

Gallagher turned his attention to Talon. This was where it would get interesting. And fun.

"Ms. Winter, has the defense finished its investigation of the case?"

The defense got to do its investigation in secret. If she found something that would be helpful in negotiating, she could tell Quinlan, but she could also wait until the last second and spring it on him. Or if the investigation turned up something seriously damaging to her client, not only could Talon keep it from the prosecutor, she was probably ethically obligated to do so. Quinlan represented the State, whatever that was. Talon represented Michael Jameson, the very real human being sitting next to her.

"No, Your Honor. We're still interviewing witnesses."

Quinlan shot a look at her, like a lover wounded by a secret. She ignored him.

"Will the interviews be complete before the scheduled trial date?" Gallagher followed up.

Talon considered for a moment. Not because she didn't immediately know the answer; she just wanted Gallagher to know her response was thoughtful. "Yes, Your Honor."

"Have you completed whatever forensic investigation you plan to do?"

Talon considered that as well. They hadn't planned on any forensic investigation. The crime was twenty-five years old. The crime scene was definitely corrupted since then. Still, when in doubt, reserve. "No, Your Honor. But any forensic investigation will also be complete before the trial."

"Your Honor," Quinlan rose to object. "I would just like to make a record that I haven't received any notice of expert witnesses from the defense."

Talon frowned. That was the one area where the defense had to give at least a little advance notice. If a defendant plans to call an expert, the prosecutor is entitled to the expert's resume and any reports he or she writes.

"We will provide those prior to trial," Talon responded, "if we decide to call any experts."

The answer was cool, but it raised a question in her mind as to whether she was missing something. Why would Quinlan get his panties in a bunch about that particular issue?

But Gallagher moved on. "Sounds good. Next is the nature of the defense." He looked down at Talon. "What is your client's defense?"

Up to that point, Gallagher had seemed impressed with her,

and decidedly not so with Quinlan. Reasonable in comparison to the whiny prosecutor. On-going interviews and secret forensics investigations. All very impressive. Surely, she had an equally impressive defense for her client, the unjustly charged Mr. Michael Jameson. There were so many.

Self-defense? Yes, he killed Jordy McCabe, but he was defending himself.

Alibi? He was at home watching movies with his elderly mother.

Entrapment? He did it, but only because the cops tricked him into it.

Duress? Kidnappers had his family and threatened to kill them all if he didn't take out McCabe.

…ugh. Talon sighed. She had nothing. Because Michael wouldn't give it to her.

"General denial, Your Honor," she admitted.

Gallagher's expression fell. "Oh," was all he said. It was all he needed to say.

After a moment, he looked up from the form he'd been filling out. "All right then. We'll confirm the case for trial in six weeks." Then he offered Talon a small frown. "Good luck, Ms. Winter."

She knew the unspoken part: *'You'll need it.'*

CHAPTER 16

Not long after the omnibus hearing, Talon was at her desk near quitting time. Quitting time for others, anyway. Not for a solo practitioner with a man's life in her hands. Trial was rapidly approaching and she still hadn't settled on a cohesive strategy. Self-defense was a tenable claim. Three armed gangsters were racing toward Michael and his brother. But the problem with self-defense was that you had to admit the underlying crime. It wasn't a defense of *'I didn't do it.'* It was, *'I did it, but it's okay. And I'd do it again.'* It was always a risky proposition to admit the crime. It spotted the prosecution nine points in a ten-point game. Plus, the jury was unlikely to be sympathetic about Michael and Ricky having to defend themselves against gangsters trying to steal the street drugs they were pushing on the Hilltop.

The more obvious defense was the one Michael had forbidden: just blame Ricky. Tell the jury Michael wasn't the shooter. Truthfully, it might not matter. The jury could still convict him as an accomplice. But there was a good chance the jury would give a pass to the younger brother who was just along for the ride.

Especially after twenty-five years.

Then again, they could . . .

"Hey, there. Don't work too late, huh?"

Talon looked up from her legal pad of half-doodled trial strategies. Greg Olsen was standing in her doorway, coat on and briefcase in hand.

"The work will still be there tomorrow, right?" he said with a friendly grin.

Talon had come to like Olsen during the short time she'd been office-sharing there. He was a conscientious office mate. He never left paper jams in the copier and he actually replaced the staples in the stapler when it went empty. On top of that, he struck the right balance between being politely social, greeting the others and confirming good weekends, and respectful of privacy—they weren't best friends after all. And they all had more than enough work to do.

All except Talon and her one case.

And even about that, Olsen was kind. He didn't tease her about staying late with only one case. Instead, he offered the advice of an older attorney not to let her work overwhelm her life, an all too common fate for a lawyer.

But she was the younger attorney, so of course she rejected the advice.

"Thanks, Greg, but I'm going to be working a lot of late nights now. Trial on that murder case is coming up. I need to be ready." She thought for a moment. "More ready than I've ever been for any trial."

Olsen nodded. "Yeah, I had a few cases like that over the years. I still remember them all. They're like milestones on my journey as a lawyer." He tipped his head toward the file on her desk. "That case may be the biggest milestone you ever have on your own road."

Talon wasn't much for poetic metaphors, but she appreciated the effort. "Right. Well, if I'm going to have a big fat milestone on my road, I'd like it to mark a win."

Olsen laughed. "Good thinking." He looked over at the clock on her wall. "So what's keeping you past five o'clock this evening?"

Talon shrugged. "I'm just trying to figure out the best way to approach the case. In law school, they called it the 'case theory.' The story you tell the jury."

"Do you have one yet?" Olsen asked. "A case theory?"

Talon frowned. "I've got too many. I'm trying to pick one, but none of them seem right."

Olsen thought for a moment, then set his briefcase down in her doorway and took a seat in her office. "I've got a little extra time tonight. Linda's picking up the kids from the Y. Why don't you run your case theories past me?"

Talon was a bit surprised. "Really?" One of the things she'd started to miss about working at a larger firm was the ability to just walk down the hall and get some advice from another attorney. Office-sharing was different. In the corporate firm, most of the attorneys spent their nine-to-fives at their desks; court was rare. But solo attorneys usually did criminal defense, bankruptcy, divorces, or some combination of those—all court-driven practices. She'd go days without even seeing Olsen. And Curt was fine for some aspects of the case, but he wasn't an attorney. "Uh, yeah. That'd be great. Thanks."

She gathered her thoughts for moment and looked down at her legal pad. "Well, I figure there are two main ways to approach it. The first is self-defense…"

So Talon explained her options, and her own opinions as to

each. She told him what Jameson had told her about the incident—the attorney-client privilege would extend to any lawyer she consulted—and how Jameson instructed her not to pursue any angle that implicated his brother. She was a bit embarrassed about that part, but she hoped Olsen could appreciate her respect for her client's wishes, even if they were misguided. She ran through how much easier it might be to go self-defense, but how she was unsure how to do it if she didn't put Jameson on the stand. And if she did, how was he going to tell the story without mentioning Ricky? She also couldn't put him on the stand for an alibi defense, because that would be suborning perjury. She couldn't knowingly have him tell a story about spending the night at Aunt Louise's beach house in Oregon when he'd already told her he was on the Hilltop running drugs with his big brother.

"So yeah," she concluded, "I don't know what to do. How do I tell a story to the jury when I know the story is a lie?"

Olsen chewed his cheek a little and nodded at her question. Then he asked a better one, "Why are you telling a story at all?"

Talon frowned. "Well, uh." She was surprised by the question. "I mean, like I said, I'm trying to come up with my case theory. My story."

Olsen thought for another moment. "This is your first criminal case, right?"

Talon inferred a little condescension in the question. She was glad she could answer, "No, actually. I defended a man against a murder charge when I was still with Gardelli, High and Steinmetz. *Pro bono*," she clarified. "He was a tribal member and, well, it's a long story."

"Was that an alibi defense?" Olsen asked.

"Uh no," Talon replied. "He kind of confessed to it."

"So you had to build a story around his confession?"

"Right."

"Did Jameson confess too?" Olsen inquired.

"No," Talon answered.

"Then why are you telling any story at all?" Olsen challenged. "Make the prosecutor try to tell the story, then rip the story down."

But Talon shook her head. "General denial? I don't know. Isn't that really just saying, 'Oh yeah? Prove it.'?"

Olsen shrugged and smiled. "Maybe. But that's not always a bad thing. Especially when they *can't* prove it."

Talon considered that for a moment.

"This is a cold case, right?" Olsen confirmed. "They might not even be able to prove a murder happened. Most of the cops are probably retired. Hell, some of them are probably dead. The ones who are left won't remember this case. Just another shooting up on the Hilltop. If they can't remember what they did, they can't testify about it. The prosecutor might not even be able to show anything happened at all, so don't get up in your opening statement and admit everything they can't prove."

But Talon wasn't convinced. "They wrote police reports, Greg. They can just use those to testify."

Olsen shook his head. "Maybe, maybe not. They can use them to refresh their recollection, but if they have no recollection to refresh, they can't just read from them. That's hearsay."

"And there's a hearsay exception," Talon countered. "Past recollection recorded. If a witness can't remember something they used to remember, and they wrote it down, they can read the report to the jury."

Olsen laughed a bit. "Sure, in a civil case, like what you're used to. But in a criminal case? No way. Some evidence rule can't trump the Constitution. Your client has a right to confront the witnesses against him—something your civil clients never had. How does he do that if the witnesses just read from their reports? Confrontation is grounded in the concept of effective cross-examination. You can't cross them if they just read from their reports for the prosecutor, and then answer, 'I don't remember, I don't remember,' to every question you ask."

Talon's instinct was to argue back. She was a lawyer after all. But she liked what Olsen was saying. "Go on."

"You're used to your client telling you what happened, then the other side finding it out through discovery. Interrogatories and depositions and stuff like that."

Talon winced at the thought of her own interrogatories, still setting on top of her file cabinet, untouched. Luckily, Olsen continued.

"But you're a criminal defense attorney now. The other side doesn't get to know anything about what your client said. If he didn't tell it to the cops when they arrested him, then they can't make him say it now. It's all on them. They have to prove it. And you don't have to let them.

"Object to the police reports. Object to the autopsy report. Hell, object to the calendar from twenty-five years ago without a witness from the calendar publishing company. Make them prove it all up, because they're going to have a lot of difficulty with that. You may never have to tell the jury any case theory story if they can't establish in the first place that a murder actually occurred. Don't spot them that. Make them prove it, because maybe they can't."

Talon was nodding by the end. She liked that approach. Maybe part of the reason she was having trouble settling on a case theory was because she shouldn't settle on one at all. Not until the prosecution put on whatever evidence they could actually muster a quarter-century later.

But Olsen had one more question. "If your guy didn't confess, how did they link him to it?"

Talon ran a hand through her hair. "That's the worst part. It was a total fluke. My guy's house was burglarized. One of the things the burglars stole was a gun. It didn't take the cops long to find the burglars and recover the stolen goods, including the gun. It's extra time if you steal a gun, but only if it's operable, so the cops test-fired it. When they uploaded the ballistics to IBIS, it came back as a match to the murder."

Olsen blinked a couple of times, then smiled. "That's ridiculous. The thinnest of connections."

Talon shrugged. "Yeah, but it's true."

But Olsen shook his head. "Irrelevant. That's the weakest link in a chain of weak links. Attack that ballistics match as hard as you can. Who's your ballistics expert?"

Talon thought for a moment. "It's some guy from the State Patrol Crime Lab. Langston or Lindstrom or something."

"No, no." Olsen shook his head. "That's *their* expert. Who's *your* expert? Who's the defense expert?"

Talon took a beat. "We don't have one."

"Get one," Olsen replied. He stood up. "I know someone."

A few moments later, he'd gone to his office and returned with a business card. He handed it to Talon.

She examined it, then looked up at Olsen. "Anastasia St. Julian?" she read the name aloud. "Really? Sounds like a comic book villain."

Olsen laughed. "Yeah, I guess it kind of does. Well, she goes by 'Ann.' And she looks more grandma than villain. But juries love the name. And they love her."

CHAPTER 17

"Anastasia St. Julian?" Curt asked after examining the business card Talon handed him. He was in the passenger seat of her Accord. They were cruising southbound on Interstate 5, toward Long Beach. Long Beach, Washington.

"She goes by Ann," Talon replied. "I'm told the jurors like the full name. Sounds sophisticated."

Curt shook his head. "I think it sounds ridiculous." But he shrugged and slid the business card into a shelf under the radio, between Talon's gum and extra phone charging cable. "But if Greg says she's good, I trust Greg."

He looked out the window at the lush rolling nothingness between the small towns that dotted State Route 101. "God, it takes forever to get to Long Beach."

Talon nodded. "Why couldn't Greg have recommended an expert from Tacoma?"

"Or at least Seattle," Curt suggested. It felt like he was about to say something more. But he didn't.

Talon sighed to herself. It was going to be a very long drive.

She was glad they were driving together this time. She wanted to talk to him. It didn't really matter about what. Anything. But words failed her. Her, the trial lawyer.

Ironic, she thought. Then she thought harder. *Or is it just coincidental?*

She shook her thoughts from that particular semantic puzzle and glanced over at Curt. He was still gazing out the window. He had a really nice profile.

But she wasn't about to tell him that. Instead, she looked out the windshield at the empty road ahead of them.

Symbolic, she told herself. Then she frowned. *Or is it metaphorical?*

Talon sighed again, audibly this time. But Curt didn't turn to look at her. She was relieved. It wasn't like she could tell him what she was actually thinking.

Yeah. It takes forever to get to Long Beach.

* * *

'Long Beach Welcomes You,' announced the sign as they finally entered the small town tucked away in the southwest corner of the state. Then a quick glance toward the ocean revealed the one landmark the town had: a large arch over the roadway that led onto the beach, adorned with the phrase, 'World's Longest Beach.'

"Hence the name," Talon muttered to herself.

"Hm? What's that?" Curt stirred from the passenger seat. He'd fallen asleep about a hundred miles earlier. The slower speed as they re-entered civilization must have brought him closer to the surface. He sat up in his seat and rubbed his eyes with his fists like a little boy. "Are we here?"

"Yup," Talon answered. "Beautiful Long Beach, Washington. Home of, uh…" She paused, unsure what Long Beach really had to offer, besides a long beach.

"Anastasia St. Julian," Curt supplied the answer. The one that mattered, anyway.

Talon nodded. "Good enough." She glanced at the GPS on her phone. "Her address is up ahead another couple of miles."

Long Beach had a main road that ran parallel to the beach. The downtown lasted about four blocks, with one traffic light. After that, it was a residential strip of old houses and new condos.

St. Julian's address was a large lot with a classic northwestern Craftsman-style house set back from the road and a large outbuilding—more shop than barn—behind the house. That's where the driveway led and that's where they found St. Julian, clearly visible inside as they parked in the gravel driveway. She didn't turn to look at them as they crunched to a halt.

Talon stepped out of the car. "Ms. St. Julian?" she called out. "I'm Talon Winter. This is my investigator Curt Fairchild."

St. Julian took another moment to finish whatever task had been holding her attention as they drove up, then she set something down on her workbench and turned around. She was a tall woman, with a thin frame wrapped in a flannel shirt and worn jeans. She had a head of thick gray hair pulled into a loose ponytail. Sharp eyes peered out through round, wire-rimmed glasses. She dusted her hands off on each other, then stepped forward to greet her guests.

"Call me Ann," she said as she extended her hand. "You're early. I like that."

Talon shook her hand. "It's always a quick drive to Long Beach."

Ann narrowed her eyes and smiled. "That," she pointed at Talon, "is a lie. So, I already know you're a good attorney. Come on, let's go inside and talk over coffee."

Ann didn't wait for a reply, but headed toward the house.

Talon wondered whether she should be offended by the lawyer comment, but there was something disarming about the woman they'd just met. She looked like that farmer grandma everyone on TV has, who knows all the answers but still somehow manages to let the kids figure it out on their own.

They entered the home through the back door, directly into the kitchen. A fresh pot of coffee was already brewed. Ann gestured toward a wooden breakfast table with three cups and saucers laid out and brought the coffee over on a tray, complete with cream and sugar.

"So, Greg says you need a ballistics expert for your case," Ann started. "Tell me about it."

"Well," Talon started, "the gun was linked to the crime from bullets left behind at the scene. What we're thinking is—"

"No," Ann interrupted. "Not the ballistics. The case. I'll figure out the ballistics. I want to hear about the case. Did he do it?"

"Uh, well," Talon started. "Does that matter?"

"It may not matter to you," Ann replied, "but it matters to me."

"Because you're an ex-cop?" Curt ventured.

"Yes," Ann answered. "But not in the way you're thinking."

"Look," Talon set down her coffee cup and leaned forward. "This is a really complicated case from a really long time ago. It's a cold case. If it hadn't been for this ballistics match, no one would ever have been arrested. Not my guy, not anyone. I have a job to do, which is to defend Michael Jameson to the best of my ability. Part of that is hiring the best experts available, and from what I hear, you're the best ballistics expert available. We need you. My client needs you. That's enough. It has to be."

Ann pursed her lips and considered. She nodded slightly to herself. She took another sip of her coffee. Then she set down her cup and leaned forward too. "But did he do it?"

Curt let out an exasperated sigh. "So this whole trip was a waste? We drive all the way down to Long Beach just to get some crappy coffee and the brush-off?"

Ann frowned into her mug. "This is excellent coffee," she assured.

"The coffee is fine," Talon interjected. "It's not about the coffee. It's just that Greg Olsen said you were a defense expert. I don't understand how you can be a defense expert if you won't help a defendant who might be guilty."

Ann leaned back in her chair again and crossed her arms. Her mouth hardened into a thin line and she appraised her guests. "I'm not a defense expert. I'm not a prosecution expert. I'm a ballistics expert. I spent twenty-five years with the State Patrol. I started out as a line trooper, driving patrol and hooking up drunk drivers. I worked my way up and over, always curious, always ready to try something new. By the time I retired, I was an expert on a lot of things. How to be a good cop, for one thing. And guns for another. If there's a problem with how they connected the bullets to your client's gun, I'll see it. And I can explain it to the jury in a way that they'll understand—and believe."

Talon ran her hands through her hair. "Perfect. That's exactly what we need. So why won't you do it?"

"Because she's a cop," Curt interrupted. "She doesn't want to help out some Black guy who may have made a mistake twenty-five years ago."

"Whoa there, young man." Ann raised a finger at Curt. "Don't bring race into this. Race has nothing to do with it."

"Actually, I think you may be wrong about that," Talon said. "I don't know if the prosecutor would go after this case as hard if it were some White guy in the suburbs who happens to have a gun in his attic that can be linked to an unsolved homicide from a quarter-century ago."

Ann raised an eyebrow. "Is that what you're going to tell the jury?"

Talon shrugged. "I don't know. I might have to if you won't help us out."

Ann steepled her fingers and tapped them together in thought. After a moment, she spoke again. "The reason I want to know if he did it isn't because I'm a cop. It's because I'm an *ex*-cop. As in retired. It's a long drive to Tacoma. The cost of living is pretty cheap down here. I can afford to be selective about which cases I take. And if I'm going to be selective, I don't want to waste time on some case where the State has a dozen eye-witnesses and a confession. Some defense attorneys think they have to call witnesses just to do *something* in their case-in-chief. But I'm not a prop. I take my reputation seriously."

Talon nodded, forcing herself to calm down. "Okay. Well, I can understand that."

"But let me say something else," Ann went on. "You're supposed to be this man's lawyer. It's your job to think clearly and plead his case. Why won't you just answer my question? Did he do it or not? You've attacked my motives and my integrity, but you won't answer that simple question. Why not?"

Talon looked over to Curt who returned her gaze. Then she turned back to Ann and shrugged. "Because we don't know if he did it. He won't tell us."

Ann took a moment. "I like this Mr. Jameson," she said with a grin. "It makes your job harder, though, I imagine."

"Oh, yeah," Curt answered.

"Or maybe not," Ann considered. "It might be easier if you don't know. No ethical qualms, that way, I suppose."

"I'll never have ethical qualms about representing my client to the best of my ability, Ms. St. Julian," Talon replied.

Ann nodded. "Good for you."

"But you're part of that," Talon went on. "The only thing the prosecutor has connecting Michael to the murder is those bullets. I need to attack that connection."

"And what if I determine the prosecution is right and the bullets came from your client's gun?"

"Then we won't call you as a witness," Curt answered.

But Talon shook her finger at him. "No. We'll still call you. We'll have you tell the jury the truth, whatever that ends up being. Because whatever you find out, you can tell the jury one thing for certain: ballistics can tell you which gun fired a bullet, but it can't tell you which person fired the gun."

Ann nodded. "That's true enough. But you don't need an expert to say that. You can just argue that in your closing argument."

"I know." Talon smiled. "And I will. But just think how much more impressive it will sound coming from Anastasia St. Julian."

CHAPTER 18

"Quinlan will never agree to release the ballistics to St. Julian," Curt complained as they drove north on Route 101. He was behind the wheel for the return trip.

"Don't be such a buzz-kill," Talon scolded from the passenger seat. "The illustrious Anastasia St. Julian has agreed to champion our cause. We should celebrate."

She chuckled at her own words. "Besides, I don't think he has any choice. The defense expert should be able to examine the physical evidence. He may be a dick about it..." She paused for a moment. "Okay, he *will* be a dick about it, but it's not his call. If he won't agree to it, I'll take it to a judge."

Curt nodded and drove on for a few moments. "*Our* cause," he repeated. "I like that."

Talon's immediate thought was to justify her use of that word in some professional, not personal, way. She was the lawyer and he was the investigator. They were part of the same team. Just like St. Julian. That's all.

Instead, she just smiled and looked out the window.

* * *

As the towns starting getting closer together and they could pick up the Seattle radio stations again, Curt returned to the subject of their partnership.

"So I was thinking," he started carefully, "as part of our team, of course."

"Of course," Talon validated with a light grin.

"As part of our team," Curt repeated, "I was thinking maybe we could stop by Shelton and talk to Oliphant."

Talon's smile dried up.

"I mean, it's on the way." Curt pointed vaguely at the road ahead. "And we agreed we should have asked Daggett about the gun. I think it just makes sense." He looked over at her with a grin of his own. "You know, as part of our team."

Talon sighed. "Look, Curt, I understand what you're saying. And it does make sense. It's just that…" But she trailed off. "I'd just rather not do that right now. I'm—I'm not really prepared for it. I should review the reports again. Really know what evidence the State has, you know? Figure out my questions in advance. All that stuff."

Curt nodded, keeping his gaze squarely on the interstate disappearing beneath the car. He didn't argue. He thought. For several moments. After an uncomfortably long time, he finally nodded again and said, "Okay, I'll do it. Alone. You can wait at a coffee shop or something. There's got to be a crappy little coffee shop somewhere near the prison."

"Uh, no. No, that's all right," Talon protested. "Really. I'll do it. It's just—I'm just not ready right now."

When Curt didn't respond, Talon insisted, "I *will* do it, Curt. We have time. Let's focus on getting the ballistic evidence to St. Julian first. Then we can circle back to Oliphant. I mean, what if St. Julian helps us get the gun evidence suppressed altogether? We won't need to ask Oliphant about the gun."

Curt thought for a moment. "You know St. Julian can't get the guns suppressed. The best we can do is have her testify the crime lab was wrong when they linked the gun to the murder. But they still made the link. As long as the prosecutor puts the crime lab guy on the stand, the gun is coming in. And anyway, guns or not, we need to talk to Oliphant. He's a witness to the crime. What if he can positively I.D. Ricky as the shooter?"

"Michael told us not to involve his brother," Talon reminded him.

"Well, I don't know about that," Curt replied, with a quick grin at her. "I recall him telling us to not *talk* to his brother. But if someone else wants to throw Ricky under the bus, we can't help that, can we?"

Talon didn't immediately respond, as she considered Curt's assertion and whether it was correct. Before she could decide, Curt went on.

"The way I see it," he said, "you have two choices. One, you can grab a cup of coffee and let me do my job. Or two, you can tell me what's really going on."

Talon crossed her arms and thought for several long moments. Finally, she uncrossed them and looked out the window again. "Fine. I could go for a mocha right about now anyway."

* * *

Curt was right. There was indeed a dumpy little coffee shop near the prison. It was called 'Grounds Zero' and featured plastic chairs and mismatched tables. But they had an espresso machine. Talon sat down at a table near the window and watched as Curt pulled out of the parking lot and headed toward the Washington Correctional Facility down the road.

She'd brought her iPad so she decided to busy herself re-

reading the police reports. Maybe she could find some weaknesses in the State's case that she'd previously overlooked. It seemed unlikely, but she had to do something. She was going to be at Grounds Zero for a few hours.

* * *

One of the problems with the Internet was that it was home to both her legal research website and every news-compiling website in the world—a siren song of distraction. And three hours was a long time to spend reading police reports, especially ones she'd already read. By the time Curt returned, she was a dozen paragraphs deep into a British article about the latest crisis in the Middle East.

Talon looked up as the bells tied to the back of the front door jingled and Curt walked in, a smile on his face and a spring in his step.

"What's a dame like you doing in a place like this?" he joked as he pulled out the chair across from her.

Talon just smiled, not sure how to respond to the anachronistic cliché. She settled on, "Dame?"

Curt laughed, then he stopped himself from sitting down. "Hold on. Let me order a coffee."

He headed back to the register and Talon switched her browser from Distraction.com to Diligently-Working-Thank-You-Very-Much.org. She could finish the article later.

Curt came back and sat down, swinging his leg over the chair to do so. A pleasant action to watch, Talon had to admit to herself.

"It went well, I take it?" Talon asked.

Curt combined a slight nod with a small shrug. "Maybe."

He was adorable when he was happy. She liked seeing him happy. But she stuck to business. "What did he say?"

"Hm, let me see…" Curt frowned in concentration and counted off on his fingers. "He said, 'Fuck you.' And, 'Fuck off.' And my personal favorite, 'Go fuck yourself.' I believe he said that one several times."

"Oh," Talon replied, a bit surprised. "So nothing, huh?"

But Curt flashed a smile. "Oh, ye of little faith. I can be quite charming when I want to."

Talon knew that was true.

"Oh, sure, it took a while," Curt went on. "But I managed to warm him up."

"How'd you do that?"

"Mostly we talked about how much cops suck and how 'The Man' is out to get people," Curt answered.

"I take it you didn't mention your stint as a police cadet?" Talon inquired.

"Strangely, that didn't come up," Curt admitted. "No need to complicate matters. It's pretty simple. When The Man puts you away for ten years for drug delivery, you're not too keen on helping The Man do it to somebody else."

"That makes sense," Talon said. "But did you really say 'The Man'? Didn't people stop saying that in the seventies? Like calling cops 'the Fuzz'?"

Curt laughed. "Well, he's in the big house for moving blow, so—"

"Okay, stop," Talon laughed. "Let's use words from this decade. What did he say?"

Curt laughed too. "Fine. He said he hates the fucking cops and doesn't want to help put anybody else in prison, even someone who killed his buddy twenty-five years ago."

"Well, that's good," Talon supposed. "But it's not like he can refuse to testify if the prosecution transports him for the trial."

"Well, he could," Curt disagreed. "The only thing the court could do is hold him in contempt and put him in jail until he agrees to testify. But he's already serving a sentence that's a lot longer than the trial would last. So, really, he could tell the judge to go fuck himself and they couldn't do anything about it."

"Is that what he's going to do?" Talon didn't try to hide her excitement at the prospect. If one of the victims refused to testify, that could really damage the State's case.

"Well, see, that's a little touchy," Curt replied. "I didn't want to encourage that. I don't need to get charged with witness tampering. It might damage my dream of being a private investigator."

"Good point," Talon agreed. "Smart."

"But I didn't tell him not to do it either," Curt assured her. "I told him it was his choice whether he wanted to cooperate with the big bad government. Then I assured him I didn't work for the government and anything he told me wouldn't get back to them."

"Did that do the trick?"

Curt nodded. "Yep. He seemed to like the idea of sticking it to The M— I mean, the government."

"Great," Talon replied. "So what did he say? Does it help us?"

"Oh no," Curt waved away the suggestion. "It's terrible. Totally hurts us. Absolutely horrible."

Talon's shoulders dropped. "Shit."

"Yeah, well, let's hope he doesn't testify," Curt said.

"So what did he say?" Talon pressed. "What was so horrible?"

Curt leaned forward and put his hands together. "Let's see... Two guys. Both young Black males. Both got out of the car. He recognized them from the neighborhood, but didn't know their names. He knew they were brothers though. It was supposed to be a drug deal, but they were gonna rob them. McCabe had a gun tucked in the back of his waistband, but he never got a chance to pull it out. The brothers could tell something was wrong. The younger one panicked, pulled out a gun, and just opened fire. Oliphant dove behind some bushes. When the shooting stopped he looked up. McCabe was on the ground, bleeding out, and the two brothers were jumping into their car and peeling away."

Talon took a moment to let it all sink in. Finally, she exhaled, "Fuck."

Curt nodded. "Exactly."

"That's about the worst possible description of events we could have gotten," Talon opined.

"Actually, it gets worse," Curt responded. "One more thing."

"What?" Talon asked. "What could possibly be worse?"

Curt grimaced. "Oliphant heard the shooter yell, 'Get in the car, Ricky!'"

Talon dropped her head into her hands. "Double fuck," she said through her fingers.

"Agreed," Curt replied.

After a few moments, Talon raised her head again and ran her hands through her hair. "Well, I guess it's better if we know this going in. Thanks for talking with him."

"Sure," Curt replied. "Thanks for trusting me to do it."

"Of course I trust you," Talon replied. "We're a team."

Curt smiled, but weakly. "You're still not going to tell me why you didn't want to go with me, are you?"

Talon smiled back, but cryptically. "I don't trust you that much."

CHAPTER 19

Talon was four pages into her Motion to Compel Production of Ballistics Evidence to Defense Expert when her phone rang. She clicked the 'save' icon on her computer and picked up the phone.

"Hello. Law Office of Talon Winter."

"Please hold for Samuel Sullivan," replied the woman on the other end.

Talon rolled her eyes. Who calls someone without actually being on the line when they answer? An arrogant, high-priced attorney, she supposed. But he was *her* arrogant, high-priced attorney, so maybe it was for the best.

"Talon?" came Sullivan's voice after a few moments.

"Hey, Stan. Thanks for calling. Has there been a development?"

She hoped maybe the other side had blinked and made a counter-offer. She was surprisingly ready to be done with the case. When they'd fired her, she'd been livid and wanted blood. Now she just wanted her rent paid and time to focus on defending an innocent man against murder charges. A probably innocent man.

Maybe.

"Have you read the motion to compel yet?" Sullivan asked.

Talon hesitated. She looked at her computer screen. "I haven't even finished writing it yet."

"What?" Sullivan responded. "No, not whatever you're working on for your little criminal case. The motion to compel filed by Gardelli High. We didn't answer their interrogatories on time. *You* didn't answer their interrogatories on time."

"Shit," Talon responded. "I'm sorry, Stan. I've just been so focused on this case." She almost said 'this little case' but stopped herself. "I forgot all about those."

She could almost hear Sullivan frown on the other end. "Sounds like you let yourself get distracted."

Talon was glad he couldn't see her shrug. "No, I know they're important. It's just—I had to go to Spokane. Then Long Beach. Now I have this motion to write. It's a lot, and I don't have three legal assistants and a paralegal to do all my work for me."

There was silence for a moment. Talon had been referring to her days at Gardelli High, but she realized Sullivan might have thought she was talking about him. *Please hold for Mr. Sullivan.*

"I just mean," she tried to clarify, "I'm used to having a lot of support staff. Now I have a receptionist to take messages and an investigator who I'm not even sure how I'm going to pay."

"Well, you're not going to pay him from this lawsuit," Sullivan scolded. "Not the way you're acting right now. I'm going to have to file a response. They want the judge to dismiss the case, of course. They're characterizing your failure to respond to their interrogatories as a failure to prosecute the case. I can file a response and probably get a short extension, but not more than a few days, maybe a week. You need to get those answers to me as soon as possible."

Talon sighed to herself. She looked at the motion flickering on her computer monitor. She needed to get the ballistics to St. Julian as soon as possible. "When do you need them by?"

"I needed them by last Friday," Sullivan replied testily.

"Right," Talon acknowledged. "But what's the latest I can get them to you?"

Sullivan sighed. He made no effort to conceal the sound. "I wish you'd told me the soonest you can get them to me, instead of asking me the latest you can. You're already past the deadline. I'm going to have to charge you for this extra work. You're not just wasting my time and the court's, you're wasting your own money."

Talon ran her fingers through her hair. She didn't need more bills. "Okay. I'll get them done right away." She looked again at her motion and considered the calendar. "Can I get them to you Monday? There's a lot of them. It's going to take me time to respond."

"Which is why you should have done them right away," Sullivan reproached, "instead of driving all over the state for some client who can't pay your investigator."

Talon didn't have a response ready for that.

That turned out to be okay because Sullivan kept talking. "I need everything by nine a.m. Monday morning. Everything. All of your responses, plus all of the documents they demanded. Your tax returns, your pay stubs, everything. Unless you've been keeping flawless records for the last ten years, that's going to take some time to gather together. You need to get started immediately."

Talon nodded again. "Right. Immediately. Got it."

Sullivan sighed again. "I hope so, Talon. These people did you wrong. You need to hold them responsible."

"I know," Talon answered. "You're right. Thanks. I'm sorry about this."

Sullivan's voice softened slightly. "Don't be sorry, Talon. Be diligent. Get me those answers by Monday. Sooner, if possible."

"Right," Talon replied. "Will do."

"Immediately," Sullivan reiterated. "Get started immediately. That's the only way you'll get them done in time."

"Yes. Absolutely. Immediately. Understood."

Sullivan acknowledged the promise, then bid his farewell. Talon half-expected his secretary to get back on the line and announce, 'Mr. Sullivan has hung up the phone.'

Talon hung up and looked over at the large envelope from Sullivan's office that had been sitting in the corner of her office since the interrogatories arrived weeks earlier. Then she looked back at her computer screen and page four of her argument about why the prosecution should be forced to surrender the firearm and bullets out from their secure property room and hand them over to a defense ballistics expert three counties away. At first blush, prudence said they shouldn't have to. But upon closer inspection, justice said they must.

She squared her shoulders to the monitor on her desk and pushed the envelope in the corner out of her mind.

'*Furthermore*,' she typed, '*Mr. Jameson's constitutional right to confront the witnesses and evidence against him mandates the release of this evidence to ....*'

CHAPTER 20

Talon arrived in Judge Kirchner's courtroom ten minutes before the hearing on her motion to compel the State to turn over the ballistics evidence to her expert. Enough time to set up her books and briefs and legal pad. Not too much time to sit there just getting nervous.

She hadn't appeared before Judge Kirchner before. Kristina Kirchner had been a family law commissioner before being appointed a judge by the Governor the previous fall. Talon had done lots of different kinds of cases, but never family law. It was the one area even more depressing than criminal. She sued and defended people over money. Family law courts terminated parents' rights for severe abuse and neglect. Talon could live a happy and full life without ever seeing children treated so badly by their parents that the law stepped in to permanently terminate the parent-child relationship.

As a result, Talon would have to go on reputation alone. And Judge Kirchner's reputation was no-nonsense, uber-professional, and the smartest one in the room. Talon liked her already.

Michael Jameson had been waiting in the hallway when Talon arrived. It was just a procedural motion, but a defendant has a right to be present at 'every critical stage' of the proceedings. If Michael hadn't made bail, the jail would have transported him in jail clothes, and he would have sat next to his lawyer, with one hand chained to his waist, the other free to take notes, and two armed guards within lunging distance. As it was, he was dressed in a dark suit and gold tie and took a seat silently at the defendant's table. He was a quiet man anyway, and knew enough to be even quieter as his champion prepared for battle.

As Talon finished organizing her materials on the defense table, the door to the courtroom opened and in walked Quinlan—along with another attorney Talon hadn't met before. A young woman, dressed in a sharply tailored dark suit and heels almost, but not quite, too high for court. She was African-American, with sharp eyes and soft curls.

"Ms. Winter," Quinlan said as they approached the prosecution table. "Allow me to introduce my co-counsel, Amity McDaniels."

Talon made sure not to let her expression betray her thoughts. And her thought was, *Damn it.* Just looking at her, Talon could tell that Amity McDaniels was smarter than Quinlan. The fact that the prosecutor's office had put her on the case meant she was an up-and-coming attorney, ready to get experience on a murder case. And Talon was cynical enough to realize Amity's race probably hadn't been overlooked in that assignment either. Jurors were real people, with real prejudices, good and bad. To the extent that Talon might be helped by a latent suspicion that the criminal justice system was slanted against African-Americans, Amity's presence at the prosecution table would work to assuage that. So yeah, *Damn it.*

"Nice to meet you," Talon said, extending a hand.

"You too," Amity replied. She had a pleasantly deep voice

for a woman. Not unnaturally so, just strong. Confident. *Double damn it.*

The ten minutes were up. Judge Kirchner's bailiff entered the courtroom from the hallway to the judge's chambers and announced, "All rise! The Pierce County Superior Court is now in session, the Honorable Kristina Kirchner presiding."

Judge Kirchner then entered the courtroom from the same hallway and climbed the steps to the bench. "Please be seated," she instructed as she, too, sat down. Her blond hair was pulled back in a tight bun, which accentuated her angular jaw and small glasses. No makeup, no jewelry, no nonsense.

"Are the parties ready in the matter of The State of Washington versus Michael Jameson?" she started the proceedings.

"Yes, Your Honor," Quinlan replied. "Eric Quinlan and Amity McDaniels on behalf of the State."

Judge Kirchner nodded down at the prosecution table. "Nice to see you again, Ms. McDaniels."

Triple damn it, Talon thought. One of the many advantages prosecutors had over defense attorneys—apart from practically unlimited resources, detectives to do all their follow-up investigation, and a general perception in the community as being the good guys—was the fact that they were constantly in court. While the responsibility of defending criminal defendants was spread out among the county's public defenders, local private attorneys, and even attorneys from Seattle and Olympia and elsewhere, every single criminal case in the county was prosecuted by the Pierce County Prosecutor's Office. As a result, the few dozen prosecutors who handled the felony cases were constantly in court, scheduling hearings, arguing motions, and getting to know—and be known by—the judges.

Judge Kirchner turned her gaze to the other side of the

courtroom. "Is the defense ready?"

Talon stood to address the judge. "Yes, Your Honor. Talon Winter on behalf of Michael Jameson, who is seated to my left. We are ready to proceed."

First impressions. So important. So impossible to gauge. As Talon retook her seat and Judge Kirchner glanced down at the papers before her, Talon hoped her legal brief had impressed Kirchner. Tailored suit and confident demeanor would only carry her so far.

"This is your motion, Ms. Winter." Kirchner looked up again. "Whenever you're ready."

'Whenever you're ready' was judge-talk for 'Go.' Talon stood up again and began her argument.

"Thank you, Your Honor. May it please the Court, the defense is asking the Court to compel the prosecution to release certain evidence for examination by an independent expert retained by the defense—"

"Ballistics evidence, correct?" Judge Kirchner interrupted.

"Uh, yes, Your Honor," Talon confirmed. "Specifically, a firearm allegedly obtained from my client's residence, and fired bullets collected from the scene twenty-five years ago."

"That's what connects your client to the crime, correct?" Kirchner followed up.

"Allegedly," Talon replied.

Kirchner raised an incredulous eyebrow, but at least she didn't roll her eyes.

"So if that evidence goes missing," Kirchner said, "the State's case would fall apart."

Out of the corner of her eye, Talon could see Quinlan nodding like a bobble-head doll. McDaniels was just sitting there attentively.

"We would stipulate to chain of custody, Your Honor," Talon answered. "The State has already examined the evidence and their expert has generated a report. That report predates this motion, so even if the evidence were lost—which, I assure you, it won't be—the State could still proceed with their report."

"And you have been provided those reports, I assume?" Kirchner asked.

"Yes, Your Honor."

"So why do you need this extra examination?" the judge inquired. "Why not just rely on the State's reports? Are you challenging the qualifications of the State's expert?"

Talon suppressed a wince. It wasn't going well. Kirchner didn't seem to appreciate the defense position, or the rights afforded a criminal defendant facing deprivation of liberty at the hands of the government. That was one of the dangers of appearing before a judge who'd spent most of her career doing something other than criminal work. But then, Talon supposed, she was new to all this too.

"No, Your Honor. We're not challenging the State's expert's qualifications. But neither are we required to accept his findings. A criminal defendant shouldn't have to rely on the opinion of someone who works for the Washington State Patrol Crime Lab. Mr. Jameson is entitled to an independent review of the evidence by someone who has an interest in challenging the State's theory of the case."

Kirchner frowned, but nodded down to her. "Continue."

"Thank you, Your Honor." Talon had to take a moment to recall where she was in her argument. Then she remembered she hadn't even started. "Criminal Rule 4.7 addresses the examination of evidence by experts—"

"I'm sorry. Ms. Winter," Judge Kirchner interrupted again.

"But I can't get past the problem of what happens if this evidence goes missing while out of police custody. You said you received the reports from the crime lab?"

"Yes, Your Honor," Talon answered. As much as she wanted to continue with her argument, she knew to answer a judge's questions promptly and directly.

"All of them?" Kirchner pressed.

"Yes, Your Honor."

"So why can't your expert just review the reports?" Kirchner asked. "If there are problems with the methodology, your expert can testify to that."

Talon took a moment before responding. Just because she knew she had to respond to the judge's questions didn't make the constant interruptions any less irritating. "Perhaps, Your Honor. But it may be impossible to see any errors in methodology if the items themselves aren't examined. It may be that the State's expert completely overlooked some important aspect of this evidence. If so, it wouldn't be in the reports and my expert wouldn't know about it precisely because the State's expert overlooked it."

Kirchner frowned, but didn't immediately reply.

"It's not a question of quality review," Talon went on. "It's about an independent examination, top to bottom, to draw independent conclusions. Those conclusions may confirm the State's expert's opinion, or they may challenge it, or they may completely contradict it. But Mr. Jameson has a constitutional right to present the best defense possible, and that requires that he be allowed to perform an independent examination of the evidence against him."

"I'm not so sure of that, Ms. Winter," Judge Kirchner returned. "We don't just do anything a defendant asks simply because he wants it. There needs to be a reason. Some sound reason, grounded in the law and the relevant science. You say your client needs to have these items examined, but you're a lawyer, not a ballistics expert. Your job is to advocate for your client, but it is for precisely that reason I can't automatically rely on everything you say."

The judge raised her gaze and scanned the courtroom. It was empty, save the participants at counsel table.

"Where is your expert?" Kirchner asked. "Why isn't he here today?"

Talon couldn't suppress that wince. *Quadruple damn it.* "Uh, she's in Long Beach, Your Honor."

Kirchner's eyebrows shot up. "Who's your expert?"

"Anastasia St. Julian." Talon couldn't say the name without feeling silly.

Kirchner considered for a moment. "And Ms. St. Julian says she needs to examine the evidence herself?"

Talon nodded. "Yes, Your Honor."

Kirchner picked up her gavel and banged it. "Motion granted." She gestured to the prosecution table. "Mr. Quinlan, make arrangements for Ms. St. Julian to pick up the evidence from the property room within the week. Whatever she wants. Understood?"

Quinlan stood up. He was clearly flustered. He hadn't even gotten a chance to argue his position. But he was also weak. And a judge had just given him an order. "Y—Yes, Your Honor. Of course, Your Honor. Thank you, Your Honor."

Talon's head was swimming almost as much as Quinlan's likely was. But she'd won. And she knew not to look a gift ruling in the mouth. "Thank you, Your Honor."

"Don't thank me," Judge Kirchner replied. "Thank Ann. And whoever told you to hire her. She's the best ballistics expert in the state."

CHAPTER 21

Talon's victory was short-lived. Or rather, her ability to bask in her victory was short-lived. Quinlan, and McDaniels, got the evidence to St. Julian within the week, as ordered. And St. Julian had called to say her initial review gave her hope of finding something helpful. But within that same week, Talon had gotten a call from Samuel Sullivan's secretary. He wanted to meet with Talon. In person.

So Talon made time in her otherwise empty schedule to go from her small, dingy office to Sullivan's bright, palatial one. When she arrived, she checked in with the receptionist who worked for just Sullivan, along with three associate attorneys, two paralegals, and a secretary in a pear tree.

"Mr. Sullivan will be with you in a few minutes," the receptionist told Talon. She was eighteen, nineteen at the most, but dressed in the conservative outfit of a middle-aged woman. It made her look like she was rapidly aging backwards.

Talon thanked the woman and took a seat in the large lobby. There were several magazines on the coffee table, but Talon passed the time examining the décor, trying to guess how much each piece of decoration might have cost.

After more than a few minutes, and definitely past the time the meeting was scheduled for, a paralegal or secretary or associate—Talon wasn't sure which—came out to take her to Sullivan's office. He was a man, probably in his late twenties, but again wearing a dark, conservative suit of someone much older than him. Talon wondered if he was Sullivan's nephew or something, but didn't bother asking, He worked there, he took her to Sullivan's office, and he left again. That was all that really mattered.

"Talon, Talon." Sullivan stood up and came out from behind his desk to greet her. "Thank you for coming. I really appreciate it."

"Of course," Talon replied, shaking his large hand.

He gestured toward the guest chairs across his desk and they both sat down again.

"I wanted to talk to you about the interrogatories," Sullivan started.

Talon cocked her head. "I finished them, Stan. Didn't you get them? I sent them over by legal messenger. If they lost them…"

But Sullivan waved his hand. "No, no. They didn't lose them. I got them. I got them and I reviewed them."

"So what's the problem?" Talon asked.

"The problem, Talon, is that I reviewed them," Sullivan answered. "And they stink."

Talon's heart sank. "Look, I may have hurried on them," she admitted. "But I got them done in time."

"No buts, Talon." Sullivan raised his hand like a traffic cop stopping a car. "You didn't get them done in time. I had to get an extension, remember? And then when you finally did answer them, they're terrible."

Talon shifted in her seat. "I wouldn't say they were terrible."

"Well, I would," Sullivan replied. "And I do. They were terrible. Half of them didn't even answer the question. Not fully, anyway. They're going to file another motion to compel full disclosure. I'm going to have to go back into court again and ask for more time to reply fully. I'm also going to have to argue against the sanctions they're going to ask for, and that the judge is going to be increasingly willing to impose."

"I'm sorry, Stan," Talon offered. "I've just been really busy and—"

"I'm busy too, Talon," Sullivan said. "You're wasting my time. Which means you're wasting your money. I'm not running a charity here."

Talon nodded. "Understood, Stan. But you'll get it all back when we get a verdict. Forty percent after trial, right? That should cover it."

But Sullivan shook his head. "No, Talon. That's not how it works."

"You took the case on contingency," Talon reminded him.

"Of course I did," Sullivan confirmed. "But that was for me to do my job. You're not doing yours, which means I have to do extra work, more than you and I bargained for when you retained me. My time is too valuable to waste it in court because of your mistakes."

"What are you saying?" Talon asked.

"You're going to have to put up a retainer," Sullivan said. "Five thousand dollars. I'll put it in a trust account. Every time I have to run to court or make a phone call because you failed to do something you were supposed to do, I'm going to charge you my hourly rate and take it out of the retainer. Then I'll send you a bill and you replenish the account. It has to stay at five thousand. Once the case is over, you'll get any unused portion back."

Talon leaned back and ran a hand through her hair. "Five thousand? Geez, Stan. I don't know if I have five thousand dollars just lying around that I can spare right now. I have rent, payroll, I have to set aside for taxes…"

"You have to make a decision," Sullivan said. "What do you really want?"

"I really want to win this case," Talon insisted.

"Do you?" Sullivan challenged. "You want your old job back? You want to be reinstated, with back pay, plus damages? Is that really what you want, to practice civil law again? Because it doesn't seem like it to me. If you really wanted to do civil litigation, you would have answered those interrogatories on time. And you would have done a hell of a lot better job on them."

He shook his head and leaned forward. "You know, the worst part wasn't even the half-answered ones. The worst part was the other answers. You answered them *too* fully. You gave them too much information, more than you had to say to be able to answer the question completely. Not only am I wasting my time on the front end going into court again and again asking for extensions, but I'm getting undercut on the back end by you making it harder for us to win the case."

He leaned back again. "It's just sloppy. You may be able to get away with that in criminal practice, but you can't be sloppy in civil practice. The stakes are too high."

"Higher than in criminal?" Talon half-laughed. "I have a man's life in my hands."

"And I have your career in mine," Sullivan returned gravely. "But I'm not going to do it *pro bono*. You have some soul-searching to do, Talon. Is this really what you want? If so, then start acting like it. But if not, then stop wasting my time. I'm not your mommy, or your nanny, or your cheerleader. I'm your lawyer. If we're going to win, it's going to be my way. But I'll be damned if I'm going to lose your way."

Sullivan terminated the meeting on that note. He stood up, Talon followed suit, and they said their good-byes. As she exited his office and pressed the down button at the elevators, Talon thought about Sullivan's parting shot.

He was absolutely right.

But not about her case.

About Michael Jameson's.

CHAPTER 22

Sullivan wasn't the only lawyer who could summon a client to a meeting. The difference was that Talon called Jameson herself, and she greeted him in the lobby as soon as he got there.

"Thanks for coming, Michael."

"Of course," he replied. "You're my lawyer. If you say we have to talk, we talk."

Talon patted him on the shoulder. "Thanks, Michael. I appreciate the helpful attitude." She directed him toward her office. "Come on. We have a lot to talk about."

The walk down the hallway was a short one and soon Talon was face to face with her one and only client. Her stubborn, well-meaning, but ultimately self-defeating client. She reached into her in-box and pulled out the stapled sheets of paper on top. She pushed it across the desk to him. "This just came in."

Michael picked up the document and looked at the top page. "What is it?"

"It's a report," Talon answered, "from our ballistics expert."

"What does it say?" Jameson asked.

Talon felt the slightest twinge of irritation at Jameson expecting her to summarize the report, rather than bothering to even look at it himself. But she realized that allowed her to control the conversation all the more.

"It says we have a chance."

Michael nodded. "Well, that's good." Then, after a moment, "How so?"

"The only way the State can link you to this murder," Talon started, "is through the gun they recovered from your house."

"They recovered it from the man who burglarized my house," Michael corrected. "Not actually from the house."

"And that may prove to be an important distinction," Talon agreed, "depending on how the testimony comes out. But you acknowledged the gun was yours once it was recovered. The gun is linked to you."

"I suppose so," Michael admitted. "And the gun links me to the murder."

Talon raised a hopeful finger. "Maybe not. That's where the ballistic report comes in."

Michael leaned forward in his chair. "Go on."

Talon took the report back from him, and raised it like a demonstrative exhibit. "We had all the ballistic evidence released to a firearms expert named Anastasia St. Julian."

She paused, half-expecting a wisecrack from Michael about the name. But Michael kept his inscrutable expression, so Talon continued.

"She examined everything," Talon said, "and she disagrees with the State's expert."

Michael raised his eyebrows. "She thinks the gun isn't linked to the murder?"

Talon couldn't tell if that was hope in his voice, or disbelief because they both knew it was linked, no matter what the expert said.

"Not exactly," Talon answered. "See, when a bullet is fired from a gun, it travels down the barrel and gets scratched by rough spots inside the gun. Those rough spots are harder than the bullet, so they remain there in the barrel, shot after shot after shot. That means every bullet fired from the same gun has the same exact scratches on the side. The rough spots aren't put there on purpose. They're just from inefficiencies in the manufacturing process—it's difficult and too expensive to try to make a perfectly smooth barrel—so every gun is a little bit different. That means every scratch pattern is unique to that gun. Like a fingerprint."

Michael nodded. "That's how they linked the gun to the shooting."

"Right," Talon said. "They compared the bullets from the crime scene to test-fires from your gun. The State's expert said it was the same gun."

Talon waved the report again. "But Ann doesn't agree with them. Not completely, anyway. Like I said, it's difficult and expensive to make a perfectly smooth barrel, but it's not impossible. And some manufacturers work harder at it than others. Glock has a barrel now that basically never leaves unique markings. So, next time you kill somebody," Talon quipped, "use a Glock."

Michael just stared at her. He didn't seem to appreciate the joke. *Understandable*, Talon supposed.

"Anyway," she continued quickly, "Ann put in her report that the markings the State's expert used to identify the gun aren't sufficient to link it conclusively to the murder. The gross characteristics are enough to identify the *brand* of gun used in the murder, but there are insufficient fine characteristics to identify your gun specifically."

"So it's not a fingerprint any more," Michael said.

"Nope," Talon confirmed. "More like a shoe print. You may have size eleven Nikes, but so do thousands of other people. It doesn't exclude you as a possible suspect, but suddenly a hell of a lot more people are included."

"So that's good news," Michael said.

"Yes," Talon confirmed. "But there's bad news. There's always bad news."

"Of course there is." Michael leaned back again in his chair. "What's the bad news?"

"It's more like realistic news," Talon clarified.

"Fine." Michael crossed his arms. "What's the realistic news?"

"There's no such thing as a free lunch."

Michael shook his head irritably. "What is that supposed to mean?"

"It means we have to pay her to testify," Talon translated.

Michael sighed and dropped his arms again. "I should have known."

"Sorry," Talon said. And she was. One of the problems with the criminal justice system—and there were a lot of them—was that it was also a business. And not just for the private defense attorneys. That much was obvious. But the prosecutors got paid too. And the judges. And the jailors. Hell, some states contracted their prisons out to private companies to run—they didn't even pretend. But everybody has to eat. Defense lawyers, prosecutors, judges. Expert witnesses, too. And there's no such thing as a free lunch.

Michael nodded. "How much?"

"Eight hundred for the initial evaluation," Talon answered. "We already owe that. But if we want her to testify, it's three-hundred an hour, including travel time. It's a three-hour drive each way and her testimony will fill the better part of a day. If it spills into a second day, we'll have to pay for her hotel. And meals."

Michael's expression didn't change. "How much?" he repeated.

"Four grand, minimum. Maybe five. It just depends."

Michael put his head in his hands. "I don't have four grand. I spent everything I had to post the bail money and hire you. I don't even know how I'm going to buy groceries this weekend."

Talon understood. But it didn't change anything. "We need her, Michael."

Michael looked up again. "I need a lot of things, Ms. Winter. I need an acquittal."

"And that's why you need Ann St. Julian."

Michael ran his hands over his face. "What do you want me to do?"

"Commit to this," Talon answered. "One hundred percent."

Michael frowned and shook his head. "That doesn't mean anything. Of course I'm committed to this."

"Then do whatever it takes. What about a second mortgage?"

But Michael shook his head. "No. Alicia will need to sell the house if I go away. Without my income, they'll need the equity."

"Stop making contingency plans to lose," Talon replied. "Invest to win."

"More words." Michael waved them away. "I have to be realistic. I can't gamble with my family's future."

"See, that comment just shows you don't get it," Talon answered. "You can't help but gamble with your family's future. You don't have any choice in the matter. You have to play. And if you don't play to win, you'll lose."

Michael closed his eyes and sighed. "I know." He took a deep breath, but kept his eyes downcast. "So what do I do?"

"You play to win," Talon answered. "You hire Ann St. Julian and you give the jury a reason to acquit you."

Michael sighed again and raised his gaze. "I just don't have the money, Talon." Then his face lit up with an idea. "Wait. Can you pay her? If we win, then I can take out that second mortgage and pay you back."

But Talon shook her head. "I can't do a contingency fee on a criminal case, Michael," she answered. "It's unethical. I'd lose my license."

"But you can front costs, right?" Michael pressed. "That's allowed, isn't it?"

Talon frowned. "Technically, yes," she admitted. "But not if I don't think you can repay me." Then Talon seized the topic and turned it back on her client. "Anyway, why should I? You're blocking our ability to win this case. I can't jeopardize my firm if you won't take my advice."

"What?" Michael was taken aback. "Of course I'll follow your advice."

Talon raised an eyebrow. "No matter what?"

Michael nodded. "Yes. We'll do whatever you say. Whatever we need to do."

"Whatever I say?" Talon pressed.

"Whatever you say," Michael confirmed.

Talon crossed her arms. "I need to talk to your brother."

Michael reacted just how she'd expected. "No." He crossed his own arms and set his jaw. "No, this isn't about him. It's about me. If I beat this by betraying my brother, I'll have to live with that for the rest of my life."

Talon was unmoved. Again, she'd expected his reaction. "If

you lose this because you refuse to let me do my job right and talk to your brother," she said evenly, "then you're going to live the rest of your life in a prison cell."

Michael crossed his own arms and looked away. "I'm prepared for that."

"Well, good for fucking you," Talon shot back.

Michael's head spun back to her.

"Is your wife prepared for that?" Talon demanded. "Is your son? Your daughter? You're putting your brother in front of your wife, and her children. How do you think that makes her feel?"

Michael didn't reply.

"What about Marcus?" Talon pressed. "Without a dad, with no faith in the system, how long until he joins you in there? And don't forget Kaylee. How long until she starts dating losers who treat her like the piece of shit she thinks she must be because you didn't do everything you possibly could to be there for her?"

Michael just sat there. He lowered his gaze.

"God damn it, Michael," Talon raised her voice. "This isn't just about you."

Then she remembered what Sullivan had told her. "If we're going to win," she echoed, "it's going to be my way. But I'll be damned if I'm going to lose your way."

Michael pushed back in his chair and looked away. He sighed heavily through his nose. Talon could see his eyes flash with anger. But one thing he didn't do was say, 'No.' She waited.

Finally, Michael turned back to her. "Okay. Fine. Talk to my brother. But," he raised a finger, "that doesn't mean we call him as a witness. You tell me what he says and I'll decide whether we use him."

Talon seized the concession, but made sure not to make any of her own. "Okay, I'll talk to him. Then you and I will talk."

Michael exhaled and ran his hands over his head. "Shit. This sucks."

Talon smiled weakly. She had no trouble agreeing with that.

CHAPTER 23

Clallam Bay.

It was about as Northwest-sounding a name as possible. Practically all of Western Washington was on some bay or inlet or another, and 'Clallam' was so typical of the sound of local Native American place names that if it hadn't been real, it should have been. The name should have evoked images of a small fishing community, half a day's drive from the hustle and bustle of Seattle and Tacoma. Instead, 'Clallam Bay' meant the Clallam Bay Corrections Center, a medium security prison tucked away on Washington's otherwise idyllic Olympic Peninsula. While perhaps not as well known by the general public as its eastern cousin in Walla Walla, it was nevertheless considered the worst prison in the state by those knowledgeable of the criminal justice system.

And by Talon Winter.

She knew the place, but had never set foot inside. Not until she went in as a criminal defense attorney. To talk with Ricky Jameson.

That is, if he was willing to talk with her.

Checking in was easy enough. Only two types of people

came to visit at a prison: lawyers and family. Talon showed the guard at the reception center her bar card and driver's license and explained she was there to speak with prisoner Richard David Jameson.

"You his lawyer?" the guard asked.

"I'm *a* lawyer," Talon answered.

The guard frowned slightly. "He expecting you?"

Talon smiled. "Probably. If he's smart."

The guard's frown slipped into a smile. "Oh yeah. Ricky Jameson's smart. Too smart sometimes."

Talon wasn't surprised to hear that, judging by his brother Michael. But then she looked up and around at her surroundings. "Maybe not quite smart enough though," she said to herself.

"Have a seat, Ms. Winter," the guard said, sliding her cards back to her. "We'll locate Jameson and bring him to one of the meeting rooms. Then we'll come get you. It could take ten or twenty minutes, depending on where he's at right now, so make yourself comfortable."

Talon took a seat in the waiting room. It was sparse, but adequate. Yellow plastic chairs and a small table covered by months-old magazines. No one else was there. Talon was thankful for that. She imagined the types of people who would be sitting in a prison waiting room. Then she caught herself and realized she was imagining the stereotype of what ignorant people thought about what kinds of people had loved ones in prison. Overweight women in too-tight clothes, a dozen kids in tow, unemployed and under-educated, cashing their welfare checks while they waited for their men to finish their time and come back home to the single-wide.

But Talon knew better.

Human beings in cages. That's all a prison was. The good people of the world—the ones who held that prison-wife stereotype—told themselves the prisons kept the murderers and rapists locked safely away from the schools and playgrounds. And there was some truth to that. But murders were usually more the result of circumstances than of men—that's why serial killers were so interesting, so rare. And half of the men in the cages were drug addicts, caught with dope in their cars or stealing something to buy more of it—no real danger to anyone's life or limb. Besides, no matter how they got there, all of those men in the cages—the murderers and the rapists, the drug addicts and thieves—they all had mothers and fathers, wives and girlfriends, friends and children, brothers and sisters.

"Ms. Winter?" The reception guard had returned. "Jameson is waiting for you in interview room B."

"Already?" Talon had gotten lost in her thoughts, but it hadn't been anywhere near twenty minutes.

The guard nodded. "He was working in the kitchen, so it was easy enough to find him. And sure enough, he said he was expecting you."

Interview Room B wasn't as comfortable as even that institutional name suggested. Indeed, even the word 'room' was a misnomer. It was an interview space, to be sure, but it was more like two closets, divided by glass and joined by telephones, one side for the visitor and one for the prisoner. The prisoner was already waiting for the visitor. His head and jaw were shaved, his arms were covered in tattoos, and the phone receiver was already in his hand.

Talon took a seat across the glass from Ricky Jameson and put the phone to her own ear. "Mr. Jameson," she started, "I'm Talon—"

"Winter," Ricky finished with a grin. "I know. I've heard a lot about you."

Talon shifted uneasily in her chair. She hated that phrase. It suggested knowledge without confirming its accuracy. Or revealing its source.

"And I haven't heard nearly enough about you," she parried. She didn't want to talk about what he'd heard about her. "That's why I'm here."

"You heard enough to know to come," Ricky answered. "I knew Mike would throw me under the bus when it got hot enough for him."

"He didn't throw you under the bus," Talon assured. "In fact, it took me forever to convince him to even let me talk to you. He's one stubborn son-of-a-bitch."

That pulled a laugh from Ricky. Talon had found that men didn't expect women to swear, so throwing out an f-bomb or an S.O.B. could really break the ice. "Yeah," Ricky agreed. That's true. That's damn true."

"But I have a job to do," Talon explained. "So I was able to convince him. I can be pretty fucking stubborn too."

Ricky didn't laugh that time. But he smiled. "So he ain't selling me out? That'd be the smart thing to do. I'm already inside. They'll just add the time to my sentence."

"How much time do you have left?" Talon asked, almost like it was a normal conversation.

"Seven months," Ricky answered. "I'm scheduled to ship out to Shelton next month to get processed out."

Talon nodded. "Well, don't change your plans," she said. "I'm not here to add time to your sentence."

"Why are you here then?"

Talon took a moment to appraise the man on the other side of the glass. He was only a few years older than Michael, Talon knew, but he seemed more like Michael's father than his brother.

He was that much more mature—harder. It wasn't just the prison tattoos on the rippling arms. It was his eyes. Ricky knew what Michael was in store for if Talon lost the case. And prison tattoos or not, he was still a big brother.

"I need your help," Talon answered. "I need to know what really happened."

"And then you'll tell the jury?" Ricky asked. "And Mikey walks?"

Talon frowned slightly. "Well, honestly, that would be my plan. But Michael won't agree."

Ricky laughed darkly. "Yeah, that sounds like him. He's always been a fucking martyr."

Talon nodded. "And what's the use of being a martyr if no one knows?"

Ricky took a beat, then smiled. "You do understand him, don't you?"

"I think so," Talon answered, with more than a little pride. "I know he cares about you."

Ricky laughed outright at that. "I've been here eight years. He hasn't visited once."

Talon took her own beat. "That doesn't mean he doesn't care. It just means..." But she trailed off.

"I know what it means," Ricky said. "I don't fit in with his world. Successful suburban dads don't want brothers in prison. Makes for awkward conversation at the PTA meetings. 'Hey, Kaylee, what did you do this weekend?'" he mimicked a child's voice. "'We went to see Uncle Ricky in prison!'"

"Well, that's better than visiting her dad in prison," Talon responded. "A murder conviction doesn't fit well with the suburban dad image either."

"Is that what changed his mind?" Ricky asked.

"No," Talon answered. "I did."

Ricky leaned back in his chair and conducted his own appraisal. "So what do you want to know, Ms. Winter? Do you want me to say I had the gun? I shot the guy? Mike wasn't even there?"

Talon shook her head. "No, I already know Michael was there. He told me that much."

"What else did he tell you?"

Talon hesitated. Not because she was afraid to tell him what Michael had said. Because she didn't want to take the time to recount it. The important part wasn't what he said, it was what he didn't say. The alleged blackout. But she couldn't communicate that part without spending the time on everything else. And that just seemed like such a waste of time—Ricky had been there, he already knew. She sighed. "Fine..." And then she told him the whole story, everything Michael had said, up to and including the alleged, and completely unbelievable, blackout at the exact time of the shooting.

When she finished, Ricky shook his head. "No one's gonna believe that."

"I know," Talon replied. "The real problem is, they're gonna believe everything except the blackout—the drug dealing, the robbery plan, everything—and they'll know what the blackout means."

"What does it mean?"

"It means Michael pulled the trigger."

"Is that what you want me to say?"

"I want you to tell the truth."

Ricky paused. Then he smiled knowingly. "Is that really what you want?"

Talon took a moment as well. Did she really want Ricky to tell the truth? She supposed that depended on what the truth was. If the truth was that Ricky shot the victim, then yes, she wanted Ricky to admit it. Then it would be a matter of convincing Michael to throw Ricky squarely under that damn bus after all.

But if the truth was that Michael pulled the trigger, well, then, that complicated things. As it stood, Talon could put Michael on the stand to tell the jury what had happened. Maybe he'd also tell them his brother Ricky had pulled the trigger, and he had no idea there was going to be any robbery, let alone a murder. Maybe the jury would let him walk. But if Talon knew the truth was that Michael was the shooter, then she couldn't put him on the stand to say it was Ricky. That would be suborning perjury. And if she put Ricky on the stand to tell the same lie, that would be more perjury — and an injustice. Ricky had done his time. He deserved to go back to Shelton and then home again. Maybe. If he was innocent. Which he might be. Or maybe he wasn't.

"I don't know," Talon admitted.

Ricky nodded, but didn't say anything.

Finally, Talon leaned forward and said into the phone, "You know, maybe we're going about this the wrong way. Let me ask you two questions."

Ricky thought for a moment, then smiled. "Okay. Two questions."

Talon took a moment to make sure her thoughts were organized. Then she asked the questions.

"Do you remember who shot Jordan McCabe?"

Ricky nodded. "Yes."

"If I put you on the stand, will you tell the truth?"

Another nod. "Yes."

And that was all Talon really needed to know after all.

CHAPTER 24

Talon took her time driving back from Clallam Bay. She could have crossed over the south end of the Puget Sound on the Tacoma Narrows Bridge—it would have been quicker and the toll was minimal. Instead, she drove around the bottom of the Sound, through Olympia. And Shelton.

She didn't stop. But she drove by. Again. And then she went home.

Or rather, she went to her home away from home. Her office. Only one case, but building a law practice was a full-time endeavor. There were plans to make, papers to prepare. Bills to pay.

The office was dark and quiet. Hannah and the rest had gone home hours ago. She had the place to herself. Herself and her thoughts.

She walked to her office, flipping light switches as she went. When she got to her office, she dropped herself into her chair and surveyed the room. But she already knew what she was looking for.

She reached into her in-box and pulled out two letters. Both of them were bills.

$5,000 for Samuel Sullivan.

Or $4,000 for Anastasia St. Julian.

Talon reached into her desk drawer and pulled out two more things: her account ledger and her checkbook.

A look in the ledger confirmed what she already knew. She had $5,801.47 in her business account. Enough to pay rent and her share of Hannah's salary for a few more months.

But her practice wouldn't last a few months more without making some hard decisions.

She opened her checkbook and started filling out the check. Sometimes the hard decisions were the easiest.

Pay to the order of ... Anastasia St. Julian...

CHAPTER 25

"Well? What did Ricky say?"

"He confirmed the story," Talon answered. "The drug deal gone wrong. Everything."

"Did he say who pulled the trigger?"

"No," Talon said. "I didn't ask him."

"What? Why not?"

"I don't want to know. I don't need to know."

"What if the prosecutor calls him as a witness? What if he says he's not the one who shot him?"

Talon shook her head. "The State can't call him. He'll plead the Fifth. They can't make him testify about a crime."

"Can't they just give him immunity?"

"They can," Talon admitted. "But they won't. If they do that before they know what he's going to say, then he just takes the immunity, says he pulled the trigger, and both of the Jameson Brothers get away with murder."

"But we can still call him?"

"Yes," Talon assured. "They can't force him to testify, but he can testify if he wants. He can be our witness and only our witness. He's our ace in the hole."

"So, all of our witnesses are ready?"

Talon nodded. "Yes. Ricky's available if we need him. Ann St. Julian is on board. The State endorsed Earl Daggett and Reggie Oliphant, but we can get good info from them on cross. The witnesses are ready."

She looked to Curt, who had been sitting silently in the corner of her office. "Are you ready?"

He nodded solemnly. "Ready, boss."

Then she turned back to face the man sitting across her desk. "Are you ready, Michael?"

Michael Jameson shook his head slightly. "Ready? Ready to go into a courtroom and do nothing while my fate is determined by a bunch of strangers? Ready to sit still while my lawyer does all the talking to a judge who doesn't know me and twelve people I'll never see again? Ready to listen to a prosecutor twist the evidence and make me out to be the worst type of person imaginable? Ready to hear a judge say everything I've done with my life for the last twenty-five years is irrelevant? Ready to sit back and watch the drama unfold, knowing there are two possible outcomes: I spend the rest of my life in prison or I walk out the door a free man? No. I'm not ready for that. How can anyone be ready for that?"

Talon frowned slightly. "No one can. But I have to be. Trial starts a week from Monday. To the extent you can, try to forget about this. Let me worry about it. You spend time this week with your family, your wife, your kids. Get everything in order. When this is over, I want you walking out that door a free man, but I can't guarantee it. No matter how prepared we are, I can't guarantee the result."

"Right," Michael acknowledged. "Of course." He looked

down for several seconds, then looked up again. His usually stoic mask had slipped. "I'm scared, Talon."

Talon's mind skimmed over several possible responses:

'Don't be. It'll turn out fine.'

'Good. That'll give us the edge.'

'You should be. It shows you're paying attention.'

'Not as scared as the prosecutors are.'

But none seemed appropriate. Or honest. Instead, she simply reached across her desk and grasped his hand. "I know."

CHAPTER 26

The night before trial, Talon was in her office, watching the sun disappear behind the Olympic Mountains, the coming night the only barrier between her and the trial of The State of Washington versus Michael Jameson.

She was busying herself with the minutiae: organizing her briefcase, double-checking her trial binders, trying not to vomit. She was to report to Judge Kirchner's courtroom at 9:00 a.m. sharp. She knew she should go home, try to get some sleep. That was more important than triple-checking that her court rules were in her briefcase. But she also knew there was no way in hell she'd be sleeping that night. Actually going home would just confirm it. Unable to relax even in her own home, she'd spend the night lying awake, her restless mind going over every angle again and again while the clock ticked the night away.

She kept hoping she'd hear the front door unlock and one of the other lawyers call out, 'Hello? Anyone here?' Then she could engage them, admit she was nervous, and ask for advice. She'd receive some gem of insight that would come to her as she began to deliver her closing argument, enabling her to rally the jury to her cause and save the life of an innocent man.

But no such luck. The office was as silent as a crypt. She'd have to come up with her own gems of wisdom for the jury. Or smoke and mirrors.

Besides, whether Michael Jameson was an innocent man was still an open question.

Talon checked her briefcase one more time, then grabbed her coat and headed for the exit. She turned off the lights and locked the door behind her.

"It doesn't matter," she reminded herself. And, a bit to her surprise, she believed it.

CHAPTER 27

"Are the parties ready in the matter of The State of Washington versus Michael Jameson?" Judge Kirchner took the bench and got right to business.

Quinlan and McDaniels both stood up. "The State is ready," Quinlan answered for the prosecution team.

Talon stood up next, gesturing slightly to Michael to stay seated. "The defense is ready as well, Your Honor."

Kirchner nodded. Her hair was pulled back in her usual bun, but she seemed to have applied the faintest layer of makeup. Jurors apparently rated higher than lawyers.

"All right then," the judge said. "Are there any matters to discuss before we bring in the panel and start with jury selection?"

"No, Your Honor," Quinlan answered again for the State. The State always answered first, an outgrowth of the State having to go first to try to prove the case against an otherwise presumed innocent defendant. Talon wondered whether, and when, McDaniels might get to speak.

"Nothing from the defense, Your Honor," Talon added. She

was anxious to get started. There was something about being back in court—real court, with juries and witnesses and verdicts. And something more. She'd tried her share of multi-million dollar tort cases, but she'd never had a man's life in her hands. It was a huge responsibility. It was also, if she was honest with herself, a huge rush.

Kirchner offered another "All right," then instructed her bailiff to fetch the panel of prospective jurors from the jury assembly room on the first floor. It would take a few minutes to bring the sixty of them up to Judge Kirchner's courtroom on the second floor. Thank God she wasn't up on the eighth floor. Of the sixty, they would only seat twelve, plus two alternates in case someone got sick or otherwise couldn't finish.

"We each get to strike six jurors," Talon explained to Michael in a whisper. "Plus two more for the alternates."

Michael nodded. They'd talked about the logistics before. "And we're stuck with the first twelve who are left. Great system. Justice by rejects."

Talon conceded the point with a shrug. Each side got rid of the jurors they thought would be best for the other side, leaving the quieter, meeker, less opinionated people to decide the fate of a man they'd never met. But if each side got to choose their favorites, every jury would end up deadlocked. Then again, that wouldn't be so bad for the defense. It would sure beat a conviction. And meek, less opinionated people were more likely to follow the rules, and favor the prosecution—the ultimate rule follower.

Talon shook her head to herself and wondered at all the subtle ways the cards were again stacked against a criminal defendant, no matter how many times the judge repeated, 'A defendant is presumed innocent...'

When the panel arrived, everyone—even the judge—stood

for their entrance. It was a nice gesture, but Talon wondered if the jurors truly appreciated it. She studied their faces as they entered, but not to gauge their approval at being stood for—that was their issue. She was getting first impressions as they filed in, holding their juror numbers, one to sixty. Talon had found her first impressions were usually right. People advertise who they are with their clothes, hairstyles, piercings, whatever. It was important to assess those nonverbal cues. Someone who's wearing an 'I love Cops' T-shirt was never getting past her and onto the jury, regardless of how perfectly they might answer the lawyers' questions. But it usually wasn't that obvious.

Other things were.

"There's no Black people," Michael whispered to Talon as the last member of the panel entered the courtroom and the bailiff closed the door to the hallway.

That wasn't quite accurate. There were three African-Americans: a young man in the first row, wearing a long-sleeved shirt and jeans; a middle-aged woman in the third row, wearing a sweater and carrying a large purse; and an old man in the last row, with white hair surrounding a bald crown and glasses perched on his nose. Talon had already done the math: twelve jurors, plus two alternates, plus eight strikes each, equaled thirty jurors. The last half were there just in case someone in the first half had to be excused 'for cause.' Maybe they knew one of the attorneys, or had read about the case in the paper and already made up their minds. Or they really couldn't miss that much work and needed to be excused. The young man was in the first twelve, so he'd be on the jury unless he got struck. The woman was Juror #29, so they might get to her if both sides used all of their strikes. But the old man was Juror #54. There was almost no way they would get to him.

"There's three," Talon answered.

"I thought I was supposed to get a jury of my peers," Michael complained.

Talon nodded as the judge asked everyone to sit down again and began explaining the nuts and bolts of the jury selection process to the jurors.

"You are," Talon answered, "but it doesn't mean you get a jury made up of people who are exactly like you."

"Well, I shouldn't get a jury with no one like me either," Michael responded. "Shouldn't there be more Black people on the panel?"

Talon had anticipated this issue as well. According to the last census, Pierce County, Washington, was approximately 4% African-American. Three jurors out of sixty was 5%. She wouldn't prevail on a motion for a new panel. And even if she did, and the numbers doubled for the next sixty, Michael would still only have six African-Americans on his jury panel; with two or three of them out of reach in the back row again.

"Maybe," Talon whispered. "But there's nothing I can do about it right now."

Michael frowned at her. "What if I tell you that you have to do something?"

Talon smiled. She really did like him. "The trial has started now, Michael. Things are going to move fast. I can't have every decision be a joint decision. You hired me for a reason." She pointed around the courtroom. "This is the reason."

When Michael didn't immediately reply, she added, "Trust me. I know what I'm doing."

And she did. Because she knew what Quinlan would do.

But first, they had to talk to the jurors.

Quinlan went first. Or rather, the prosecution—as always—went first, and Quinlan stood up to talk, not McDaniels. He was the man, after all. And he was White. Talon wondered whether he even realized he was tokenizing McDaniels. More importantly, she wondered if the jurors realized it. If Quinlan couldn't even see the implicit bias in the White guy always getting to talk first, how many of the jurors might not see it either? After all, the D.A. is supposed to be a White guy in a suit.

And the defendant is supposed to be a Black man.

The questioning alternated in twenty-minute blocks. Quinlan wasted the prosecution's first twenty minutes on icebreakers.

"How did you feel when you got your jury summons?"

"Has anyone served on a jury before?"

"What makes a good juror?"

When he was done, Talon stood up and cut to the chase.

"By show of hands," she asked, "who walked into the courtroom, looked at my client, and thought, 'I wonder what he did?'"

Only a few hands went up, and even those were tentative.

"Remember," she reminded them, "you all took an oath to tell the truth."

At that, almost all of the other jurors raised their hands too. Talon made note of the few who didn't—they were liars. Then she started talking to the panel. She started with Juror #1.

"How can a criminal defendant get a fair trial," she asked the young woman in the first seat, "if as soon as his jurors see him, they already assume he must have done something wrong?"

Talon knew there was no easy answer to her question. Juror #1 stumbled through a response about The System, and The Constitution, and Following the Law. But the answer didn't matter. The import was the question. And how it set up the real question, posed to Juror #2.

"How," Talon asked the middle-aged White man, "does a Black man get a fair trial when everybody assumes he's guilty just for being here?"

Again, the answer didn't matter. Not really. If someone had said something overtly racist, then yes, that would have been helpful to get them excused for cause. But no one was going to say that. Juror #2 agreed it was a concern, a challenge even, but assured Talon he could be fair. Same for Juror #3, another middle-aged White man. Then she got to Juror #4.

The young Black man.

"What are your thoughts on that?" Talon asked him.

The man took a moment to answer. He shifted in his seat and exhaled deeply. Then he glanced around at the jurors seated to either side.

"I think," he started slowly, "that most of the people probably mean well, but they don't know what it's like to be Black in America. And certainly not what it's like to be a young Black man."

That sent a ripple of discomfort through the room. Talon knew already there was no way Quinlan was going to let Juror #4 on the jury—in fact, she was counting on it. But whatever jurors would eventually make it onto the jury were all sitting in that room, and they would all hear what Juror #4 had to say.

"What is it like?" Talon asked.

The young man paused again. Then he pointed toward where Michael was sitting. "It isn't just sitting at the defendant's table. It's everywhere. It's everything. It's when you're walking down the street and the person ahead of you keeps looking over their shoulder at you. It's when you're sitting on the bus and people choose to stand in the back instead of taking the empty seat next to you. It's when you get pulled over for a defective taillight or some other made-up crap and you have to keep your hands visible at ten and two so you don't get shot."

Talon nodded thoughtfully at the response. "What did you think," she asked Juror #4, "when the judge told you Mr. Jameson is charged with murder?"

The juror offered a pained smile. "I thought of all the cops who shoot unarmed Black men and don't even get fired, let alone charged with murder." He paused, then added, "And I thought, I don't feel comfortable sitting on a jury where the defendant—the accused—is Black, I thought, I bet some of the White jurors feel too comfortable, because it fits the stereotype that all crime is committed by Black people and all Black people are criminals."

Yep, no way Quinlan wouldn't strike Juror #4.

Talon smiled inside. But only inside. Those were important concepts. Ones the other jurors needed to hear, and ones she couldn't touch on so candidly once the trial started.

"Thank you, sir," she said earnestly.

The room was still charged from the comments. Like the leftover tingle after the adrenaline rush subsides. Talon moved on to a few more areas, spoke to a few more jurors, but soon enough her twenty minutes were up and she sat down again.

Then, to her dismay, Amity McDaniels stood up to conduct the State's second round of questioning.

"Good morning, everyone," she started in a smooth, pleasant voice. "I'd like to start by thanking everyone for their honesty, and encouraging it to continue."

She glanced briefly at Juror #4, then expanded her gaze to the rest of the panel. "Who's ever heard the term 'Black-on-Black violence'?"

Talon suppressed a wince. That was the one racial angle that could help the prosecution. Yes, Michael Jameson was African-

American. But so was Jordy McCabe.

Several of the jurors raised their hands, including all three African-Americans.

McDaniels pointed at Juror #12, a middle-aged White woman who'd raised her hand. "What's Black-on-Black violence?" she asked.

"It's when an African-American commits a crime against another African-American," the juror answered, with that pleased expression the smart kid in school always had whenever they answered a question.

McDaniels nodded. She pointed at Juror #26, a young Asian man. "So what's Black-on-White violence?"

The juror hadn't raised his hand in response to McDaniels's lead-in question, but he could figure out the answer. "It's when an African-American commits a crime against a White person?"

McDaniels nodded again. "Right. So...," she glanced over her audience, "which one is worse?"

Talon squeezed her pen tighter. McDaniels was good. Talon just hoped Quinlan's ego would keep her mostly sidelined during the actual trial.

There was no right answer to McDaniels' question, of course. So the jurors hesitated. Finally, someone in the third row mumbled, "They're the same." That was followed by a murmur of approval throughout the jury panel.

"They're the same?" McDaniels repeated. "Or at least, they should be, right?"

"Right," answered several jurors.

McDaniels raised a hand to her chin. She narrowed her eyes slightly and tapped her lips thoughtfully. After a few moments, she took her hand away again and pointed to her audience. "Has it always been, though?"

Again, a wave of unease flowed through the room, followed by several independent 'No's, popping up like timid whack-a-moles.

"No?" McDaniels asked.

"No," answered several more jurors, more confidently.

McDaniels singled out a specific juror again. Juror #9, a twenty-something White woman. The juror information sheet said she was a first-grade teacher. "Say, twenty years ago," McDaniels asked her, "do you think the police might have worked harder to solve a Black-on-White crime than a Black-on-Black crime?"

The juror frowned. "Well, I don't think they should have. But, yes, I think that might be true. Sometimes."

McDaniels pivoted to Juror #18, an older African-American woman with a large purse and staid expression. "What do you think, Juror Number Eighteen?"

The juror nodded thoughtfully and straightened up a bit in her seat. "I think," she started slowly, "that it will be a long time before White people will care as much about Black victims as they do about White victims."

"So you don't think the problem might have been worse twenty or thirty years ago?" McDaniels tried to clarify. She didn't care—at least professionally—if things were fair now. She was just trying to suggest that the jurors would have a chance to right a long-ago racial injustice, if they would just convict Michael Jameson of murder.

Juror #18 shrugged. "I'm not sure how much things have really changed." She gestured toward the front of the courtroom. "I mean, just look. The defendant is Black. And you too, but you're clearly the assistant prosecutor. Everyone else is White."

Talon stood up immediately. It wasn't her turn to talk, but she'd take the objection. "I'm Native American," she informed the juror.

The juror was taken aback for a moment, but then her surprised expression melted into a warm smile. "Well, that's good, I think."

Talon returned the smile. "I think so too," she agreed. Then she sat down again, all without any objection from Quinlan, or his 'assistant.' Probably because it happened too quickly.

McDaniels gathered her thoughts for a moment. Then she returned to open-ended questions for the panel. "Let's assume we haven't reached the point quite yet where the criminal justice system treats everyone fairly regardless of race," she said. "Should we wait to prosecute crimes against Black people until that happens?"

Of course not, Talon knew. After a moment, a few of the jurors said as much. Quietly.

"And should we ignore," McDaniels finished up, "cold case crimes against Black victims if they occurred when people cared even less about Black-on-Black crime?"

And again the answer was, "No." "Of course not."

McDaniels smiled, then thanked the jury panel and sat down again, her point made.

"Any further questions, Ms. Winter?" the judge asked.

Talon hesitated. She was a lawyer. Lawyers liked getting the last word. But there was a limit to how much back and forth the jurors would tolerate. Even people who love to watch tennis are waiting for a player to miss and the point to be scored.

Talon stood up. "No, Your Honor. Thank you."

She'd make her own point in opening statement.

But first, she had an objection to make.

* * *

Actually, the objection had to wait for the objectionable

conduct to occur. But it didn't have to wait long.

Once the jurors were excused from the courtroom, Quinlan exercised his first peremptory strike against Juror #4. Ordinarily, the lawyers didn't have to give any reasons for exercising a peremptory strike. That was the whole point of them—getting rid of people who just rubbed you the wrong way, even if they didn't quite qualify to be excused for good cause. But there was one exception to that rule.

"The defense objects to excusing Juror Number Four," Talon interjected. "Pursuant to *Batson versus Kentucky.*"

Batson v. Kentucky was the United States Supreme Court decision that first held jurors can't be struck from a jury panel just because of their race. The holding was later extended to other protected classifications. Saying '*Batson* objection' was the lawyer equivalent of shouting 'Racist!'

But if the objection fits…

Quinlan recoiled. An appropriate response, really, at being called a racist—even in code. "Your Honor," he stammered, "I am shocked. I would never strike a juror because of their race or ethnicity." He took a moment to gather his thoughts. "Besides, I have a race-neutral reason for wanting to excuse Juror Number Four."

That was the one way to overcome a *Batson* objection. Point to a race-neutral reason for excusing the juror. That is, any reason other than, 'He's African-American' or 'She's Asian.'

Judge Kirchner looked dubious. "Okay, Mr. Quinlan. What's your race-neutral reason for excluding Juror Number Four?"

Quinlan stood up straight. "The State is concerned about his answers regarding systemic racism and the inability of an African-American man to receive a fair trial in the United States."

Kirchner looked to Talon. "Any response, counsel?"

"That answer," Talon responded, "is anything but race-neutral. It's inextricably intertwined with the juror's race."

"Race-neutral means a reason other than the juror's race," Quinlan interjected. "The reason I gave was something over and above his race."

Judge Kirchner raised an eyebrow. "'Over and above'?" she repeated. "So, race was part of it?"

Quinlan's face blanched. "That's not what I meant, Your Honor. I meant, it was what he said, not his race. Not at all."

Kirchner frowned. She took a moment then looked again at Talon. "Anything further, Ms. Winter?"

"I think Mr. Quinlan's responses speak for themselves, Your Honor," Talon answered. "He struck the juror because of his views on race and justice in the United States—views which are necessarily impacted by his experience as an African-American man in the U.S. The Court should sustain my objection."

The judge nodded thoughtfully. "This is challenging," she admitted. "Generally speaking, the case law on this issue suggests that any reason other than, 'Because he's Black'—or Asian or whatever—will overcome a *Batson* objection. But Ms. Winter makes a valid point. If the views expressed by a juror are the basis for the challenge, but those views are informed by the juror's race, what then?" She tapped a finger on her chin for several seconds. "Okay, here's what I'm going to do. I'm going to reserve ruling. Let's move on to your other challenges and we'll see where we end up."

Talon was willing to accept that. And for the same reason that Quinlan objected.

"But, Your Honor," he complained, "that could have a chilling effect on my other challenges."

Kirchner cocked her head at him. "Not challenging jurors for racial reasons will have a chilling effect on you?"

Quinlan shifted his weight. "Again, that's not what I mean,

Your Honor."

"Good," Kirchner ended the exchange. "Let's move on."

And they did, each side striking potential jurors who they thought might not be fair, or receptive to their side of the case. Then they reached Juror #18.

"The State would thank and excuse Juror Number Eighteen," Quinlan tried to sound nonchalant as he challenged the only other African-American whose juror number was low enough to make it onto the panel. It didn't fool anyone.

Talon didn't even need to object.

"You're challenging the only other African-American juror?" Kirchner asked with no effort to hide her incredulity.

"Uh, well, yes," Quinlan admitted, "but not because of her race."

"And what's your race-neutral reason for this challenge," the judge demanded.

Quinlan cleared his throat. "The juror stated she thought the system wasn't fair because Your Honor and I and Ms. Winter are all White."

Kirchner shook her head. "That's not exactly what she said."

"And I'm not White," Talon added.

"Right," Kirchner agreed. "Ms. Winter informed the juror that she's Native American."

"Well, I'm not sure that matters," Quinlan started.

"It matters to me," Talon interjected.

Quinlan closed his eyes and exhaled. "The juror's concerns about the fairness of the system still stand. That's a race-neutral reason to excuse her."

Talon considered arguing that Juror #18's views were just as impacted by her race as were Juror #4's. But she knew that she didn't need to. Kirchner got it.

"I'll tell you what, Mr. Quinlan," the judge said. "I'm going to let you excuse either Juror #4 or Juror #18, but not both."

Quinlan blinked up at her. "That hardly seems fair."

"I disagree," Judge Kirchner replied. "You're not going to sanitize this jury of all African-Americans—especially for the reasons you've given. You can strike one of them, but not both. Choose."

Talon wasn't sure allowing 50% of State-sponsored racism was the best solution, but she was willing to accept it at that point. It beat having neither juror on the jury.

Quinlan sat down and held a whisper conference with McDaniels. After several minutes, McDaniels stood up and informed the court, "The State would strike Juror Number Four, Your Honor."

It seemed a little late to be adding McDaniels to the mix. It just confirmed her 'assistant' role that she hadn't been permitted to make the arguments, but Quinlan made her voice their decision.

And with that decision, both sides had exercised all of their peremptory challenges. The first twelve of the remaining jurors, including the woman who thought it was good that Talon was Native, would be their jury. Talon could live with that.

Judge Kirchner looked at the clock. "That took longer than I'd hoped," she admitted. "I don't want to start opening statements this late in the day. I want to move directly to witnesses, not have the jurors spend the night thinking about the openings and not hear the first witness until the next morning."

Talon liked that. The jurors would be told 'the lawyers' remarks, statements, and arguments are not evidence.' But without any actual evidence to consider, the jurors wouldn't be able to help but start weighing who told a better story.

Quinlan, apparently, agreed. "That sounds fine, Your

Honor. We'll have our first witness here at nine o'clock, ready to go as soon as we finish openings."

The judge looked to Talon. "Any objection to that procedure, Ms. Winter?"

"None at all," Talon answered with a small shake of her head. "We'll look forward to starting the trial in the morning."

With that, Kirchner called the jury panel back in and excused all but the lucky—or unlucky, depending on your point of view—twelve who took their spots in the jury box. Eight men and four women; one African-American, one Asian American, and ten White Americans. About what Talon had expected.

Kirchner swore them in and then excused them for the day. The attorneys were next, freed from further presence before Her Honor. Talon didn't bother saying good-bye to Quinlan. She and Michael walked out into the hallway to touch base.

"Did that go well?" Michael asked. "I can't really decide."

Talon smiled weakly. "Me either. And we won't know until it's over and they've returned a verdict. If it didn't go well, it'll be too late to undo it."

Michael frowned. "That's not very encouraging."

"I'm not about encouragement," Talon answered. "I'm about hard work."

She reached out and clasped his arm. "And I have a lot of it to do before tomorrow" she said. "Go home. See your family. Get some sleep. I'll see you first thing tomorrow."

"Okay. But I'm not going to get any sleep tonight."

Talon nodded. "Me either."

CHAPTER 28

There was a lot to consider when it came to opening statement. It wasn't as simple as just standing in front of the jurors and telling them what you thought they should do. Talon sat in her office contemplating her options, weighing the conflicting, sometimes contradictory, philosophies of what made a winning opening statement.

The first decision, at least for a defendant, was whether to give an opening statement at the beginning of trial, right after the prosecution, or reserve it, and give it after the State rested its case. The advantage to waiting was the ability to tailor your case to whatever evidence the prosecution actually put on. The disadvantage was, that advantage was pretty obvious to the jury. It also sacrificed the opportunity to orient the jury to the defendant's theory of the case before hearing the evidence. When a State's witness testified, would you want the jury to only have the State's version of events in their head, or both the State's and the defendant's? If they had only heard from the prosecutor at the outset, it was a pretty good bet that prosecution witnesses' testimony was going to fit into what the prosecutor said in opening statement. But if the jurors heard from the defense attorney, too, now they had something to test a witness' testimony against—a different lens through which to view a witness' testimony. But they could only look through that lens if Talon gave it to them before the witnesses started talking.

No, there was no way she was going to reserve argument. As soon as Quinlan—or, God forbid, McDaniels—sat down, Talon would be on her feet to give the jury her competing version of events. The true version of events.

Or at least, that's what she'd tell them.

Which led to the other major consideration: the format of opening statement. What made for the most compelling opening statement? The structure most likely to convince the jurors that maybe, just maybe, the prosecution got it wrong? That maybe, just maybe, this great nation of ours does occasionally charge citizens with crimes they didn't commit? That 'innocent until proven guilty' was more than a catch phrase?

Fortunately, there was a general consensus that the best way to deliver an opening statement was to just tell a story. Opening statement was supposed to be a preview of what the lawyer expected the evidence to show, not an argument as to why the jury should return a certain verdict. Any such attempt would be objectionable as 'argumentative.' So just tell a story. Convert those thousands of pages of police reports and witness interviews into a compelling narrative that explained to the jury what happened, why they were there, and what they were about to hear. And also suggested a particular verdict without actually asking for it.

Unfortunately, that was usually a lot easier for the prosecution. The prosecutor already had a story: the defendant committed a crime. It was the same, case after case. But the defense might be anything from alibi, to self-defense, to 'prove it.' And 'prove it' wasn't much of a story. The only thing that kind of opening statement would communicate was that there *was* no defense story—which strongly suggested the accuracy of the prosecution story the jurors just heard.

For every stage of a trial—jury selection, opening statement, witness testimony, closing argument—there was a lawyer who would swear, 'You win the case in jury selection,' or 'You win the case in closing argument.' Talon figured it probably depended on the facts of a given case. But if she had to pick one segment of a trial being the one that, above all others, determined the outcome, she would have put her money on opening statement. Whichever attorney gave the better opening statement went into the rest of the trial with a lead. The question was whether it would be a one-run lead, a two-run lead, or—if she really knocked it out of the park—maybe even more. The kind of opening that, when a witness testified differently, the jurors doubted the witness's word.

That happened when the story was so good, so rich, so compelling, the jurors felt like they were experiencing it themselves. So that the witness's inconsistent testimony didn't just contradict the lawyer's opening statement, it contradicted the juror's own (false) memory of the event.

"So," Talon wondered aloud, "what's my story?"

* * *

Talon was so focused on her opening statement that she didn't think to look at the caller I.D. when the phone rang a little before 6:00 p.m.

"Talon Winter," she answered, almost absently, her eyes and concentration still on the notepad on her desk.

"Talon? Oh, I thought I'd get your voice mail."

It was Sullivan. Talon's heart dropped. "Oh. Hey, Sam. Uh,

no. Working late tonight. Opening statements in the morning.

Although she would have preferred to keep the conversation on her murder trial, she knew that wasn't why Sullivan was calling.

"You must be pretty focused on that," he replied. "You forgot to pay me the retainer."

Talon hesitated. There wasn't much point in lying. "I didn't exactly forget," she admitted. Besides, the truth would make the conversation go faster.

"I know," Sullivan answered.

He didn't say anything else for a moment. Talon wasn't sure what to say either. Finally, Sullivan broke the silence.

"So, are you ready for your opening statement?"

Talon smiled weakly to herself, surprised by the question, but not by what it meant. "I'm getting there."

"Do you have a plan for the trial?" Sullivan asked.

Talon thought for a moment. "Yeah. I think so."

"Good, good," Sullivan said.

After a few more moments of awkward silence, Sullivan asked, "You're not going to pay the retainer, are you?"

Talon frowned. "No," she admitted. "Not right now. I can't."

She could practically hear him nodding over the phone. "Okay," he said simply. "I knew that. I have a plan, too."

"You do?" Talon asked.

"Of course," he replied. "But don't worry about it right now. Worry about your opening statement. I'll take care of our case."

Talon closed her eyes and felt at least some of her stress lift off her shoulders. She didn't ask what his plan was. "Thanks, Sam."

Sullivan laughed just slightly. "Don't thank me yet. I'll call you in a week or so. Focus on your murder trial. Forget about this case until then."

That was exactly what Talon had already done. But she didn't say that much. "Sounds good, Sam. I will."

Sullivan hung up first and Talon returned the receiver to the cradle and considered.

She considered wondering what Sullivan's plan was. She considered spending time trying to guess what it might be or how it would affect her. She considered caring about it.

But she couldn't. She didn't.

She stood up and stepped over to the mirror she had finally hung up on the wall.

"Ladies and gentlemen," Talon said to her reflection, "let me tell you Michael Jameson's story…"

CHAPTER 29

The next morning, Michael Jameson was waiting for Talon outside the courtroom, sitting on the bench in the hallway, holding his wife's hand. They stood up and Michael shook her hand when she reached them.

"Talon," was all he said. What more was there to say really?

Alicia just smiled. No words for the spouse of a man on trial for murder.

"Are you ready?" Talon asked. It was for both of them.

Alicia looked down and shook her head slightly.

But Michael looked Talon in the eye. "Ready? Of course I'm not ready. How could anybody be ready for this?"

Talon nodded. "You prepare," she answered. Then she grabbed a hold of the courtroom door. "And then you execute."

Ten minutes later, Talon and Michael were seated at the defense table, Alicia was behind them in the gallery, and Quinlan and McDaniels were at the prosecution table. Judge Kirshner entered and took the bench.

"Mr. Quinlan," the judge got right to it, "is the State ready for opening statements?"

Quinlan stood up. He didn't look as nervous as Talon had hoped he would. "Yes, Your Honor."

Kirchner looked to the defense table. "Ms. Winter, is the defense ready for opening statements?"

Talon stood up as well. Time to execute. "Yes, Your Honor. The defense is ready."

Judge Kirshner nodded to her bailiff, who stood up and fetched the jurors who had been told to arrive thirty minutes earlier and were already waiting in the jury room. As soon as the jurors were all seated in the jury box, Judge Kirshner addressed them.

"Ladies and gentlemen of the jury," she said, "please give your attention to Mr. Quinlan, who will deliver the opening statement on behalf of the prosecution."

And they were off.

Quinlan had remained standing while the jurors filed in and sat down, knowing he would be speaking first. He nodded up at the judge and stepped out from behind the prosecution table.

"Thank you, Your Honor. May it please the Court, counsel, ladies and gentlemen of the jury."

It was an overly formal, outdated way to begin an opening statement. *Good,* Talon thought. Anything to get in the way of Quinlan actually establishing a bond with the jurors. He took up a spot directly in front of the jury and probably one step too close to the jury box. Then he began his opening statement in earnest.

Talon had allowed herself to hope, maybe even expect, that Quinlan would do a poor job in his opening statement. Unfortunately, as much of a jerk as Quinlan was outside of court, there was still a reason he was allowed to try murder cases. He could turn on the charm when he needed to. And right then, unfortunately for her, he needed to.

"Justice delayed," he began, then pausing to exploit the attention he was afforded by the formality of the situation, "is still better than justice denied."

Talon frowned inside. It was a good opening line. Memorable, but not too cheesy. And it encapsulated the strongest argument for the State's case, namely that it was never too late to hold someone accountable for murder.

Talon knew what she had to do. The only question was when to do it. But she had faith in Quinlan…

He continued. "Almost twenty-five years ago, a young man named Jordan McCabe was murdered just a few short blocks from this very courthouse."

Talon knew that wasn't exactly true. The County-City Building was near the top of the steep hill up from the Tacoma waterfront, near the edge of the aptly named Hilltop neighborhood where the shooting had taken place. But it was still outside of it. And the murder had happened deep inside the Hilltop. It was a small inaccuracy, Talon knew, but those could add up, if Quinlan kept choosing dramatic effect over the factual precision.

"He was shot twice in the chest," Quinlan continued, "and left to bleed to death in the middle of Cushman Avenue. His killer disappeared into the night, never to be found. Literally, getting away with murder. Almost."

Quinlan turned and pointed at Jameson.

"Until twenty-five years later, the killer was finally identified. That man. The defendant. Michael Jameson."

Talon had made a point of looking down to take notes, rather than watch Quinlan as if he were actually interesting or something. That was in case a juror or two happened to glance over at her. But the naming of her client guaranteed all the jurors would be looking over at the defense table. No one likes being called out in a crowd, let alone singled out as a murderer. Michael looked appropriately distressed, but Talon patted his arm confidently and shook her head just the right amount. 'No, he's not,' she was telling the jury.

Quinlan turned back to the jury box. "You're going to hear from a lot of witnesses during this trial."

Talon went back to sort of taking notes. But she was listening intently, waiting for it.

"You'll hear from the first officers who were dispatched to the scene. You'll hear from the original detectives who investigated what few leads they had back then. You'll hear from the current detective who picked up the case once the trail became hot again. And you'll hear from the victims."

Talon looked up.

"Well, not the murder victim, of course," Quinlan corrected, "but the victims of the other crimes the def—"

"Objection!" Talon pounced. "Objection, Your Honor!" she repeated as she stood and slapped the table.

All eyes turned to her. Quinlan's were wide. Kirchner's were curious.

Before the judge could say anything, Talon added, "I'd like to be heard outside the presence of the jury."

Quinlan let out an exasperated sigh. "This is opening statement," he complained, as if that alone should result in the objection being overruled.

"I'd prefer not to interrupt Mr. Quinlan's opening statement," Kirchner echoed his sentiment. "You'll have your chance to speak, Ms. Winter."

"Based on what Mr. Quinlan just said, the damage may be irreparable by that point, Your Honor," Talon answered. "I'm trying to protect the integrity of this trial."

That sounded pretty good in front of the jury.

Kirchner could see showmanship for what it was. But she wanted to protect the trial as much, or more, than anyone. And she was experienced enough, she could probably guess what Talon's objection was. The judge sighed herself, then looked to the jurors.

"I'm going to ask you to retire to the jury room for a moment, ladies and gentleman," she explained. Quinlan's shoulders dropped and he stepped back toward the prosecution table. "My bailiff will bring you back into the courtroom very shortly."

The jurors stood and filed out of the courtroom, curious, but mindful not to speak. The lot of the audience as the drama played out in front of them. When the door to the jury room closed, Quinlan beat everyone to the verbal punch.

"This is outrageous, Your Honor! I was in the middle of my opening statement. The only valid objection in opening statement is that it's argumentative, and I was nowhere near arguing the case. I was simply explaining to the jurors who they were going to hear from. Ms. Winter objected for the sole purpose of interrupting my flow."

Talon couldn't help but smirk at Quinlan having a 'flow.' But she knew to wait for the judge to take control of the discussion before speaking.

"I understand why you're upset, Mr. Quinlan," Judge Kirchner said. "And I share your concerns. But I'd like to hear from Ms. Winter first." She looked down at Talon. "What's your objection, counsel, and why couldn't it wait until Mr. Quinlan had finished his opening statement?"

"My objection, Your Honor," Talon answered, "is that the prosecutor just told the jury that my client committed more crimes than he is charged with, thereby prejudicing him by inviting the jury to convict him of murder regardless of the actual evidence as to that one and only charge."

Kirchner's face scrunched into thought as she tried to recall exactly what Quinlan had said.

Quinlan didn't bother thinking. "I said no such thing, Your Honor," he insisted.

"He said," Talon was ready to answer, "the jurors would hear, not from the victim of the murder, but the victims of the other crimes my client allegedly committed. Or he was about to when I objected. There are no other crimes charged. Telling the jury Mr. Jameson committed other crimes is a textbook case of hoping jurors will convict a defendant because they think he's a bad person generally, rather than because of whatever evidence might have been presented." Then a jab: "Obviously, Mr. Quinlan knows he won't be able to prove the charged crime beyond a reasonable doubt and is already hedging his bets and lowering expectations."

"I am not," Quinlan shot back. "And your client did commit other crimes. He was dealing drugs, for one thing. That's why this happened in the first place."

"He's not charged with drug dealing," Talon answered.

"That's because the statute of limitations on drug dealing ran years ago," Quinlan said. "The only crime that doesn't have a statute of limitations is murder and that's why it's the only crime he's charged with."

Judge Kirchner stepped in. "Counsel, stop arguing with each other and direct your comments to the bench. Ms. Winter, I understand your point, but if this case arose out of a drug deal gone wrong, how can the State explain the evidence without mentioning the crime of unlawful delivery of a controlled substance?"

Talon nodded. "In all candor, Your Honor, that's not my problem. The State is the one who chose to bring the charge on the flimsiest of evidence. They could sanitize it and have their witnesses simply say it was a business transaction without mentioning drugs."

"That won't work, Your Honor," Quinlan started, but Kirchner cut him off.

"Wait your turn, Mr. Quinlan," she instructed. He nodded in compliance, and the judge turned back to Talon.

"Isn't the drug dealing part of the res gestae, Ms. Winter?" the judge asked. "It's just part of what happened. Gunshots aren't usually fired at your run-of-the-mill business transaction, but it's not uncommon that a drug deal can turn violent very quickly."

Talon shrugged. "Maybe, Your Honor. Maybe not. The State hasn't endorsed any expert witnesses to discuss the statistics of drug deals gone wrong. But regardless, the State can't call it a crime. My client is charged with one crime: murder. And that's the only thing in this trial that should be labeled a crime."

"I think the jury will know," Kirchner pointed out, "that selling drugs is a crime."

Another shrug. "Maybe," Talon conceded, "but the State can't be allowed to call it that. It's irrelevant. Would you allow the State to say Mr. Jameson committed a crime if he'd had some marijuana in his pocket? It was a crime then, but isn't now. What was illegal then is irrelevant unless it's charged now. And nothing is charged except murder. The State cannot be allowed to smear my client by claiming he committed other crimes that are uncharged and for which I haven't been put on notice I would need to defend against. It violates his right to prepared counsel and a fair trial."

It was a good speech. But speeches by defense attorneys were usually discounted. A defense attorney had an obligation to argue every possible point in favor of their client, but that made each argument suspect. The judge turned to Quinlan.

"Response?" she invited.

Quinlan huffed. "I'm not even sure how to respond, Your Honor. It's not like Ms. Winter didn't know I was going to tell the jury that Jordan McCabe was shot during a drug deal gone wrong. If she was going to object, she should have made a motion in limine before I started my opening. The horse is out of the barn now, I think."

Talon raised an eyebrow at the metaphor. "If I might, Your Honor," she interjected. "I didn't make a motion in limine because I didn't think Mr. Quinlan would be so careless and brazen as to accuse my client of crimes he's not charged with."

"You knew I was going to talk about a drug deal," Quinlan shot at her.

"I didn't know you were going to call it a crime," Talon returned.

"Drug dealing *is* a crime," Quinlan responded in a raised voice.

"Enough!" Judge Kirchner raised her own voice even more. "I told the two of you to address your comments to me, not each other. I won't tolerate another outburst like that."

Both attorneys apologized. Talon took a moment to glance at Amity McDaniels. She was still seated, her hands folded on the table, and her eyes focused attentively on the judge. Very professional. Unlike her co-counsel. Or Talon, for that matter. But Talon's outbursts were also strategic. The jury had been out for over five minutes already. Hardly a short recess. One of them had probably already started a chain reaction of using the bathroom while they waited. Even if Kirchner ended the arguments right then, it'd be at least another five minutes before Quinlan was back in front of them, picking up wherever it was he'd left off.

Mission accomplished.

"Anything more, Ms. Winter?" the judge asked.

"I believe I stopped Mr. Quinlan before he finished his sentence accusing my client of uncharged, undefendable crimes, so I don't believe the Court needs to strike any comments by Mr. Quinlan or instruct the jury to disregard anything. I would simply ask the Court to instruct Mr. Quinlan not to use the word crime when discussing anything other than the one and only crime alleged here, the murder of Jordan McCabe."

Judge Kirchner looked to Quinlan. "Can you live with that?"

Quinlan didn't seem to appreciate just how much time the entire argument was taking up. Rather than agree and move on, he replied, "No, Your Honor, I can't. The defendant did commit other crimes that night. The fact that the statute of limitations prohibits their prosecution doesn't mean they weren't crimes at the time."

Kirchner exhaled and considered. "What crimes do you want to tell the jury Mr. Jameson committed?"

"Well," Quinlan hesitated. "Selling drugs for one."

"Can't you just tell them he was selling drugs without calling it a crime?" the judge asked.

"But everyone knows selling drugs is a crime," Quinlan repeated his earlier argument.

"So why do you have to say it then?" Judge Kirchner asked.

Quinlan opened his mouth, but didn't have a reply ready. "Uh…"

Kirchner looked at the clock. Almost ten minutes now. "Okay," she announced, "I'm going to sustain the objection. Mr. Quinlan, you can tell the jury what facts you think the evidence will show, including describing conduct which would have been criminal, but you can't call it a crime or accuse the defendant of committing any crimes other than the one with which he is charged."

"Your Honor," Quinlan started to protest.

"Do you really want to turn this into a half-hour argument, Mr. Quinlan?" she interrupted. "Should we adjourn your opening statement for an hour or two while you go look up some case law? I would think you'd like to get back into your flow."

The judge said the last word the same way Talon felt about it.

"No, Your Honor," Quinlan replied meekly. "Thank you. I'm ready to proceed."

Kirchner looked at Talon again. "Ms. Winter?"

"Nothing further," Talon answered. "Thank you."

And thank you, Mr. Quinlan, she thought. He'd been slick when he'd started. She guessed he was rattled now. Not just about having been objected to on that one subject, but wondering what else Talon might object to. He hadn't seen his comment as objectionable. Were there more landmines buried in his prepared remarks? He didn't know.

It was sneaky, maybe even dirty. But she had a life in her hands. There was no going back to civil litigation.

Judge Kirchner called for the jury, but, as expected, it took nearly five more minutes before everyone was seated again and Quinlan could pick up where he'd left off. And not even quite there, given Talon's sustained objection.

"As I was saying," Quinlan tried to rally himself, "you will hear from many different witnesses during this trial. Police officers, civilians, forensics experts."

His voice had lost its confident edge. He was still loud enough, still delivering his words in the right order, without hesitation or stammering. But it wasn't the same. His voice didn't grab the jurors; he didn't have the room any more. He plodded through the rest of his opening like an exhausted parent reading a bedtime story so the kid will go to sleep, not because it's interesting.

"Twenty-five years after Jordan McCabe was murdered," Quinlan said, "the gun that killed him was recovered from a burglar who had burglarized the defendant's home. He'd kept the gun all those years. When the gun was test-fired, the ballistics matched those found at the scene of the murder. The killer had finally revealed himself."

Quinlan stood up a little straighter, ready to deliver his parting lines. "The defendant kept the gun as a souvenir, but it was the justice system that never forgot. Never forgot about Jordan McCabe. And never gave up on holding his killer responsible."

He pointed again at Michael Jameson. This time Talon kept her eyes riveted on Quinlan. She was Michael's champion, and Quinlan was his attacker. The jury needed to see that too.

"At the end of this trial," Quinlan concluded, "I will stand up again and ask you to return a verdict of guilty to the crime of murder in the first degree. Thank you."

Quinlan strode back to the prosecution table and sat down. McDaniels gave him an encouraging nod, but he didn't return it. He was obviously still shaken by Talon's gambit.

But Talon didn't have time to gloat.

"Now, ladies and gentlemen," Judge Kirchner announced, "please give your attention to Ms. Winter, who will deliver the opening statement on behalf of Mr. Jameson."

CHAPTER 30

Talon stood up and took her place before the jurors. There was a quiet that seized a courtroom when an attorney was about to deliver an opening statement. Part of it was artificial: the rules said no one else was supposed to talk. But part of it was organic: the jurors really did want to hear what the attorneys had to say. They may have been able to infer some things from the questions during jury selection, but these were the first direct statements of the case. And like any first impression, they tended to stay with the jurors throughout the trial.

No pressure.

New attorneys often employed what was called 'the ramble.' The attorney would thank the judge and jurors, then re-introduce themselves by name and which side they represented, then maybe an explanation about what opening statement was supposed to be. A lot of words whose only real purpose was to calm down the speaker. In the meantime, the jurors, who wanted nothing more than to hear that side of the story, sit there, thinking, but unable to say, 'Get on with it!'

The better tactic—the one they taught at trial advocacy clinics—was what was known as the 'attention grabber.' A phrase or line designed to grab the jurors' attention. Like a catch phrase for a movie or the first line of a novel. Quinlan had done a good job with his—that was why Talon had to interrupt his flow. Talon needed one too. A better one.

She'd given a lot of thought to it. What was the case really about? What was the single most important part? What was the one thing she wanted the jurors to think about throughout the entire trial, even when they were home, brushing their teeth and getting ready for bed?

Well, that was easy.

"Michael Jameson," Talon began. And she, too, gestured at her client, but with an open hand, not an accusatory finger.

"He's sitting right there," she went on. "Look at him. He's a real person. With real emotions and real thoughts and a real story."

Opening statement was all about storytelling. Talon was going to tell them her story. Michael's story.

"In fact, Michael has many stories. We all do. Stories that capture a snapshot of who we are, who we were, who we hope to be."

She stepped to one side and opened her body slightly toward her client. It was an invitation to look at Michael again, but to join Talon in her ruminations as they did so.

"Think back," she said, "about the person you were when you were still in high school. Now think about the person you are now. For some of us, those seem like two pretty different persons."

There were several nods and at least one light chuckle from the jury box. Good, Talon thought. They were listening. More importantly, they were experiencing.

"But you're still the same person." A subtle shift from 'him' and 'we' to 'you.' You, the jurors. "It's all the same story, just a different chapter.

"Stop and think for a moment. Think back to your best friend in high school. Or your first girlfriend or boyfriend. Maybe even a rival on the football team or in the math class. Someone who knew you back then. Now, think about the story they might tell about you. One that really summed up who, to them, you were."

She took a step back toward her original position. It told the jurors to pay closer attention. To her, to what she was about to say.

"Now, imagine your best friend now. Your spouse or significant other. That co-worker who always seems to look at you sideways. What story would they tell?

"Think about your kids. Or even your grandchildren. What story would they tell if someone asked what you were like?

"Now, put those stories next to each other. The person your best friend in high school knew, the person your spouse knows, the person your boss knows, your kids know, your neighbors know. Would they even be recognizable as the same person? Would your prom date recognize the story from your grandkids?"

Talon smiled. "For some of us, the answer may be yes. There may be some thread of similarity that connects eighteen-year-old us to forty-five-year-old us, to eighty-year-old us. But for most of us, life is about changes, about growth. About pain and loss and falling off the horse, if only to see if we can get back up again. And when we do, when we climb back up on that horse after being thrown, we're not that same person who let a horse throw him off."

Some of the jurors were still looking at Michael. Some of them were looking at her. And a lot of them were looking down, walking down their own path of memories, recalling the horses that threw them, and how they were different for it.

Talon let them wander a few moments more. Then she

brought them back to the courtroom. Back to Michael Jameson.

"So, Michael has more than one story. Or rather, more than one chapter to his story. I'm going to tell you two."

She turned and slowly walked toward the near side of the jury box. Pacing was never good during an opening statement—or closing argument—but was common. Good trial lawyers were like ducks: calm on the surface but paddling like hell underneath. If you're not nervous when you're talking to a jury, then you're not paying attention. The trick was to convert that anxiety into energy for the presentation. Like gasoline exploding hundreds of times per minute to drive the race car forward.

But proper placement in the courtroom could underline and emphasize points of the argument in ways no words could. Talon would stand near her client when she told the jury about who Michael was now. But she'd stand at the other end of the jury box when she addressed the earlier chapter of his story.

"First, I'm going to tell you about the Michael Jameson I know. The Michael Jameson who sits before you today. Go ahead, look over at him again." Another warm gesture toward her client. "*That* Michael Jameson."

She smiled at him. He was clearly uncomfortable with everyone staring at him. Good. That's what a normal person would feel, how a normal person would look. Talon hadn't warned him. That would have ruined it.

"Michael is a computer programmer. He works at a company called DigiDream International, based right here in Tacoma. They create apps for smartphones, graphic design software for architecture firms, and a lot of other things that the rest of us don't completely understand, but are glad exist. He's worked there for over ten years and is a supervisor now, responsible for both programming and managing other programmers."

So, the Black man in the defendant's chair actually had a job. A good one. One that required brains and hard work. Talon wondered how many of the jurors were a little surprised, and if any of them realized their surprise was part of what she was fighting.

Talon nodded to the woman in the gallery sitting two rows behind Michael. No one was allowed to sit directly behind a defendant.

"Michael is married," Talon went on. "He met his wife, Alicia, in college. They have two wonderful children. A son named Marcus, who graduated from high school this year, and a daughter, Kylee, who's about to start high school herself."

So, the Black man in the defendant's chair was not some absentee father who'd impregnated several different women and left them to raise his children alone. The only thing remarkable about all this was that it could be remarkable.

Alicia couldn't quite manage a smile—not under these circumstances—but she did give Talon a nod. Talon provided the smile, sending it to her over the rail that separated her from her husband.

Talon turned back to the jurors. "They live in University Place. A four-bedroom house, yellow with white trim, and the cars in the driveway because the garage is filled with Michael's workbench and storage boxes full of memories. He goes to the same Home Depot, and Subway, and Baskin Robbins, like everyone else in U.P."

So, the Black man in the defendant's chair didn't live on the Hilltop—not anymore, anyway. He wasn't relegated to that part of town the rest of the city's residents could avoid by taking Schuster Parkway along the water, or State Route 16 around back.

"In short," Talon said, "his story now isn't really any different from what the rest of us have, or want, anyway. It's the

American Dream. It's what makes this country great."

She'd give the jurors a beat to feel good about themselves. But only a beat.

"Or at least, that's what we want to tell ourselves. But while that chapter may look like it's happy and idyllic, there were a lot of chapters before that. A lot of chapters the rest of us don't have to read, let alone live."

Several of the jurors shifted in their seats. It was about to get uncomfortable.

"Michael moved out of the Hilltop, went to college, met Alicia. They fell in love, got married, started a family, and bought a beautiful house in the suburbs. They never looked back. Until now."

Talon dropped her voice a notch. "But now they have to look back."

She walked away from her client and took that spot on the other side of the jury box. The one that required the jurors to look away from Michael. Turn away from the Michael Jameson he was now in order to learn about the Michael Jameson he was then.

But that wasn't what Talon wanted to talk about. She wasn't about to tell them about young Michael Jameson, driving his brother around to deal drugs on the Hilltop. It wasn't about that. It was about the very act of looking back.

"They have to look back," Talon repeated. "Past Marcus' high school graduation. Past Kaylee's gymnastics tryouts. Past the last promotion and that family trip to Hawaii. Past signing the mortgage, and planning the wedding, and popping the question. Past the twenty hours Alicia was in labor with Marcus, and the emergency C-section she had with Kaylee. Past everything they've built, everything they stayed up late worrying about, everything they fought for to have a successful life in a culture that isn't comfortable with too many people like them getting too successful."

Talon wondered if Quinlan might object, but she almost wished he would. Let the middle-aged White guy in the suit object. He stayed quiet and Talon went on.

"Michael has to look back to the time before all that. Before that good job, when money was scarce. Before that house in U.P., when he lived up in the Hilltop. Before Marcus and Kaylee when Michael's own dad was gone. Before Alicia, when he was just another skinny kid trying to survive both the gangs and the cops."

Talon returned to her spot in front of the jurors, but just a little closer than she'd been before. Not too close—not crazy, threatening close. More, 'this is important' close.

"Because, let's not forget. Things have changed a lot since then. Maybe not for your typical White kid from the Brown's Point or Proctor neighborhoods. But a lot for your typical Black kid from the Hilltop."

It was Talon's time to point the accusing finger. Directly at Quinlan. "The prosecutor isn't just asking you to look back twenty-five years to what happened that night on Cushman Avenue. He's asking you to forget about all the progress we've made since then. All the progress Michael's made since then."

Talon clasped her hands and looked directly at the jurors, making eye contact with each of them as she spoke.

"But that story, the one from twenty-five years ago…"

The one the jury really wanted to hear.

The one that was actually relevant and unobjectionable.

The one she couldn't tell the jury because it implicated her client.

"…that story is best left in the past."

She took one step back and opened her hands to the jurors. "This case isn't really about what happened to Jordan McCabe twenty-five years ago. It's about what should happen to Michael

Jameson now. The truth is, the prosecution doesn't really know what happened that night. They certainly won't be able to prove it. Which means, at the end of this trial, you won't really know what happened either."

She looked again at her client. "You won't really know what Michael was like back then. But you will know what he is now:

"A father.

"A husband.

"A neighbor.

"A co-worker.

"And most importantly, not guilty of murder.

"Thank you."

The silence she'd started with also enveloped her as she returned to her seat. But rather than a silence of expectation, it was a silence of reaction, as the jurors—and everyone else in the courtroom—digested what they'd just heard.

They'd listened. That was all Talon could really have hoped for. They would view the evidence through a lens alright—the lens of Michael Jameson.

The battle was joined.

Finally, Judge Kirchner broke the silence.

"Mr. Quinlan," she boomed. "Call your first witness."

CHAPTER 31

Instead of Quinlan, McDaniels stood up to announce, "The State calls Joanne McCabe-Johnson to the stand."

Jordy McCabe's mother.

Talon wasn't surprised. The prosecution didn't have to tell her the exact order of their witnesses, but they did have to provide a complete list prior to trial. Joanne McCabe-Johnson's name was buried almost exactly in the middle of the alphabetical list of witnesses whom the State intended to call. She'd seen the name and knew she might be first.

Every good murder story starts with a body. And someone to identify it.

Joanne McCabe-Johnson walked into the courtroom and up to Judge Kirchner to be sworn in. She looked to be in her early 60s, with soft gray curls and plastic-rimmed glasses hanging from her neck on a beaded chain. Her gait was slow and deliberate as she made her way to the witness stand. Once she had fully settled into the chair and looked up, McDaniels began.

"Could you please state your name for the record?"

She did. Her voice was smooth and strong.

McDaniels nodded in acknowledgment of the response. A common tick of trial attorneys. "Did you know Jordan McCabe?"

Mrs. McCabe-Johnson nodded as well. "Yes, I did."

"How did you know him?"

"He was my son." The answer was delivered simply. No tears. No catch in the throat. Just, *He was my son*. The words were weighty enough on their own.

She didn't have any information about the murder. She didn't see what happened, how, or by whom. She really was there just to identify the body. That, and to tug on the jurors' heartstrings. A murder charge required at least some proof that an actual, living breathing human being had been killed. A conviction required the jury to care.

McDaniels took a respectful moment to allow the response to sink in, then fetched an 8" x 11" photograph from her table. Per the court rules, she showed it to Talon first, who nodded, then gave it to the witness.

"I'm handing you what's previously been marked as State's Exhibit Number One," McDaniels said for the record. "Do you recognize the person in this photograph?"

Now there was a catch in her voice. "Yes," Mrs. McCabe-Johnson answered. "That's Jordy."

"How old was he in this photograph?" McDaniels followed up.

"Seventeen," came the response. "That was his yearbook photo from his junior year at Stadium High School."

McDaniels looked up to the judge. "The State moves to admit Exhibit Number One, Your Honor."

Kirchner looked to Talon. "Any objection?"

"No, Your Honor," Talon answered.

"Exhibit Number One is admitted," Judge Kirchner declared.

"The State moves to publish, Your Honor," McDaniels continued the exhibit dance.

Talon wanted to object, of course. The last thing she wanted was for the jury to see a smiling school photo of the young man gunned down on that fateful night twenty-five years earlier. One of the last things she wanted, anyway. But it was relevant, and it was coming in, so there was no reason to make the jury think it bothered her. "No objection," she offered.

McDaniels stepped over to the projector tucked between the counsel tables and a few button pushes later, the photo of an awkward and innocent-looking seventeen-year-old Jordan McCabe was blown up on the wall opposite the jury box.

"That's your son, Jordan?" McDaniels confirmed.

Mrs. McCabe-Johnson took a moment. She smiled a terrible, painful smile. "Yes, ma'am."

Then McDaniels grabbed a second photograph off her table. The one that really mattered. Again, she showed it to Talon. Again, Talon nodded and wished she could object but knew she couldn't. Not successfully anyway.

Get on with it, she thought.

"I'm going to show you another photograph," McDaniels warned Mrs. McCabe-Johnson. "I'm sorry."

That last bit was probably objectionable. But when the jury was in the room, objections were strategic. Objecting to kindness wasn't good strategy.

"Do you recognize the young man in that photograph?" McDaniels asked.

Mrs. McCabe-Johnson looked at the photo. She grimaced slightly, but otherwise maintained her composure. She looked away as she answered, "Yes."

McDaniels took the photograph back and again asked the judge to admit and publish it. Again, Talon didn't object, and a few moments later the screen that covered the wall was filled, not with the smiling face of a high school junior, but the bloody crime scene of a long-ago murder.

It was a medium-wide shot of Cushman Avenue, houses in the background, crime scene tape everywhere, and a body in the foreground. There was no sheet over it. It was Jordy McCabe, dead and sprawled out for all the world—and the jury—to see.

McDaniels asked a few more questions. A little background on Jordy, He went to Stadium High School. He liked watching sports and hanging out with his friends. He played videogames and tinkered with computers. Not surprisingly, no mention of gang affiliations or drug dealing.

McDaniels thanked Mrs. McCabe-Johnson and sat down. It was Talon's turn.

She had a few options.

The easy thing to do was nothing. No questions. She was the victim's mother after all; it was hard to imagine a more sympathetic witness. Thank her for coming and sit down again. After all, she hadn't really done any damage. The fact that her son had been murdered wasn't really at issue. The question was, who did it? Or rather, could the State prove Michael Jameson did it?

The lazy thing to do was to go after her. The stereotypical attack cross-examination. *You didn't see what happened, did you? Your son was dealing drugs, wasn't he? Your son probably shot first, didn't he? Answer the question!*

But the smart thing to do was to use the witness—every witness—to support her own case theory. Her story.

Talon stood up and offered an understated nod to the

witness. "Good morning, Mrs. McCabe-Johnson," she began.

As Mrs. McCabe-Johnson returned the greeting cautiously, Talon stepped out from behind her counsel table and took a very specific spot at the bar: not too far away to seem sheepish, but not too close to seem aggressive. Confident, but not attacking. You don't attack the dead boy's mother.

"Your son's birthday was March eleventh, right?" she confirmed. Easy enough to read from the police reports, or the death certificate. "How old would he have been this year?"

Mrs. McCabe-Johnson thought for a moment. "Forty-two."

"So he was seventeen when he died, correct?"

"Right," Mrs. McCabe-Johnson answered, her voice and expression guarded against the woman representing her son's killer. Well, alleged killer anyway.

"You mentioned during direct examination," Talon continued, "that he was interested in computers?"

Mrs. McCabe-Johnson frowned slightly. "Yes. He was always tinkering on them."

"Was he taking them apart too?" Talon asked. She wasn't quite leaning on the bar, but she had assumed a conversational affect. "Or just the on-screen stuff."

"No, he definitely was taking them apart," Mrs. McCabe-Johnson remembered with a faint smile. "He had circuit boards and whatever else those things are called all over his room. He'd get old parts from the computer repair shop and was always wiring them up together to make some new super computer or something. I didn't really understand it, to be honest."

"But Jordy understood it, huh?" Talon followed up.

"I think so," she replied with a stronger smile and a shrug. "It seemed like he was always working on something or another."

"That's a good field," Talon said. "Was he interested in

doing computer programming or something in the computer field for a living?"

"I was hoping he would," Mrs. McCabe-Johnson answered. "Something that could help him be successful."

"That's what every mother wants, right?" Talon asked. Not, *'So he could get out of the Hilltop.'* You don't insult where the dead boy's mother raised him. "For her child to be successful."

"Or happy," she countered. "I wanted him to be happy. Being successful can help with that."

Talon nodded. "Easier to be happy if your bills are paid, huh?"

She knew that well enough herself. And she knew most, if not all, of the jurors did too. Just a small moment of bonding. She was going to need them to trust her when she finally got up in front of them again for closing argument.

"I suppose so," Mrs. McCabe-Johnson answered. "But we got by, and we were happy."

Oops. Don't insult the dead boy's mother's financial situation. Time to move forward.

"So, Jordy was interested in computers, and he would have been forty-two this year," Talon recounted. "Do you ever think about what his life might have been like if he were still alive?"

Mrs. McCabe-Johnson smiled sadly. "Every day."

Talon acknowledged the sadness with another simple nod. "Tell me."

Talon waited for a moment while Mrs. McCabe-Johnson gathered her thoughts. Everyone did. That gave the jurors a chance to refocus and lean forward a bit for the answer. It also gave McDaniels a chance to object. There were several possible objections, including 'calls for narrative' and 'relevance.' But McDaniels didn't interrupt. You don't interrupt the dead boy's mother. Especially when she was about to talk about her dead boy.

"Grandkids," Mrs. McCabe-Johnson started. "I'd have grandkids. Lots of them. Jordy loved kids. He was always playing with the little kids in the neighborhood, and he loved it when his baby cousins came over on holidays. So, yeah, for starters, he'd have kids."

"And they'd live nearby?" Talon said. "You'd want your grandkids nearby, right?"

"Right," Mrs. McCabe-Johnson answered. Not right next door. "A man needs his privacy from his mother. But not too far either. Tacoma area, definitely."

"Maybe Lakewood?" Talon suggested. "Or University Place?"

"Yeah, somewhere like that," Mrs. McCabe-Johnson agreed. "Someplace with good schools. My grandbabies should go to good schools."

"So, married with kids, living nearby, with good neighborhood schools," Talon summarized. "And maybe a job working as a computer programmer?"

"Sure, computer programmer," Mrs. McCabe-Johnson said. "That sounds good. Or maybe a teacher. Anything really. Whatever made him happy."

Talon took a moment before her next question. She let her expression tighten from encouragement to discomfort. Sadness. The moment was to allow Mrs. McCabe-Johnson's vision of her son's future to settle into the jurors' minds. It was any of them wanted for their own children, for themselves. Most of them had probably made it too.

"But your son never got to do any of that, did he?" Talon asked after another moment. "That's part of what makes this all so tragic, isn't it? He could have had all that. He should have had the chance. But because of what happened that one terrible night, it was all taken away from him. His wife, his kids, his house nearby with the good schools. It was all taken away, wasn't it?"

Mrs. McCabe-Johnson frowned. "Yes. It was."

"And that's just not right, is it?"

"No," Mrs. McCabe-Johnson agreed. "It's not right."

Talon nodded, offering a last pained smile. "Thank you, Mrs. McCabe-Johnson. No further questions."

Judge Kirchner looked to the prosecution table. "Any redirect examination, Ms. McDaniels?"

Talon had returned to her seat. She knew the answer. Redirect was to show how the defense attorney has twisted the facts with unfair and misleading questions. It wasn't for what Talon had just done.

"No, Your Honor," McDaniels stood to reply. "Thank you."

Judge Kirchner turned to Mrs. McCabe-Johnson. "You are excused, ma'am. Thank you."

You thank the dead boy's mother.

Mrs. McCabe-Johnson returned the thanks, then made her way down from the witness stand. When she'd reached the door to the hallway, Judge Kirchner turned again to the prosecution.

"You may call your next witness."

This time Quinlan stood up. "The State calls retired detective Harold Halcomb."

CHAPTER 32

McDaniels fetched the witness from the hallway while Quinlan took his spot at the bar, a little farther away from the witness stand than Talon had just stood. More sheepish, even with his own witness. Or at least, that's what Talon hoped it communicated to the jurors.

Halcomb entered the courtroom and strode up to the judge, his right hand already raised by the time he stopped walking right in front of the bench. Judge Kirchner swore him in and a moment later he threw his large body into the witness stand.

Retirement seemed to agree with him. He was stout, with a large belly and fat hands. Rosy cheeks and a pink, bulbous nose rested between his white moustache and what was left of his thinning white hair. He'd worn a tweed blazer over an open-collared shirt, but the sleeves were a little short anymore. Talon guessed it had been a few years since he'd had to wear a jacket anywhere, especially court. He seemed very relaxed. Especially for a murder trial.

Quinlan started with the usual name, rank, and serial

number.

"Harold Halcomb."

"Detective Sergeant, Tacoma Police Department."

"Homicides and major crimes."

"Retired twelve years ago in May."

Then they moved on to the case at bar.

"Were you involved in the investigation of the murder of Jordan McCabe?" Quinlan asked.

"Yes, sir," Halcomb answered. He'd been trained, like all cops, to deliver his answers to the jury. Jurors usually appreciated it when a witness looked at them while explaining something or recalling an incident. It felt forced when the witness looked at the jurors, but said 'sir' back to the lawyer he wasn't looking at.

"How were you involved?"

"I was the lead detective," Halcomb told the jurors. That was more natural. Talon considered how she might use his training against him.

Then Quinlan took the witness through the crime scene and early investigation. It was important, and it took a while, but it wasn't substantially different from what either Quinlan or Talon had said in opening statement. No bombshells. Jordan McCabe was shot twice in the chest and bled out in the middle of Cushman Avenue. That much was not in controversy. Throughout, Halcomb delivered his answers to the twelve people in the jury box who were going to decide Michael Jameson's fate. He was affable enough and the jurors seemed to like him. Talon would need to undo that.

Halcomb explained all the steps he took, but ultimately the leads dried up and the case went cold. He retired before it was solved. But, he made sure to tell those rapt jurors, he never forgot about poor Jordy McCabe.

"No further questions," Quinlan advised the judge and he

returned to his seat.

"Cross-examination?" Judge Kirchner asked Talon.

Talon stood up and tugged her suitcoat into place. "Yes, Your Honor." *Oh, yes.*

In truth, Talon didn't have that much to ask him about. It wasn't going to be so much what he said, as how he said it. She took a spot at the bar, a little closer to the witness, but not quite as close as she might have otherwise. It needed to be an unremarkable place to stand; she didn't want him to notice her proximity. That would ruin it.

"Good morning, detective," she started.

"It's retired detective now," he told the jurors with a smile.

"Of course," Talon replied. "As I said, good morning."

Halcomb hesitated, then returned the greeting. "Good morning." But it was delivered more to the jurors than Talon.

"You were in charge of the investigation into Jordan McCabe's murder?" she confirmed.

"Yes, ma'am." Again, though, Halcomb looked away when saying 'ma'am.'

"So you decided what investigative steps to take, correct?"

"Correct."

"What evidence to send to the crime lab, whom to interview, which leads to pursue? Those were all your decisions."

"Yes, ma'am." Again, an affable smile to the jurors. And Talon was sure to notice a few smiles in return.

"So, the decision to terminate the investigation was also yours, correct?"

Halcomb shrugged his shoulders equivocally. "It wasn't a matter of terminating the investigation exactly," he told the jurors. "It was just a matter of running out of leads."

"Well, who decided there were no more leads to follow?"

Talon asked. "That was you, right? You were the lead detective."

"I was the lead detective," Halcomb confirmed. "But the leads dried up on their own."

"Well, there's also the question of resources, right?" Talon asked. "You had other cases as well, right?"

"I did have other cases," Halcomb told the jurors. "We have plenty of crime here in Tacoma. Especially back then and especially up on the Hilltop."

"You mean especially in the Black neighborhood," Talon challenged.

If a record had been playing, it would have scratched to a halt. Halcomb turned away from the jurors to finally look directly at Talon. "That's not what I said."

"It might not be what you said," Talon agreed. "But it's what you meant. The Hilltop. That's the Black neighborhood, right? Especially 'back then'?"

"It was a high crime area," Halcomb answered grimly. Then he remembered to look at the jurors again. "It doesn't matter who lives there."

"Doesn't it?" Talon asked. "Would you have given up on the case so easily if it had been a young White teenager gunned down in the middle of Proctor Avenue, the nice neighborhood?"

"We didn't give up on the case," Halcomb told the jurors, but without the previously ubiquitous smile. "The case gave up on us."

"You didn't answer my question, Detective," Talon pointed out. "Can you honestly tell these jurors that, twenty-five years ago, you would have let the case go cold if the victim had been a White teenager from the rich neighborhood instead of a Black teenager from *that* neighborhood?"

"I would never do that," Halcomb assured the jurors.

"Are you sure, Detective?" Talon pressed. "Is it possible you did it without even realizing it? That you had some unconscious bias you didn't even know about that enabled you to let go of that case a little bit easier than if the victim hadn't been just another young Black man gunned down on the Hilltop?"

"I don't have unconscious bias," he told the jurors.

"Oh really?" Talon asked. "Then why have you refused to give me the common decency of looking at me when you answer my questions? Is it because I'm a woman of color?"

"No," Halcomb insisted. "Of course not." But he couldn't decide whom to address, and his head swiveled back and forth like an owl. A startled owl.

"Isn't it common decency to look at the person you're talking to?" Talon demanded.

"Well, yes, but," Halcomb started.

"And aren't I the one asking you questions?"

"Yes, but my training—"

"You were trained to ignore women? To ignore minorities?"

"No, of course not. I was trained to look at the jurors when testifying."

"So, you're using a parlor trick to make the jurors like you more?"

The jurors weren't smiling any more.

"No, no," Halcomb told them. Then he made sure to look at Talon again. "It's to help them understand my testimony."

"To understand, for example" Talon challenged, "that there was just a lot of crime *up there*, in *that* neighborhood, with *those* people?"

"That's not what I said," Halcomb repeated.

Talon ignored his answer. "Do you have any idea how disrespectful it is to look away from a woman when answering her questions?"

Halcomb caught himself. "No," he admitted. "I'm sorry. I didn't realize."

"Just like you didn't realize the reason you closed the Jordy McCabe case so easily was because it was just another Black-on-Black shooting back then, in that neighborhood."

"I didn't do that," Halcomb maintained.

"But you just admitted," Talon pointed out, "that you didn't even realize it was rude to turn your back on me when answering my questions. How can you be so certain you didn't have some unconscious bias when you closed this case with no further investigation?"

"I'm certain," Halcomb answered.

"You're certain you're not biased?" Talon asked.

"Yes. Absolutely certain."

Talon stepped into his comfort zone finally. "That's how we know you're lying."

She turned her back on him. "No further questions."

Quinlan popped to his feet before the judge even asked if he had any redirect. He couldn't let that stand.

"Detective," he stated, "did you close the Jordan McCabe murder investigation early because Mr. McCabe was African-American?"

"Absolutely not," Halcomb answered. He made sure to respond directly to Quinlan.

"Did you address your answers to the jury because you were trying to disrespect Ms. Winter?"

Again, "Absolutely not."

That seemed to be enough for Quinlan. "Thank you, Detective. No further questions."

Talon stood up. Re-cross. She retook her position within his personal space.

"Mr. Quinlan is a White male, correct?" she started.

Halcomb hesitated, but there was only one answer. "Correct."

"And you just looked directly at him to answer his questions, didn't you?"

"That's because—"

"Didn't you?" Talon interrupted. "Answer my question, sir, even if I am a woman."

Halcomb set his jaw. "Yes, I looked directly at him."

"And you didn't correct him just now when he called you 'detective' instead of 'retired detective,' now did you?"

Halcomb thought for a moment. "I guess I didn't notice he said that."

"But you noticed it when I did," Talon pointed out. "And you felt it was appropriate to correct me about the exact way I addressed you—in the middle of a murder trial."

"I'm sorry," Halcomb offered. "I didn't realize."

"You didn't realize you might be doing things that are biased, even though you had the best of intentions."

"Right," Halcomb conceded.

"That's all I wanted you to realize, Retired Detective Halcomb," Talon thanked him. "Nothing further."

Quinlan stood up as Talon returned to her table, but then he demurred. There was no good way to rehabilitate that. "No further questions, Your Honor."

And Retired Detective Harold Holcomb was done.

CHAPTER 33

Following the testimony of *Retired* Detective Harold Halcomb, Judge Kirchner looked at the clock and decided to adjourn the trial for the day. Talon checked in with Michael, then sent him home; every day at home with his family was a gift. She packed up her things in silence while Quinlan and McDaniels did the same. No amiable small talk between attorneys after the judge and jury left the courtroom. Some attorneys could do that: drop the advocate's role like an old cloak and grab drinks with the enemy. But not Talon Winter. Trial was like a drug to her. Her adrenaline was flowing and her synapses were in overdrive. She couldn't just turn it off with the bang of the gavel. She was in her zone. And it was a small zone. There wasn't really room for anyone else.

Which made it all the more jarring when she headed for the exit and found Curt standing at the doorway, waiting for her.

"Ruthless," he commented, leaning against the wall next to the doors, arms crossed and biceps bulging. "That's a compliment, by the way."

"Of course it is," Talon rejoined, concealing her surprise at seeing him. She'd been so focused on her own performance in the trial, she'd almost forgotten about her investigator. "What are you doing here?"

"I wanted to see you in action," he returned with a calm smile. "I like to watch."

The double entendre wasn't wasted on Talon. If anything, the adrenaline of the trial made her more susceptible to it. She was jacked up, in more ways than one. But she wanted to stay focused on the trial. Mostly.

"Good to know," she said. "I just hung a mirror in my office."

Curt raised an interested eyebrow, but before he could say anything, Talon announced, "Dinner." It wasn't a question.

"But a quick one," she added. "I have to prep for tomorrow."

Curt pointed first at Talon, then at himself. "Wish. Command."

Talon smiled and reached out to pat him—firmly—on the cheek. "Good boy. I like a man who knows his place."

"Under you, right?" Curt continued the flirtation.

Talon's smile deepened as her adrenaline rush spread further through her body. "Depends on my mood."

She pushed the doors open and strode into the hallway. She didn't have to tell him to follow her.

CHAPTER 34

Trials could take a long time, and murder trials even more so. After Halcomb, the prosecution called a series of witnesses from the original investigation. Beat cops who'd been the first called out, forensic technicians who'd photographed the scene, and the like. Talon minimized her cross-examination of these lesser witnesses. She wasn't going to convince anyone that Jordy McCabe hadn't been murdered. She just had to convince them that Michael Jameson didn't do it. Or rather, she needed to convince them the State hadn't proven he'd done it.

So when the witnesses turned to those who might connect her client to the murder, she was ready.

"The State calls," Quinlan stood to announce their next witness, "Detective Sarah Jefferson."

Jefferson was the new lead detective, the one who'd reopened the case after the ballistics from Jameson's gun were found to match the casing left at the scene of Jordy McCabe's murder. She was in her forties, with straight reddish-brown hair, and wore the dark blazer and slacks combo favored by detectives whenever they testified.

Once she was sworn in and seated, Quinlan set to work. And Talon prepared to do the same.

"Could you please state your name for the record?" Quinlan started. It was the usual biographical and professional background all the cops provided. Years on the force, units and divisions, awards and distinctions. Then, finally, into the case.

"How did you become involved in the investigation of Jordan McCabe's murder?"

Detective Jefferson nodded at the question. She looked to the jury, but only briefly in acknowledgement, and turned back to Quinlan to answer. Obviously, Quinlan and McDaniels had retrained their witnesses after Talon's little attack on Halcomb.

"I was contacted by Detective Kevin Brewer of our cold case unit," Det. Jefferson said. "There are too many cold cases for Detective Brewer to handle them all, so the rest of homicides help out sometimes when he gets a new break on an old case. Well, anyway, Detective Brewer called me and told me—"

"Objection!" Talon sprang to her feet. "Hearsay."

Jefferson knew not to continue until the lawyers and the judge worked out the objection. Quinlan looked more put out than surprised. "It's not hearsay, Your Honor," he almost whined.

"The witness was about to recount what another person told her," Talon pressed. "That's the definition of hearsay."

"Actually," Judge Kirchner corrected, "the definition of hearsay is an out-of-court statement offered to prove the matter asserted therein." She looked at Quinlan. "How is what another detective told her about the case not hearsay?"

"Uh, well," Quinlan thought for a moment. "I'm not offering to prove what Detective Brewer said was true, just that he told it to Detective Jefferson."

"Relevance," Talon added to her objection.

But Judge Kirchner raised a hand to her, as if to say, 'I got this.' "Why is that relevant?"

"It explains why she took the steps she took next," Quinlan said. "It's a classic non-hearsay use: effect on the listener."

"Can't she just explain what she did next without telling the jury whatever Detective Brewer might have told her?" Kirchner asked.

Quinlan hesitated. "I suppose so," he admitted, "but it won't make as much sense without the context."

Kirchner thought for a moment. Quinlan decided to interrupt her thoughts. "I could always just put Detective Brewer on the stand to say what he told her."

Talon shook her head. "That would be hearsay too," she pointed out. "Anything someone says out of the courtroom, even if the witness said it himself."

Kirchner nodded. "She's right. You don't avoid the objection that way either, Mr. Quinlan. I'm going to sustain it. Ask another question."

"I can't ask her what Detective Brewer told her?" Quinlan whined.

Judge Kirchner didn't mind a healthy exchange of ideas, but she didn't take well to being challenged—at least not in front of the jurors, who had remained in the jury box to listen in on the legal discussion. "The objection is sustained. Ask another question."

Quinlan took a few seconds. In part, to gather his thoughts. In part, Talon guessed, to figure out another question to ask.

"Uh, okay," Quinlan ramped up again, "so, what was the first thing you did after you spoke with Detective Brewer?"

Jefferson nodded. "I ordered the original file from archives. It took a few days to arrive. While I waited for that, I read the reports from the burglary of the defendant's home."

"And what did you learn from those reports?" Quinlan asked.

Talon popped to her feet again. "Objection! Hearsay."

Quinlan threw his hands down. "I'm asking about what was in the reports, not what someone told her," he told the judge.

"It's still hearsay," Talon rejoined. "Those reports were drafted out-of-court. This witness can't tell the jury what other witnesses learned."

Kirchner looked at Quinlan. "She's right. It's hearsay. Objection sustained."

Quinlan lowered his gaze to floor as he considered his options. "Your Honor, could I be heard outside the presence of the jury?"

He wanted to make a fuller argument. Talon guessed it was one that would involve telling the judge exactly what Detective Jefferson would say, if allowed. He couldn't do that with the jurors in the room. It would undercut Talon's objection, and Judge Kirchner's ruling. Kirchner knew it too. But that didn't mean she had to let him. "No," she said simply. "Ask another question."

Quinlan sighed audibly. He looked up at Jefferson, his expression betraying his growing frustration. "So, you read the burglary reports, and I assume you read the cold case file when it arrived. What were your next steps?"

"Well, the thing that really jumped out for me," Jefferson said, "was the ballistics match between the handgun from the defendant's residence and the fired cartridges from the murder scene, so—"

"Objection!" This time Talon slapped the table. "And I have a motion."

'I have a motion.' That was defense attorney for *'The prosecutor*

just stepped in it. And I'm going to make him pay.'

Quinlan threw those hands down again, and spun away from Jefferson in frustration. This time, the jury was definitely going out of the courtroom. Jefferson would be waiting in the hallway, too, as the attorneys discussed what she could or couldn't say.

As soon as the doors to the hallway and the jury room closed, Talon spoke. "The defense moves for a mistrial, Your Honor. And for a dismissal on double jeopardy grounds. The State's misconduct precipitated the mistrial and—"

Kirchner raised another hand to Talon. "Let's not get ahead of ourselves. We'll deal with the mistrial motion first. What's the basis?"

The judge knew the basis, but Talon had to say it out loud. Besides, she wasn't sure Quinlan understood. "The State elicited hearsay testimony from the witness despite my repeated objections, objections which the court sustained. Mr. Quinlan knew Detective Jefferson would not be permitted to tell the jury what other witnesses had told her, and yet they still went ahead and had this witness—not the ballistics expert—tell the jury that the handgun from my client's residence matched the crime scene. I don't know how many times I have to object, but at some point I shouldn't have to any more. We'd reached that point, but Mr. Quinlan did it anyway. There's no way to unring that bell. The only remedy is a mistrial. Strike this jury panel and start all over. Although, again, when the State causes a mistrial, double jeopardy bars a new trial. This case should be dismissed."

Kirchner frowned. No judge wants to dismiss a murder trial. Especially not based on a stupid mistake by the prosecutor. She sighed and looked to Quinlan. "Response?"

Quinlan stood up from where he'd been pouting in his chair.

The smart thing to do would have been to admit the mistake, apologize for it, then explain why it didn't require mistrying the entire case. But Quinlan had rarely been accused of being overly smart.

"Again, Your Honor, I don't believe Detective Jefferson's statement was hearsay," he protested. "As I explained before, she was recounting what she learned so the jury would understand the steps of her investigation, not to show that any of it was necessarily true."

"You told the jury in opening statement," Kirchner reminded him, "that the ballistics matched. Are you saying now that you don't intend to argue that?"

"Of course I do, Your Honor," Quinlan replied. "But not based on what this witness says."

"Then why have her say it?" the judge challenged. "Especially after I had told you twice not to have this witness testify as to what other people told her."

Quinlan shifted his weight. "Well, perhaps Ms. Winter should have objected again instead of moving directly to mistrial."

"I shouldn't have to object again," Talon interjected. "The court was clear."

Kirchner's hand raised again. "You'll get your chance, Ms. Winter. Please be patient."

Talon nodded. "Yes, Your Honor."

Back to Quinlan. "Ms. Winter makes a valid point. Did you not understand my rulings?"

Quinlan raised his chin a bit. "Of course I understood them."

"Then why did you elicit more hearsay?"

Quinlan hesitated. "Well, I, I mean, I don't think I did really. I didn't really ask her what someone told her. She just kind of volunteered it when I asked her what she did next."

Talon frowned inside. That was actually true. Kirchner looked to her. "Ms. Winter, what about that?"

Talon considered conceding the point. But she wasn't very good at conceding. "He knew what she did next and why. He knew what she would say when he asked that seemingly innocuous question. In fact," she realized, "that's what makes it even more troublesome. After having been objected to, and sustained, twice, Mr. Quinlan formed a question that didn't give me the chance to object. If he'd asked, 'Did you receive a ballistics report and what did it say?' then I could have objected in time. Instead, he took my ability to object away by leading the witness to the inadmissible testimony and letting her carry it across the goal line herself."

Kirchner smiled slightly at that. "Any further response, Mr. Quinlan?"

Quinlan took a moment. Causing a mistrial on a murder case would be difficult to explain to his superiors, let alone Mrs. McCabe-Johnson and the rest of Jordy's family. And Talon was right, a mistrial caused by the State could very well lead to a dismissal. The court would have to find that things weren't going well for the State and that the mistrial was caused to try to get a do-over, but Talon would be able to argue that, especially after the way she'd gone after Retired Detective Halcomb. "I would ask the court to deny the motion for mistrial. This was an inadvertent mistake. We plan to call the ballistics expert later in our case and he will testify to his findings, first-hand."

"That doesn't mean it wasn't hearsay from this witness," Kirchner pointed out.

"Understood, Your Honor," Quinlan offered meekly, "but I think it goes to the prejudice, if any, suffered by the defendant. If at the end of our case-in-chief, we haven't gotten that information to the jury through other means, then the court could reconsider the motion for mistrial. But at this point, the court should deny it. We ask the court to deny it. Please."

Judge Kirchner drummed her fingers on the bench. "Is there anything this witness will testify to that isn't hearsay?"

Quinlan frowned. "Well, that's kind of what a lead detective does, Your Honor. They read reports written by other people and assign tasks to other people who report back to them later."

"So, no?" Kirchner asked to confirm.

Quinlan thought for a moment. Talon figured he was trying to remember what testimony he was planning on eliciting from the detective. When he didn't have any ready, Kirchner went ahead and made her decision.

"All right," she said. "Here's what we're going to do. I'm going to deny the motion for a mistrial. I do that in part because Mr. Quinlan has represented that the information about the ballistics match will come in later through a proper witness. If that doesn't happen, I will entertain a motion to reconsider the mistrial."

Talon was disappointed, but not surprised.

"But let me make one thing perfectly clear, Mr. Quinlan." Kirchner pointed a stern finger at him. "If this witness provides even one more word of hearsay, I will grant the mistrial and we'll schedule the motion to dismiss for one week from today. Do you understand?"

Quinlan nodded tightly. "Yes, Your Honor."

"Good," Kirchner replied. She looked at her bailiff. "Get the jury."

As the bailiff did that, McDaniels fetched Jefferson from the hallway. A few minutes later, the jury was back in the jury box, the detective was back on the witness stand, and all eyes were back on Quinlan.

He had used those few minutes to decide what to do.

He looked up at the judge. "No further questions," he announced.

Talon was only a little less surprised than everyone else in the courtroom. It was the safest thing to do, but it left the jurors hanging. It also presented Talon with a decision. Should she do any cross-examination? But that was actually a fairly easy decision.

"No questions, Your Honor," she stood to say.

Any questions could invite more hearsay from Jefferson, and she could hardly object to her own questions. More importantly, though, the abrupt, mid-sentence end to Jefferson's testimony, immediately after a closed-door session of judge and attorneys, let the jury know that either Jefferson had done something wrong, or Quinlan had. Maybe both. That was good. It took at least some of the attention off of that bad thing her client was accused of doing.

Point, Talon. Battle of Jefferson won.

But the war continued.

"Call your next witness," Judge Kirchner instructed the prosecutors.

Quinlan obliged. "The State calls Sergeant Mark Brennan."

CHAPTER 35

Talon frowned. Brennan was their bridge witness. He had nothing to do with the murder investigation. But he had everything to do with the burglary of Michael Jameson's home.

Brennan walked into the courtroom in a short-sleeved patrol uniform, Tacoma P.D. badge on his chest and sergeant's stripes on his arm. He was in his late thirties, tall, with thick arms and short black hair over a clean-shaven jaw. He just looked trustworthy.

Damn.

After the preliminaries, Quinlan got right to the point, "Were you involved in the investigation of the murder of Jordan McCabe?"

"No, sir," Brennan answered. "Not directly."

Talon frowned. *Nice editorializing.*

"Were you involved in a more recent case," Quinlan followed up, "involving the burglary of the defendant's home?"

"Yes, sir," Brennan said. "I was the supervisor on that call."

"And who called the police?" Quinlan clarified.

"The defendant's wife, Alicia Jameson."

Quinlan paused. "Please don't tell me anything Mrs. Jameson told you," he warned his witness, lest there be another hearsay objection and motion for mistrial. "But did you ever speak with the defendant here, Mr. Jameson?"

By evidence rule, statements of a criminal defendant were never hearsay if elicited by the prosecution. They meant that 'everything you say can and will be used against you' stuff. So Talon couldn't object to what Michael had told Brennan.

"Yes," Brennan answered. "I spoke to him when I was first dispatched to the home for the original report. I also spoke with him again after the burglary suspects were apprehended and the stolen items were recovered."

"What did he tell you when you first spoke with him?"

Brennan thought for a moment. He was testifying without a copy of his report in front of him, which meant he'd memorized it before coming to court.

"He simply advised us that the home had been broken into while the family was away on vacation. They had come home to find a back window broken out and the interior of the home ransacked."

"Did he report what was stolen?"

"Yes." Brennan ticked off the items on his fingers. "A flat screen television, a laptop, some of his wife's jewelry, and a small amount of cash."

Did he report any firearms being stolen?" Quinlan prompted.

Brennan hesitated. "*Mr.* Jameson?" he confirmed. "Not at that time, no."

Great, Talon thought. So, everyone knew Alicia had reported the guns stolen, and Michael had confirmed it later. All without the witness actually saying it, so she had nothing to object to.

"Did he mention the firearms later?" Quinlan followed up.

Brennan nodded. "Yes, we were able to locate the stolen items rather quickly using our PawnStop program."

"What is the PawnStop program?" Quinlan interrupted for the benefit of the jury.

"It's a program we have with most of the area pawn shops," Brennan explained. "We upload serial numbers into the system and the pawn shops self-report if they've accepted any of the stolen items for pawn. In this case, the Jamesons had kept excellent records of their personal electronics. By the time we uploaded the serial numbers for the T.V. and the laptop. They had already been pawned at the Pawn Super-Xpress on South Tacoma Way."

"Is Pawn Super-Xpress part of the PawnStop program?"

"Yes. As soon as we got the match, Pawn Super-Xpress notified us and we went out to take a report and recover the property. Every pawn shop in town takes a photocopy of photo I.D. on every transaction. They all have interior surveillance cameras as well. We were able to positively identify the burglary suspect based on the driver's license and store video."

Quinlan nodded. "And what items had the suspect pawned?"

"Both the television and the laptop."

"Anything else?"

"Yes."

"What?"

Here we go, Talon knew.

"Two handguns," Brennan answered. "A thirty-eight caliber revolver and a nine millimeter semi-automatic."

"So the same suspect pawned all four items at once?"

"Yes, sir."

Quinlan allowed a smile. "So, what did you do next?"

"I seized the items as evidence and transported them back to police headquarters."

"Evidence of the burglary?" Quinlan clarified.

"Yes," Brennan confirmed. "At first."

Ugh. This isn't going well, Talon worried. Brennan was a good storyteller in his own right.

"Did you return the items to the Jamesons?"

"We returned the electronics right away," Brennan explained, "but we kept the firearms for further processing."

"What kind of processing?" Quinlan asked. "And why?"

Talon probably could have objected to the compound question, but it was easily overcome and she didn't want the jury to know how much Brennan was hurting her.

"We sent the firearms to the State Patrol Crime Lab for operability testing."

"Why would you do that?" Quinlan followed up.

Brennan nodded. "That's a good question." He turned to the jury to give his explanation, but it made sense to do so, since Quinlan likely would already know what he was about to explain. "You see, burglarizing a home is called residential burglary. But if you're armed with a deadly weapon when you do it, that raises the offense to burglary in the first degree. You can be armed for the purposes of the burglary statute even if you enter without a weapon if, during the course of the robbery, you take a firearm or other deadly weapon. Plus possessing a stolen firearm is a crime in its own right. But the firearm has to be operable, and not just a collector's piece or a cigarette lighter or something. So, we needed to know if the firearms actually worked. The way we do that is, we send them out to the Crime Lab and they test fire them."

"And what were the results of the operability testing?" Quinlan asked.

Finally. "Objection!" Talon interrupted. "Calls for hearsay."

Quinlan threw his hands up. "Really?" Not professional, but honest.

"Yes, really," Talon answered. "Unless this witness performed the operability tests himself."

Kirchner raised an eyebrow at Quinlan. "Did he?"

Quinlan shook his head. "No, Your Honor. That was Mr. Langston."

"Then this witness can't speak to the results. Objection sustained."

Talon smiled slightly and sat down again. Quinlan thought for a moment. Then he walked over to the clerk and requested one of the exhibits. The only type of exhibit you had to request because they weren't going to let it just sit out on the bar with the reports and photographs. Not in a murder case anyway. The bailiff unlocked the door behind him and removed the 9 mm semi-automatic handgun with the exhibit tag hanging from its trigger guard.

Quinlan took it and walked it over to Sgt. Brennan.

"I'm handing you what's been marked as State's Exhibit Number Thirty-Seven," he said for the record as he gave the firearm to Brennan. "Do you recognize this?"

"It's a handgun," Brennan answered.

"Can you identify it as related to your investigation of the burglary of the defendant's home?" Quinlan followed up.

Brennan took a moment to inspect the handgun. After a moment he looked up. "Yes. I recognize the serial number. This is the same handgun that was recovered from the pawn shop and returned to Mr. and Mrs. Jameson."

Quinlan took the handgun back from the witness and returned it to the bailiff. "No further questions," he announced not a little triumphantly.

Talon knew his strategy. Brennan identified Exhibit #37 as Jameson's gun and then Langston would identify Exhibit #37 as the gun that fired the bullets recovered from the murder scene. Good lawyering, but nothing too special. That was how it was supposed to work. But in his irritation at Talon and satisfaction with himself for figuring out how to do it the right way, he forgot to ask the one more question that would have sealed the connection: 'Did Mr. Jameson confirm the gun was his when you returned it?'

As it was, Talon had some wiggle room. Brennan had testified to Jameson admitting a gun or guns had been stolen, and Exhibit #37 was from the pawn shop. But there was no direct evidence linking Exhibit #37 to Jameson. It was inferred, but not explicit. Something to exploit in closing argument. But not now. If she asked Brennan herself, of course he'd confirm it. And if she asked even one question, Quinlan would be allowed to conduct re-direct exam, and ask the question he'd forgotten to ask,

She stood up and took a calculated risk. "No questions, Your Honor."

She knew that would leave everyone in the room curious. Was she confident, or stupid?

Maybe both.

But Quinlan lost his opportunity to connect that last dot as Brennan was excused and McDaniels stood to announce their next witness. As interesting as it might have been to see the alleged murder weapon paraded through the courtroom, it would pale in comparison to eyewitness testimony from the survivors of the attack.

"The State calls Earl Daggett."

CHAPTER 36

Talon looked at her client, who seemed as surprised as she was. Daggett was on the State's witness list, and Talon had prepared a cross-examination of him, but when Quinlan had left behind the closing of the case and started into the re-opening of it with Jefferson, she'd let herself hope that maybe they hadn't found him at that meat-packing plant outside Spokane. Still, hope for the best but prepare for the worst. She was ready. She just needed to make sure Michael was too.

"Don't look at him," she instructed in a whisper. "There's no good way to look at someone who testifies against you. Someone on the jury will think you're staring him down, no matter what your expression."

Michael nodded. "Okay," he whispered back.

"And if he identifies you as the shooter, don't shake your head. Don't scoff. Don't react at all. I'll handle it on cross. No one can I.D. someone twenty-five years later."

"He knew me back then," Michael reminded her.

"I'll handle it on cross," Talon repeated. "Got it?"

Michael nodded again. "Got it."

She patted his arm, fully aware that at least some of the jurors had been watching her and Michael's whisperings, rather than Earl Daggett walking to the witness stand to be sworn in— which happened in short order. McDaniels stepped forward to begin her direct examination.

Talon wondered whether Quinlan was assigning McDaniels to do all the African-American witnesses. But she supposed they wouldn't be that obvious. Would they?

"Please state your name for the record," McDaniels began.

"Earl Jeremiah Daggett," came the quiet reply.

"Thank you for being here today, Mr. Daggett," McDaniels said. Again, that was objectionable. But again, it was kind. It might be ingratiating to the jury, or it might come across as trying too hard and off-putting. Either way, no objection from Talon.

Daggett just shrugged in response.

So McDaniels continued. "Did you know a person named Jordan McCabe?"

Daggett nodded.

"You need to answer out loud," McDaniels explained. "For the record."

"Yeah," Daggett complied. "I knew him."

"How did you know him?"

Another shrug. "Just from around the neighborhood, you know?"

"Was he a friend?" McDaniels suggested.

"I guess," Daggett answered. "We all just kinda knew each other, you know? It was a long time ago."

McDaniels nodded. "How long ago?"

Daggett thought for a moment. "We were in high school. So, what, twenty-something years ago. A long time."

Talon studied Daggett's demeanor. He didn't seem engaged. That was good. It made McDaniels's job more difficult. More importantly, he didn't seem like he had it out for Michael. And if he didn't care, why should the jurors?

"What about the defendant?" McDaniels gestured toward the defense table. "Did you know Michael Jameson back then?"

Daggett peered over at Michael, squinting his middle-aged eyes. "I knew a Mikey Jameson back then. I don't know if this gentleman is him. Could be, It was a long time ago."

Talon was sensing the theme: *It was a long time ago.* She liked that theme.

"Let's talk about the night Jordan McCabe was killed," McDaniels soldiered on. "Were you there that night?"

Daggett nodded slowly. "Yeah, I was there."

"And did you see Mr. McCabe get shot?"

Daggett frowned. "Yeah. I saw it."

Ok, Talon thought, *here we go. The million-dollar question.* She kept her eyes down, ostensibly taking notes.

"Did you see who shot him?"

Another slow nod. "Yeah, I saw who shot him," Daggett replied.

Damn.

"But I don't remember who now," he finished.

Un-damn. Talon couldn't keep her head from popping up at that addition.

McDaniels managed to keep her poker-face, but Talon knew it was body-blow. She was reeling, as evidenced by the next question McDaniels grabbed from her brain and threw at the witness. "What were you doing that night?"

A terrible question. They were dealing drugs. Or buying them at least. And maybe robbing the other drug dealers. That question could open the door to a very long discussion about hobbies Jordy McCabe's mother didn't know about, or at least didn't testify about. But it would depend on Daggett's answer.

"Just hanging out, you know?" he answered. "Nothing special."

Okay, McDaniels is safe.

"Hanging out?" she questioned. "At two in the morning?"

Or maybe not.

Daggett took a moment. "Like I said, it was a long time ago. I don't remember exactly what we were doing. I don't remember exactly what happened. I know Jordy got shot and I know I got the heck out of there. Life went on. For me, at least."

"And for Jordy's murderer?" McDaniels pointed out.

"I suppose so," Daggett agreed. "I been through a lot since then. I'm not looking to go back."

McDaniels paused. She was both obviously irritated and obviously trying to hide it.

"So you don't remember who shot your friend Jordy?"

"He wasn't really a friend," Dagget answered. "And no, I don't remember."

"And you don't remember what you were doing when Jordy was shot?"

Daggett looked ready to offer another 'it was a long time ago,' but Talon stood up before he could answer.

"Objection, Your Honor," she said calmly. "Counsel is leading the witness. Also, asked and answered."

Good procedural objections, likely to be sustained. Which was guaranteed to further irritate McDaniels.

"The objections are sustained," Judge Kirchner ruled without even asking McDaniels for a response. "Rephrase your question, counsel."

McDaniels thought for a moment. Talon knew she was considering impeaching Daggett with his prior statements to the police—25 years ago. But she also knew Daggett didn't I.D. the shooter back then either, not by name anyway. And telling the jury he was a gang member buying drugs probably wouldn't really help McDaniels's case after all.

"No further questions," she said.

Talon stood up at Judge Kirchner's invitation to cross-examine. She waited for McDaniels to return to the prosecution table, then replaced her at the bar.

"It's been a long time," Talon repeated his words back to him. "Hasn't it?"

Daggett nodded. "Yes ma'am."

"Are you the same person you were twenty-five years ago?"

A faint smile and a shake of the head. "No ma'am." Talon opened her arms to the whole courtroom. "Are any of us?"

"Objection!" McDaniels interrupted. "Calls for speculation."

'Relevance' would have been the better objection.

"It's permissible lay opinion," Talon argued.

But the judge didn't buy it. "Sustained."

It didn't matter. The jurors knew the answer.

"No further questions," Talon said.

McDaniels didn't redirect. Daggett was excused.

That went pretty well, Talon thought as she sat down again next to Michael, but she made a point of not letting the thought show on her face. Good thing we talked to him before he testified. He must have liked us.

Quinlan stood up. "The State calls Reginald Oliphant."

CHAPTER 37

"But first, Your Honor," Quinlan continued, "perhaps we could take a brief recess."

Talon knew why and was a little disappointed that Quinlan knew too. Oliphant was still in prison. He could be transported from prison easily enough with a few orders faxed to the right people. But the jury wasn't allowed to know he was in prison. So he'd be dressed out in civilian clothes, and would testify without the handcuffs. But until he was on the stand, those handcuffs were staying on. Leg irons too, most likely. And two corrections officers in the courtroom, close enough to tackle him if he made a run for it.

All that meant the jury had to go out of the room long enough for the guards to bring Oliphant in and get him set up on the stand. Then the jury would be brought back in. As if they wouldn't notice this one witness was already on the stand and those two uniformed officers were suddenly there, but gone again after he was done testifying.

It was so much window-dressing and willful ignorance, but it was required. If they marched him in wearing prison garb and belly chains, it'd be a mistrial. And a mistrial caused by the State—it wasn't Talon's job not to screw that up—which would present another argument for dismissal.

So Talon was disappointed Quinlan had been sharp enough to ask for the recess after calling the witness. His plan was to have the jury out just long enough to get Oliphant on the stand, then get them back in before they had too much time to think about it.

And since that was Quinlan's plan, Talon decided to mess it up.

She didn't object to the recess, but as soon as the jurors were safely inside the jury room, she said, "Your Honor, could we take a longer recess? I wasn't aware the State would be moving from the new lead detective immediately back to witnesses from the original crime. I was able to conduct cross-examination of Mr. Daggett without my notes, but I don't think I should have to examine Mr. Oliphant as well without my materials. I'd like to go back to my office to get my information on Mr. Oliphant."

Judge Kirchner nodded. "That seems reasonable. Any objection, Mr. Quinlan?"

"Actually, yes, Your Honor," he answered. "We would object. I have two officers standing by to bring Mr. Oliphant to the courtroom. If we don't bring him now, they'll have to book him back into the jail. I don't know how long it will take to get him out again. And besides, the jury is expecting to hear from Mr. Oliphant. We just announced we would be calling him."

Exactly, Talon thought.

"Ms. Talon?" the judge invited a response.

"If Mr. Quinlan had the foresight to notify the guards to have Mr. Oliphant waiting in the wings," she answered, "I would think he could have let me know as well. I understand why he wanted to surprise me, but I'm asking to not be completely ambushed. I just want an opportunity to go to my office and round up my materials and my investigator."

"Investigator?" Quinlan gasped. "Why does she need her investigator? We didn't receive any notice that her investigator had interviewed Mr. Oliphant."

"I didn't say he had," Talon answered. "And if he did, I don't have to tell you. It's defense work product."

"I object, Your Honor," Quinlan said. "We should have been given discovery about this."

Talon was about to explain why that wasn't true, but the judge beat her to it.

"Discovery is not reciprocal in Washington, Mr. Quinlan," Kirchner explained, a bit impatiently. "You know that. The defense only has to provide information about a witness if they intend to call them. I presume, Ms. Winter, you weren't planning on calling an eyewitness to the murder your client is charged with committing?"

"Correct, Your Honor," Talon confirmed.

"Correct," Judge Kirchner echoed. "So let's address the real issue. How long do you need, Ms. Winter?"

"Not long," Talon answered. "Two hours should be enough."

"Two hours?" Quinlan wailed. "That's far too long, Your Honor. Like I said, I have everyone on notice and waiting."

"Not everyone," Talon reminded the court.

The problem with complaining and expecting things to go exactly the way you want them to—a professional hazard for prosecutors—was that it could irritate the person who was actually in charge: the judge.

"Two hours seems reasonable," Judge Kirchner ruled. "We will reconvene at four o'clock."

Which was another bonus. It would jam Oliphant's testimony up against the end of the court day. If it was difficult to bring him in once, it would be even more so to have to bring him back again tomorrow morning. Quinlan might feel pressure to cut corners to finish in time.

As it turned out, that wouldn't be a problem, but Talon wouldn't know that until after she returned from her office, and Curt's.

* * *

"Knock, knock," Talon announced as she entered Curt's office across the hall from her own office suite. She realized she hadn't been there before. It just seemed more natural that he would come to her. "Curt? You here?"

It was similar to her set-up, with a receptionist's desk by the front door and small, individual offices beyond. Only, there was no receptionist—not right then anyway—and it sure looked like most of the offices were unleased.

"Curt?" she repeated.

"Talon?" Curt called back. He stepped out into view and approached the front door. "What are you doing here? Aren't you in session today?"

"Yes, we're in session," she answered. "Quinlan just called Oliphant to the stand. I came back to get my materials."

"What materials?" Curt asked.

Talon reached out and rested a finger on his chest. "You."

Curt cocked his head askance.

"I want you to sit through his testimony," she explained. "Tell me if he says anything different. If he does, I'll call you during our case-in-chief to impeach him."

"Unless what he says now is better than what he said then, right?"

"Of course." Talon smiled. Her finger was still on his chest. "Smart boy."

He looked down at her finger and she finally removed it. "I should probably dress for court then, huh?" he asked. He was wearing a tight-fitting T-shirt and well-worn jeans.

She liked how it looked on him, but not for court. "Yeah," she agreed. "Clean yourself up. Then meet me in court in an hour and a half."

* * *

Ninety minutes later, they were both in the courtroom. Talon at counsel table with Michael, and Curt—in a blue blazer and open-collared shirt—in the gallery one row behind Alicia, who was sitting through every single witness. Eleven minutes later, Judge Kirchner took the bench.

"Are we ready to proceed?' she inquired.

Talon stood up to answer, "Yes, Your Honor. Thank you."

The judge looked to Quinlan. "Is the State ready?"

Quinlan also stood to address the court. "Yes, Your Honor. If I could just have a moment to call the jail, I will have Mr. Oliphant transported."

Kirchner assented and after a whispered phone call and few more minutes' wait, three uniformed corrections officers brought Reginald Oliphant into the courtroom. He was deposited onto the witness stand and the corrections officers fanned out: one by the door to the hallway, one next to the jury room door—there was an exit to the outside hall through there—and one directly behind the witness box. Nothing said 'not in custody' like an armed guard looming over the witness' shoulder.

Kirchner's bailiff went to fetch the jury as Quinlan approached Oliphant. If Talon hadn't known better, it looked like he was introducing himself. Had he not talked to Oliphant in advance?

When the jury was seated, Judge Kirchner bade Oliphant to stand and raise his right hand to be sworn in.

Oliphant declined. "No."

Kirchner raised an eyebrow, then looked to Quinlan, who seemed as surprised as anyone else. She turned back to Oliphant. "You won't swear to tell the truth?" she asked.

"No," Oliphant answered. "Because I ain't testifying."

Talon felt her heart race, but tried to keep her elation off her face. Fake note-taking wasn't appropriate either though. This was too out of the ordinary not to pay attention.

"You have to testify," Judge Kirchner said. "You've been compelled to appear by the State."

"They can compel me to appear wherever they want," Olpihant said, "but they can't compel me to say anything."

Kirchner thought for a moment. "I could hold you in contempt until you agree to testify."

"Oh, what, and hold me in jail?" Oliphant laughed. "Been there, done that. I ain't testifying. Not for the State. I ain't a snitch."

Talon might have preferred something more affirmative, like, 'Michael Jameson didn't shoot anyone,' but she'd take this turn of events. Quinlan, on the other hand…

"Your Honor," he squeaked, "perhaps another brief recess would be in order?"

Kirchner didn't seem enamored at the suggestion. "We all just got back in here, Mr. Quinlan. If the witness refuses to take the oath to tell the truth, he can't testify. How do you want to proceed?"

Quinlan thought for a moment. "I'd like a recess to speak with the witness, Your Honor."

Talon stood up. "I'd object to that, Your Honor," she said. "The witness is on the stand, sworn or not. It would be inappropriate for either side to have a private conversation with him at this point."

"I agree with Ms. Winter," Kirchner said. "We're not going to do that. You called the witness. The witness is on the stand. You can ask me to hold him in contempt or you can call another witness."

Quinlan considered. He didn't bother to look back at his co-counsel. Talon hoped the jurors were catching that too. "The State would ask you to hold the witness in contempt, Your Honor," he said.

"Denied," Kirchner replied. "You should have known this was going to happen, counsel. I'm not going to penalize a witness who would have told you he wasn't going to testify. Especially for the reasons given."

That last bit didn't help as much. The judge understood going back to prison with a 'snitch jacket' would mean real physical danger to Oliphant. But confirming it as a valid reason did sort of suggest that Jameson was guilty. You don't snitch out an innocent person. Still, she'd take it. And quickly, before Quinlan got the judge to change her mind.

"May I excuse my investigator then?" Talon asked. She didn't actually need permission to do that, but she wanted to end any further conversation about Oliphant actually testifying.

Judge Kirchner was visibly irritated at this turn of events. Quinlan looked bad, but it spilled onto her a bit too when a witness refused to take the oath she was trying to administer. "Yes, counsel." Then she looked at the clock. "And we will adjourn for the day."

They needed to get the jurors out of there before they could transport Oliphant back to the jail. Judge Kirchner narrowed her eyes at Quinlan. "Be ready to call your next witness first thing tomorrow morning," she instructed, "and make sure they're actually going to testify."

"May I ask who the next witness will be?" Talon interjected.

"Arnold Langston," Quinlan practically snapped. "From the crime lab."

The ballistics expert, Talon knew. And probably their last witness. *Smart way to finish*, she had to admit. Or it would have been, if Det. Jefferson had been allowed to preview the ballistics match, then Daggett and Oliphant had identified Jameson as the shooter.

"Thank you," Talon chimed.

"Court will be adjourned until tomorrow morning at nine o'clock." Judge Kirchner banged her gavel. She stepped down and headed for her chambers as the bailiff crossed the courtroom to lead the jurors out. Talon checked in with Michael to make sure he would be there bright and early the next morning, and offered a reassuring pat to Alicia's shoulder. Then she stepped up to Curt, who'd remained standing after the judge and jurors had left.

He gestured at his clothes. "All dressed up for nothing. I guess."

But Talon took a moment to gaze at her investigator's solid frame wrapped in something worthy of a night on the town—and what might come after.

"No," she disagreed with lowered lids. "Not for nothing."

CHAPTER 38

'All dressed up and no place to go' might have been the better expression from Curt. No matter how good he looked in that outfit, there was no way Talon was going to spend the night before the State's key witness doing anything other than preparing her cross-examination. There was a lot more to that than just writing out questions. There was anticipating what Quinlan's (not McDaniels, she assumed) direct examination would be. There was reviewing the exhibits. And it was knowing that even when she thought she was done, she wasn't. There was always more

After court, Talon went directly back to her office. Alone. She only left twice. Once around 6:30 to grab some takeout, and again a little after 9:00 to go home. She spent a couple more hours refining everything before finally going to bed shortly before 11:00. Getting enough sleep was part of good preparation too

The next morning she arrived at the courtroom 20 minutes before 9:00, which was five minutes after her client.

"Good morning, Michael," she greeted him as she set her briefcase down on the table. She offered a nod to Alicia as well in the front row.

"Morning, Talon," Michael answered. "Are you ready?"

Talon thought for a moment, recalling all the work she'd done the night before, and throughout the preceding weeks and months. "I hope so."

Michael seemed to accept that answer. Talon supposed he was hoping she was ready too.

Then Talon checked in with the one other observer in the courtroom. The most important one, Alicia's personal interest in the outcome notwithstanding. Alicia cared about the result, but Anastasia St. Julian could affect it. Hopefully.

"Ann," Talon greeted her expert as she walked up to her spot in the last row of the gallery. "Thanks for coming up early to sit through Langston's testimony."

Arnold Langston, the ballistic expert from the Washington State Patrol crime Laboratory. The State's expert. The one witness who could link Michael Jameson to the murder of Jordan McCabe.

"Of course," St. Julian replied. She stood to talk with Talon. "I always prefer to listen to the testimony of my opponent. Albert's a good guy, but he's not always as careful as he should be, in my opinion."

"Well, it's your opinion that matters," Talon said.

"We'll see," St. Julian replied.

Talon shrugged. "Either way, thanks for being here."

"I'm billing you for this time as well," St. Julian responded. "You and your client understand that, right? I bill all my time, including travel and preparation."

Talon nodded. She was well aware. She realized she hadn't heard back from Sullivan yet. But she didn't have time for such thoughts. "We understand."

St. Julian smiled. "Good. Now, let's get started. I can't wait to hear what Arnold has to say."

Talon knew what he was going to say. She just needed St. Julian to say he was wrong. She thanked St. Julian one more time then returned to her seat next to Michael.

There wasn't any small talk as Talon set up her materials on the table. Michael had his ever-present legal pad in front of him, pen in hand, fresh page waiting for the next—and last—State witness. McDaniels arrived next, but there was no greeting between the opponents. When Quinlan arrived a few minutes later, he and his co-counsel exchanged hushed hellos, but nothing more.

There was an anticipation in the room that seemed to silence its occupants. Even when the bailiff and court reporter took their stations, their entrance was muted. The quiet was only shattered when the judge emerged from her chambers and took the bench, to ask, "Are the parties ready to proceed?"

"Yes, Your Honor," Quinlan answered.

I hope so. "Yes, Your Honor," Talon echoed.

"Good," Kirchner replied, then she called for the jury.

Once the jurors were seated, McDaniels stood to announce their final witness. "The State calls Arnold Langston to the stand."

Talon wondered absently whether Langston was African-American, but when he walked in he was as White as the majority of jurors. She was surprised Quinlan let McDaniels handle this vital witness. Then again, maybe he didn't want to be bothered with the science of it all. She decided that was it; something bad. She didn't want to give Quinlan credit for anything. Another emotional side effect of trial. The enemy was evil, period. She could be dissuaded later, after the verdict. For now, every motivation of Quinlan's had to be either evil of stupid.

Langston entered the courtroom and took his place on the witness stand. McDaniels wasted no time. The sooner they got through this, the sooner Jameson was linked to the murder and the sooner they could rest their case, a huge accomplishment.

"Could you state your name for the record?" The standard beginning.

"Arnold Langston," the expert replied. He was tall, thin, with graying hair struggling to cover the top of his increasingly bald head. He wore a blue shirt, navy blazer, and yellowish tie—none of which really looked that good together. It just added to the 'scientist' vibe he was throwing off.

"How are you employed, sir?"

"I am a forensic scientist at the Washington State Crime Laboratory." He was addressing his answers to the jury. He must not have gotten the memo after her attack on Halcomb. Talon didn't suppose the same tack would work on this very different witness, but she added it to her arsenal of possible weapons for cross-examination.

"Do you have an area of specialization?"

"Yes," Langston nodded. "I work in the ballistics division. Most of my work relates to comparing ballistics from crime scenes with ballistics from known weapons."

McDaniels had a script in front of her, Talon could see, but she read from it naturally, as if she were thinking of each question on the fly. "Let's break that down a bit," McDaniels said. "When would you have a known weapon and why compare it to evidence from a crime scene?"

Again, Langston turned to the jury. "That's actually a very common scenario. A crime occurs and evidence is collected at the scene, like casings and projectile, but there's no firearm because the shooter fled with it. Then later, we get a hold of the firearm somehow. So we compare the evidence from the scene to see if it matches the firearm that's recovered later."

"And how do you make a match?"

Langston became a bit more animated. Most people like to talk about their work. "Well, you see," he told the jurors, "every firearm is unique and leaves unique markings on the bullets and casings that pass through it."

He then explained the basics of firearm operation and manufacture.

"I avoid the term 'bullet' because different people mean different things at different times when they use that word. Instead, I refer to projectiles and casings. The projectile is housed in the casing until it's fired from the firearm and the casing is discarded. When the projectile is still inside the casing, prior to being fired, we call that a cartridge.

"When the firing pin hits the back of the casing, it punctures a small disc of gunpowder, causing it to explode. The projectile travels down the barrel and out of the firearm, and the casing remains behind. In a revolver, the casing stays in the rotating cylinder. In a semi-automatic, the casing is ejected with an ejecting pin. In both cases, the firearm loads the next cartridge into position to fire another shot."

"So if a person fires a semi-automatic, the casing might be left behind at the scene?" McDaniels asked from her script.

"Exactly," Langston agreed. "Casings from the same firearm will have matching scratches on them from the ejecting pin. It will strike every casing in the same place, so if we find casings at a scene, even if we don't have the firearm, we can sometimes confirm they were all fired from the same firearm because the ejector pin markings match."

"What about markings on the projectile?"

It was a Ballistics 101. Enough for the jury to understand, but not enough for them to question. That was what Prof. St. Julian's Ballistics 201 class would be for.

"Those are also unique to each firearm," Langston confirmed. "When a projectile travels down the barrel, it's actually touching the inside of the barrel, or at least part of it is. Bullet's spin, just like a well-thrown football, which is why they cut through the air and can be so accurate. The way it's accomplished is a process called 'rifling,' which is where the term rifle comes from. Think of those old-fashioned musket ball guns from Revolutionary times. Those balls were wildly inaccurate. They just flew out and could go in any number of directions. Like a knuckle-ball in baseball."

Talon wondered if all the jurors were getting the sports references. But she supposed enough of them were. Langston continued.

"Well, the interior of a rifled barrel has ridges, usually four to six of them, with depressions in between. The ridges twist inside the barrel and the bullet, because it just barely fits and is right up against those ridges, it twists too as it goes down the barrel, so at the end, it comes out of the barrel spinning, ready to go perfectly straight."

"Why does that enable you to match bullets to a particular firearm?" McDaniels wasn't even looking up from her script any more. Quinlan didn't trust her; he trusted Langston.

"Different manufacturers use different numbers of ridges and depressions—which are actually called lands and grooves—and different directions of the twist. So one manufacturer might use five lands and grooves and twist to the right, while another might have six lands and grooves and a twist to the left. A projectile with marking of five lands and grooves cannot have been fired down a barrel with six lands and grooves."

"Can you match a projectile to a specific firearm?"

"Yes," Langston answered. "When the barrel is bored out, there are small imperfections left behind, little tiny bits of metal that stick up and scratch the bullet as it travels down the barrel. These bits of metal are different for every individual firearm, The scratches left on a bullet are therefore unique to that firearm."

"Is the same true for casings ejected by the ejector pin?"

Langston shrugged a bit as he answered, "It's not as specific for ejector pins, but the location and length of the marks can vary widely from firearm to firearm, so if ejected casings from a crime scene match known casings ejected during a controlled test fire, we feel confident there's a match."

So, no, Talon thought. But that didn't help with the bullet extracted from Jordy McCabe's body. The same bullet McDaniels then retrieved from the bailiff, along with the casings from the crime scene and Exhibit #37, the handgun stolen—maybe—from Michael's home.

"I'm now handing you several exhibits," McDaniels announced for the record. "Did you examine these in relation to this case?"

Langston took the combination of plastic evidence bags and the handgun from McDaniels. He took a moment to confirm the markings on the various evidence tags, then confirmed, "Yes."

"And what are these items?" McDaniels asked.

"These," Langston held up a small plastic bag with both red and blue evidence tape and numbers and letters marked in various places in Sharpie, "are two spent casings, reportedly recovered—"

"Don't tell me where they might be from," McDaniels interrupted, to avoid the objection. The collecting evidence officers had testified days ago about collecting and packaging the casings, just like Brennan had testified about recovering the handgun, Exhibit #37. "Just what they are. Other witnesses have already identified where each item came from."

"Oh, okay," Langston replied. He seemed a little surprised.

Talon supposed not all defense attorneys held the State to the strict letter of the hearsay rules. And there were allowances for experts, but McDaniels wasn't taking any chances after the mistrial threat.

"What about the next bag?" McDaniels prodded.

"Ah, this." Langston held it up for the jury to see. It had the same blue evidence tape on one edge, and black identifying marks, but no red tape. "This is a spent projectile, recovered— Oh, well, it's just a spent projectile."

McDaniels nodded. The Medical Examiner had already testified that it had been removed from Jordan McCabe at autopsy. The cause of death was never in question, just the causer.

"It's partially deformed from impact," Langston added.

McDaniels nodded. Everyone knew that already too. Its tip was pancaked from lodging in McCabe's spine. The second gunshot had been a through-and-through, its bullet never recovered, flying off into that long ago night.

"And Exhibit Thirty-Seven?" she prompted.

Langston held up the handgun. "This is a nine millimeter semi-automatic handgun which I examined in relation to this case."

"Did you attempt to determine whether the projectile and casings from the other exhibits had been fired from this handgun?" McDaniels asked from her script.

"Yes," Langston nodded.

"How did you do that, exactly?"

"I fired the same type of ammunition through the firearm and then compared the test-fires with the recovered evidence to see whether the markings matched."

"Did the markings appear to match?"

"Yes, they did."

Says you, thought Talon. Not that she could phrase her cross-examination quite so juvenilely.

In contrast, McDaniels dropped into the formalistic questions-and-answers used to elicit the final expert opinion without, she undoubtedly hoped, objection.

"Do you have an opinion as to whether the projectile in Exhibit Number Thirteen was fired from the handgun that is Exhibit Thirty-Seven?" she asked.

"Yes, I do."

"And do you have an opinion as to whether the casings in Exhibit Number Five were ejected from the handgun that is Exhibit Thirty-Seven?"

"Yes, I do."

"What are those opinions based on?"

"My opinions are based on my examination of the unique markings on these exhibits when compared microscopically to the markings on the test-fired projectiles and casings from Exhibit Thirty-Seven."

"And what is your expert opinion, Mr. Langston?"

"It is my expert opinion," he turned again to the jury, holding up the exhibits for emphasis, "that this bullet and these casings were in fact fired from this handgun."

"Thank you, Mr. Langston," McDaniels said. "No further questions."

She returned to her seat next to Quinlan and waited for Talon to start her cross-examination. Talon didn't hurry. She had a script, too, one prepared the night before with input from St. Julian. It wasn't as long as McDaniels's script, but then again, the better cross-examination was often the shorter. Focused on the weaknesses of the State's evidence, rather than going over it all again. So if she wasn't going to talk as long, she could let Langston sweat a little as she got herself up to the bar and into position. There were three things she needed the jury to understand.

First, "The markings on Exhibit Number Thirteen are not as complete as those on your test-fired projectiles, are they, Mr. Langston? Because the exhibit is deformed from impact, right?"

Langston could hardly argue with that. "That is correct," he admitted. "But they were still sufficient to form a match."

"In your opinion?" Talon clarified.

"Yes, in my opinion."

"It's easier to make a match between two non-deformed bullets, isn't it?" she asked.

"Yes, of course."

"And the more deformed a projectile is, the harder it can be to make a match, correct?"

Langston thought for a moment. "I think that's a fair statement, yes."

"In fact," Talon pressed, "some projectiles can be so deformed as to make it impossible to match it to a specific firearm, isn't that true?"

Langston nodded. "That can happen, yes."

"So whether a deformed projectile is too deformed to be of value, that's a matter of opinion, isn't it?"

"A matter of expert opinion," Langston half-joked. "Yes."

Talon smiled weakly at the joke. "And experts can disagree, isn't that right, Mr. Langston?"

Langston shrugged. "Sometimes."

Second, "Ejector pin markings are not anywhere near as unique as the markings left on a projectile from the inside of a barrel, correct?"

"Yes, I believe I already testified to that," Langston answered.

"And so again, using ejector-pin markings to determine whether a particular casing was ejected from a particular semi-automatic is difficult to impossible, correct?"

"I wouldn't say that," Langston defended. "You can determine whether it's consistent with other evidence."

"Like the fired projectile?" Talon asked.

"Exactly," Langston confirmed.

"So your opinion that those casings were ejected from that handgun was based at least in part on your independent opinion that the deformed projectile was fired from that handgun?"

Langston thought for a moment. "I'm not sure I'd say that exactly. I try to look at all the evidence—"

"Evidence you didn't collect?" Talon interjected.

"Uh, correct," Langston admitted.

"I mean, you weren't there when these casings were allegedly collected, right?"

"Right."

"And you weren't there when this projectile was collected, were you?"

"No, I was not."

"But you were told, weren't you, by the detectives and the prosecutors that they believed the projectile and casings were from the same handgun?"

Langston shifted in his seat a bit. "I'm not sure I was told that, exactly. I was asked to do a comparison to see if they matched."

"Mr. Langston," Talon stepped into his space, "when you did your examination, you knew the prosecution's working theory was that this handgun fired this bullet and ejected these casings, didn't you? Yes or no."

Langston paused. "Yes," he admitted.

"And Mr. Langston," Talon continued, "if they had simply given you the handgun and the casings—alone, without the projectile *they told you was from the autopsy of the victim*—and asked you if they matched, you would have said you couldn't make an actual match from ejector-pin markings, right?"

"Uh, well, I'm not sure…"

"They told you the bullet was from the autopsy, didn't they?"

"Yes."

"And they gave it to you at the same time as the casings, didn't they?"

"Yes."

"They could have asked you to do the examinations separately," Talon insisted, "or not told you they were related, or had two different people at the crime lab do the testing independently, couldn't they?"

Langston frowned. "I suppose so."

"But instead they gave you the casings along with the bullet pulled from the spine of the dead man and asked, 'Hey, these are from the gun, too, right?'"

"That's not how they asked it," Langston defended.

Talon ignored the response. "Ejector-pin markings are very generic and the same markings can actually be made from a variety of different individual weapons, isn't that right?"

Langston shrugged again, but nodded. "Yes, that is technically correct."

"But it's your expert opinion that these casings are from this handgun, right?" Talon confirmed.

"Correct." He could hardly change his opinion now.

"But experts can disagree, right?" Talon asked again.

"Yes, they can."

Third, "Do you know Anastasia St. Julian?"

Langston raised his eyebrows at the name. "Yes. Yes, I do."

"She's also a firearm expert, isn't she?"

Langston nodded slowly. "Yes, she is."

Talon looked him right in the eye. "She thinks you're wrong."

Langston tried not to seem rattled. "Is that a question?" he huffed.

"No," Talon grinned at him. "No question about it."

She turned then and headed back to her seat, gathering her papers from the bar methodically and making no hurry to return to her seat. When she finally arrived, she looked up at the judge. "Nothing further."

Kirchner looked to McDaniels. "Any redirect?"

Talon could see McDaniels considering the points Talon had made:

The markings on damaged bullets were less reliable than on perfect bullets.

Casings can't really be linked to a specific handgun absent additional information.

Experts can disagree.

There wasn't anything to rehabilitate there.

"No, Your Honor," McDaniels answered. "Thank you."

The judge excused Langston, his irritation at Talon poorly concealed as he stomped his way out of the courtroom. When he'd left and the door closed behind him, Kirchner looked again to McDaniels. "Any further witnesses, counsel?"

But Quinlan popped to his feet. "No, Your Honor," he answered. "The State rests."

CHAPTER 39

Judge Kirchner wasn't about to make Talon put her case on immediately upon the State resting theirs. Professional courtesy was to adjourn for the day and start fresh in the morning with the defense case. As was typical for a murder case with over thirty prosecution witnesses, it had taken the State weeks to put on their case-in-chief. One more night wouldn't make a difference. Not for the State anyway. But maybe for the defense.

After Langston's testimony, Talon and St. Julian had conferred one more time back at her office. St. Julian would be there at ten to nine. Talon would bring her second script, the one St. Julian had all but drafted.

"Ask me these questions, in this order," had been her directive. And while Talon wasn't usually one for taking directives, she knew when to make exceptions.

The next conference was with Michael. There wasn't much strategy for that. It was just a check-in. "How are you holding up?" "Do you have any questions?" Things like that. There was only one strategic decision to make.

"Is he going to testify?" Curt asked after Talon sent Michael home for the night, to spend time with his wife and kids. She left off the 'while you still can', but it was implied.

"No," Talon shook her head. "I can't put him on the stand."

They were alone in her office. The workday hadn't quite ended but people were trickling onto the street and into the roadways for the commute home.

"Why not?" Curt asked. "He's articulate and likeable. And the jury's going to want to hear him say he didn't do it."

Talon put her feet up on her desk. It had been a long day, a long trial. "Well, that's the problem, isn't it? I don't know if he'll say that."

Curt frowned. "He should still say it, even if it's not true."

"Yeah, I'm not supposed to suborn perjury, remember?"

"It's not perjury if you don't know whether it's true," Curt replied. "You taught me that."

"Sure," Talon agreed. "But telling someone to testify to anything qualified by 'even if it isn't true' is a little too close for me. Anyway, it doesn't matter. He told me he won't testify. His brother won't testify. All I have is Anastasia St. Julian."

"That's nothing to sneeze at." Greg Olsen had appeared in the doorway. "I told you she was good. The jury will think so too."

Talon dropped her feet to the floor again. "I don't doubt it. I just hope the jury doesn't vote based on how long each side's case was. Theirs was four weeks. Mine will be forty minutes."

Olsen waved the idea away. "Nah, she'll take longer than that. A few hours at least, depending on cross."

"Followed by a meek, 'The defense rests,'" she answered. She shook her head. "I wish we had more to put on, but..."

"But it's not your job to put on evidence," Olsen opined. "It's theirs. You don't have to disprove the allegation; they have to prove it—beyond a reasonable doubt."

"I know how it works," Talon joked. "I'm just not sure the jury will stick to the script. It was a murder, for God's sake. Somebody's dead. And my guy isn't going to take the stand and say he didn't do it."

"Most defendants don't," Olsen observed.

"Most defendants are convicted," Talon replied. "Right?" She was still new to this criminal stuff, after all.

Olsen shrugged and smiled. "Right," he conceded.

"Did you make a half-time motion?" he asked.

"Do those ever work in criminal cases?" Talon asked.

"What's a half-time motion?" Curt added.

Olsen answered Curt's question first. "It's a motion you make after the State rests. You argue they didn't prove the case and the Court should dismiss it right then."

"Do those get granted?" Curt repeated Talon's question.

Olsen thought for a moment. "No," he laughed. "Not usually. It's more for the show of it. Personally, I'm not a big fan. To make it sound credible, you have to point out all the stuff the State forgot to prove. But if you do that, they can always re-open their case."

"I thought there was something magical about resting your case," Curt said.

"Maybe in a shoplifting case," Olsen answered. "But no judge is going to dismiss a murder case because the prosecution forgot some small detail. It'd have to be huge."

"They forgot to say my guy identified the murder weapon as his gun," Talon offered up.

Olsen raised his eyebrows. "That's pretty big."

"That's why I didn't make the motion," she replied.

"Because you might win?" Curt asked, incredulously.

"That's crazy."

"That's brilliant," Olsen disagreed. "They don't know they missed that, do they?"

Talon smiled. "Nope. That's the downside of four weeks of witnesses. You can't keep track. Neither can the jury or the judge for that matter. But I caught it. And I'll be sure to point it out in closing argument. But not sooner."

"But the judge might dismiss the case," Curt protested. "Isn't that worth it?"

Talon and Olsen both shook their heads. "No, Curt," Talon said. "Greg's right. Defendants are guilty, prosecutors are whiny, and judges are elected. Even if Kirchner agreed it was a fatal flaw, she'd let them fix it, and then I'd lose it for closing. No, I'm going to let them think they did such a great job that I didn't even bother making a half-time motion. When I point it out in closing, it'll be way too late to recall Sergeant Mark Brennan, Tacoma P.D."

CHAPTER 40

Talon sent Curt home so she could get some rest. Her direct examination of St. Julian was already scripted, so she didn't need to prepare, but she didn't need any unnecessary adrenaline rushes from protected flirting either. Not yet. An expert ballistic witness was about precision, not emotion. Now, closing argument? That might be a different story…

She shook the thought out of her head.

"Are you okay?" Michael asked her. They were seated in the courtroom, ready for battle. St. Julian was waiting in the hallway. Quinlan and McDaniels were in place next to them, also at the ready.

Talon smiled. "I'm perfect." She lowered her voice. "Last chance. You're sure you don't want to testify?"

Michael didn't smile. But he nodded. "I'm sure."

"I know," Talon answered. "But I had to ask one more time."

The judge came out then and took the bench.

"Is the defense ready?" she asked once everyone was seated

again.

Talon stood. "Yes, Your Honor."

Kirchner looked to her bailiff. "Fetch the jury." He did and a few moments later, Talon announced, "The defense calls Anastasia St. Julian."

Curt was in the courtroom again—he was as emotionally invested as anyone. Well, almost anyone. Alicia Jameson might disagree. He stood up as Talon announced their witness and retrieved her from her seat on the benches in the hallway. St. Julian had exchanged her blue jeans and flannel from their first meeting for a muted gray pantsuit. She carried a binder of papers under her left arm so she could raise her right hand and swear to tell the truth, the whole truth, and nothing but the truth.

This time Talon got to go first. She took a comfortable spot at the bar, and began their predetermined dialogue.

"Please state your name for the record," she said. "And spell your last name for the court reporter.

"Anastasia St. Julian," she answered. Talon had told her about the 'don't disrespect me by looking away' thing with Halcomb, so St. Julian made sure to give her answers back to Talon, with an occasional glance to the jury to confirm she knew they were important too. "S-T, new word, J-U-L-I-A-N. My friends call me Ann."

Talon knew it was just background, not an invitation. "Ms. St. Julian, could you please state your education, training, and experience in the field of ballistics examination?"

So she did. Starting with her B.A. in mechanical engineering and ending with her retirement from supervising the Washington State Patrol Crime Laboratory. Where Arnold Langston worked.

"Have you had an opportunity to examine the evidence in this case?" Talon asked.

"Yes."

"Did you examine it yourself or just read the reports of others?"

"I examined it myself."

"Did you also review the reports of Arnold Langston of the Crime Lab?" Talon continued along their script.

"Yes, I did," St. Julian answered.

"And did you have the opportunity to listen to his testimony yesterday?"

Again, "I certainly did."

"What do you think?" Talon asked.

"I think he's wrong."

Nice, Talon thought. But they weren't done.

"What was he wrong about?"

"His opinion isn't supported by the evidence."

Again, good, but in need of more explanation. "Could you explain, please?"

St. Julian nodded. This time she did look to the jury. After all, she was asking them to trust her over him. "He isn't wrong about what he observed, but what he observed isn't sufficient to support his conclusions."

That sounded kind. He's not dumb, just stupid.

"Mr. Langston made it sound like the matching of striations on the sides of fired projectiles is purely objective. Like on television when a computer program superimposes the patterns and then a large green sign pops up, flashing 'Positive Match!' But it's not like that in real life. Especially not when you're dealing with a deformed projectile." She turned back to Talon. "May I use the easel?"

"Why, of course," Talon answered. What a wonderful, not at all pre-planned idea. Every courtroom in the courthouse had a portable easel and a large pad of butcher paper for witnesses to draw diagrams when necessary. It was typically used for drawing things like car crashes and the like. But a picture was worth a thousand words, whether it was car crashes or deformed projectiles.

She positioned the easel so the jurors could see while she drew on it. She started with a normal projectile.

"This," she explained as she drew a profile of it, square at the bottom, pointed at the top, "is a fired, non-deformed bullet. I'm just going to call it a bullet. We don't have to say projectile. We all know what we're talking about."

Informative and *folksy*. *Perfect*. The jurors were paying attention.

"This can happen any time the bullet doesn't hit anything hard enough to smash the metal. It might pass through a series of soft materials, flesh, fabric, wood, until it loses enough velocity to come to rest without deforming. In the lab, we fire into water or a special jelly that stops the bullet without deforming it."

Then she drew a series of unevenly spaced lines down the side of the bullet.

"These are the scratches the bullet received when it travels down the barrel of the gun. Now if we get a second non-deformed bullet from the same gun..."

She drew another bullet next to the first and added the same pattern of uneven lines on it.

"...you can see how we can identify it as being fired from the same weapon. These lines are identical and are almost certainly unique to a particular firearm. But..."

Underneath the first pair of bullets, she drew two more: one normal-looking, the other smashed down like a mushroom.

"...if you compare a non-deformed bullet with a deformed bullet, well, that's something different altogether."

She replicated the scratch pattern on the first, normal bullet.

Then she started drawing lines on the mushroom bullet.

"When the metal of the bullet is deformed, so is the pattern of scratches. It twists and turns and expands. Lines that were parallel on the non-deformed bullet may get pressed together into a single line, or may end up pushed far apart from each other. It's like taking an impression from silly putty, then stretching it. They won't line up when they're super-imposed. There's no 'Perfect Match' to flash on something like this."

"So does an analyst make a match?" Talon asked.

St. Julian looked at her drawings and shrugged. "Honestly, it's a guess. At this point we move from science—precise measurement and repeatability—to art—interpretation and conjecture. Do these lines look like they could have been the same if we stretch the silly putty back into its original position? But, of course, you can't stretch a bullet back into its regular position. And the more damaged a bullet is, the more difficult it can be to make this kind of judgment. But no matter what, that's what it is: a judgment. A guess."

"Thank you," Talon said. It was a signal for St. Julian to re-take the witness stand while Talon fetched Exhibits 5, 13, and 37 from the bailiff.

"You said you had the opportunity to examine these items of evidence?" Talon asked as she handed them to St. Julian.

"I did," St. Julian confirmed.

"Did you also test-fire bullets from Exhibit Thirty-Seven?"

"Yes."

"Did you compare them to the fired bullet that is Exhibit Thirteen?"

"Yes."

"And what was your conclusion?" Talon asked.

"The bullet is too damaged to determine whether or not it

was fired from this particular handgun."

"You mean, you couldn't tell?" Talon followed up.

"No," St. Julian clarified. "I mean it is scientifically impossible to determine whether it was fired from the handgun. It is too deformed to be able to make that determination. It's not that I couldn't do it. It's that no one could make that determination."

"Arnold Langston did," Talon pointed out.

"Arnold Langston is wrong," St. Julian replied. "You can't rule the weapon out. It has five lands and grooves with a right twist, and even in its deformed state, those gross characteristics are decipherable. But the fine difference in striation patterns is too compromised in the deformed bullet to be able to match it to any individual handgun."

So far, so good. But there was more. It was necessary for the jury to hear St. Julian say Langston was wrong, but it wasn't sufficient. They needed a reason to believe it.

"Why would Mr. Langston say they matched when you say a match can't be made?" Talon asked.

"It's not Mr. Langston's fault," St. Julian offered, not directly in response to the question, but directly in line with the script.

"Why not?" Talon provided the next line.

"Mr. Langston works for the *Washington State Patrol* Crime Laboratory," she answered. "It's a law enforcement agency, not a purely scientific lab. They don't take the precautions a more objective lab would take."

"What do you mean?"

"At a purely scientific lab, all testing should be independent," St. Julian explained, "and it should be conducted with no knowledge of why the testing is being requested. Also, there should always be a control. For example, in this case, the fired bullet in Exhibit Thirteen should have been submitted with another, random deformed bullet that was definitely not fired from that handgun. That way, if the analyst found that both were fired from the same gun, we could know the analyst was going too far in his conclusions. As it is, Mr. Langston was provided a bullet and asked to confirm what detectives already suspected. That's called confirmation bias. Law enforcement doesn't submit bullets and a gun to the lab just for fun. They only do it if they already suspect there's a connection. The analyst knows that and therefore may see confirmation where there really is none. That's why a known control sample is so important, but it wasn't done here."

"Interesting," Talon said. "Anything else?"

"Yes," St. Julian answered, not surprisingly. "They submitted both the casings and the bullet to the same analyst. So again, the analyst not only knows the detectives want a match between the bullet and the gun, they also want a match between the casings and the gun. So first the analyst stretches to connect the bullet to the gun, then uses the casings to confirm his already biased conclusion about the bullet. Because, you see, the analyst knows where all the items are from."

"Wait," Talon faux-interjected. "Are you saying the detectives told Mr. Langston where each item of evidence was collected and what their theory was as to how they were all connected?"

"Exactly," St. Julian said. "They could have just said: 'Here. This is a gun, and this is a bullet, and these are casings. Tell us if they're related.' But they don't. The lab request they send has the case number, the crime, the suspect's name, the victim's name—"

"It lists all that?" Talon asked. "Even the crime? So Mr. Langston knew it was for a murder case?"

"He knew it was for a twenty-five-year-old murder case," St. Julian expanded. "The case number starts with the year of the incident. Just from the lab report, Mr. Langston knew he was being asked to link those items together to solve a cold case homicide, which is pretty much the holy grail of forensic science."

"He had a chance to be the hero," Talon posited.

"To solve an unsolvable crime," St. Julian added. "To bring closure to the victim's family and praise upon himself and his colleagues in law enforcement."

Talon shook her head. "What should they have done?"

"They should have sent the bullet to one analyst, with a control bullet," St. Julian answered. "They should have sent the casings to another analyst, again with known control casings from a different handgun. And they never should have told either of them why they were asking, or what case it was for, or whether it was even for a case rather than just a random quality control check for the lab to keep its accreditation."

"They could have done all that, couldn't they?" Talon asked.

"Of course they could have," St. Julian answered.

"Why didn't they?"

St. Julian paused. "I can't say for certain, but I have an opinion."

Talon suppressed a smile. "What is your opinion based on?"

"My years of experience as a forensics ballistics examiner, including my time as the supervisor for the Washington State Patrol Crime Lab."

"Anything else?"

"And my personal examination of the evidence in this case," St. Julian added.

"And what is your opinion?"

St. Julian turned to the jury. This needed to have its full force. "The crime lab was created to solve crimes. Detectives send evidence there to solve crimes. Analysts draw conclusions to solve crimes. In this case, Mr. Langston gave the detectives what they wanted. He solved the crime."

"But?" Talon prodded.

"But he was wrong."

Talon closed her binder. The script was finished. "No further questions, Your Honor."

She returned to her seat and St. Julian squared her shoulders to the prosecution table. Kirchner looked there as well. "Cross-examination?"

Quinlan hesitated, then stood up. "Uh, could we have a brief recess, Your Honor?"

Wow, thought Talon. *Did it go that well?* Objecting was like saying 'ouch' in front of the jury, even if it sometimes had to be done. But asking for a recess before cross-examining a witness? That was like holding up a severed limb and asking if it was noticeable.

But it was smart, maybe. It would give Quinlan a few minutes to gather his thoughts and plan an attack. After all, prosecutors were way more used to directing witnesses they called than crossing defense witnesses. A lot of criminal defendants never called any witnesses. And good cross-examination was difficult even with practice. Plus, it would provide an opportunity for St. Julian's testimony to fade a bit from the jury's mind.

At least it would have, if Judge Kirchner had granted the recess.

"No recess, counsel," she responded. "The witness is on the stand and the jury is in the box. Do you have any questions?"

"Uh, yes," Quinlan replied weakly. "Yes, Your Honor."

He could hardly let that testimony stand. But he didn't seem to know how to attack it either.

"You're getting paid by the defense, isn't that true, Ms. St. Julian?"

That was weak, but predictable. Make her look like she's a paid mouthpiece. Or, in less polite terms, a whore.

"I'm paid for my time, not my opinions," St. Julian replied. "Just as part of Mr. Langston's job duties are to testify when called by the State. That doesn't mean he provides a particular opinion in exchange for money. And neither do I."

Quinlan thought for a moment. "And now that you're retired from the crime lab, you testify only for the defense, is that right?"

"Now that I'm retired?" St. Julian confirmed. "Well, yes. The prosecution gives its work to the crime lab and calls those analysts as witnesses. I have been consulted by the State, but when I am, and when I provide an opinion such as the one I provided here, the prosecution doesn't usually proceed."

Talon had to keep herself from clapping. Quinlan needed to watch himself or he was going to lose another limb.

He seemed to sense it.

"Uh, so you disagree with Mr. Langston?" he tried, a bit softer.

"I do," St, Julian answered, not softer at all.

"But experts can disagree, correct?" Quinlan tried. "That's not completely uncommon, is it?"

St. Julian thought for a moment. "No, it's not uncommon. In fact, it's part of science for experts to disagree and then try to figure out why."

"And a jury is free to choose which expert to believe," Quinlan said, "isn't that true?"

Talon started to rise to object. It was inappropriate to ask a witness to tell the jury how they should deliberate. Jury deliberations were sacrosanct. Lawyers weren't even supposed to suggest how to deliberate in their closing arguments. But she sat down again. Anastasia St. Julian had it.

"A jury is supposed to decide whether the prosecution proved each and every element of the charge beyond a reasonable doubt," she answered. "They should keep that in mind when deciding whether to believe an analyst employed by law enforcement whose conclusions are demonstrably inaccurate."

Quinlan blinked at the answer. He turned to McDaniels. She had nothing.

"No further questions," he conceded.

Kirchner looked to Talon. "Any re-direct examination?"

Oh, hell, no, Talon thought. But she stood up. "No, Your Honor. Thank you."

Kirchner looked to St. Julian. "You're excused." Then back to Talon. "Any further witnesses?"

Yes, Your Honor. The defense calls Michael Jameson to say he didn't do it.

Yes, Your Honor. The defense calls Ricky Jameson to say he was the shooter.

Yes, Your Honor. The defense calls ...

"No, Your Honor. The defense rests."

Now it was time for that release.

CHAPTER 41

Closing arguments were scheduled for the next morning. Again, a professional courtesy to allow the attorneys time to collect their thoughts, prepare their comments, organize their exhibits.

And work off their anxiety.

In that order. Roughly.

Talon sent Michael and Alicia home to spend time with each other. If there was a quick verdict, and if it was a conviction, Michael would be arrested in the courtroom, his bail revoked by the verdict. He wouldn't get out again.

She thanked St. Julian in the hallway. Profusely. If she was only going to call one witness, she couldn't have asked for a better one.

She ignored Quinlan and McDaniels. Screw them. They were the enemy. She wasn't going to shake hands. Not unless it was an acquittal and she made them shake hers.

And she told Curt to be at her office at 6:00 p.m. sharp. He didn't ask why. *Good boy.*

It was a sort of ritual of hers when she was in trial. The night before, she needed the edge off. In the past, she had always been dating someone or another, so there had never been an issue. But since she was fired from Gardelli High, her life had been turned upside down. She'd been so busy with Michael's case, and her own, she hadn't even tried to date, Kyle the barista notwithstanding.

But Curt would do.

In fact, he would more than do.

That was the part that scared her.

He arrived at exactly 6:00. Everyone else had already gone home for the night. Even Olsen, although Talon had to shoo him out of the office for fear he might linger after hours as he was wont to do.

Curt walked directly into her office. He didn't ask why he was there. He didn't say anything at all. He wasn't stupid. But he was gorgeous. Dressed for business in a tight T-shirt and perfect jeans.

He closed the door behind him. She got out of her chair and sat on the edge of her desk, spreading her skirt and her legs to him. He stepped up to her and put his arms around her waist. But when he leaned in to kiss her, she turned her face away. Instead, she grabbed the back of his neck and pulled his face into her neck.

A few deft moves later, her skirt was above her hips and his pants were around his ankles. It was quick and it was rough. Talon looked at herself in that mirror on the wall. She looked at them both. They looked good.

He finished first. But he didn't stop. He pulled his face from her neck and looked into her eyes. She wanted to look away, but didn't. He lowered his hand and made sure she finished too, their eyes locked the entire time.

When her body stopped wracking, he pulled himself away from her, his eyes the last thing to let go. He pulled up his pants, then leaned in again to kiss her.

She let him.

He stopped at the door and smiled. It lit up his entire face. And hers. "I'll see you in court, Ms. Winter."

CHAPTER 42

The next morning the courtroom was packed. Alicia had been there every day. Curt had come a few times. St. Julian had watched Langston's testimony. But otherwise, the courtroom had been mostly empty throughout the trial, save the participants. Not every murder case caught the public interest. But most of them did catch the attention of the prosecutor's office, and the local defense bar, and the police. So it was only natural they would show up for the big show at the end: closing arguments.

Junior prosecutors and senior detectives came to watch Quinlan and McDaniels. Curious defense attorneys came to see the new defense attorney doing that cold case murder trial. A few others probably just followed the crowd in. Either way, every seat in the courtroom was taken.

Quinlan and McDaniels seemed nonplussed. Talon wasn't about to let it affect her either. Michael seemed a bit disquieted. But it was the jurors who were truly surprised when they walked out from the jury room to a sea of expectant faces, all standing when they entered.

If they had perhaps concluded from the heretofore empty courtroom that no one cared about this case after all, that notion was dispatched immediately. It was evident on their faces. There was a human tendency to normalize things and try to get comfortable. Photos of murdered teenagers gave way to bonding with fellow jurors, stories about weekend activities, and jokes with the bailiff about the morning's donut selection. But that time was over. It was back to work.

Judge Kirchner bade the jurors to sit, then explained what was about to happen.

Ladies and gentlemen, we have reached the point in the trial where the parties are ready to deliver their closing arguments. Prior to that happening, I am going to instruct you on the law. The bailiff will hand you each a copy of the jury instructions. I want you to read along as I read these out loud to you."

There were 34 different instructions, Talon knew. She and Michael had copies too. So did Quinlan and McDaniels. They were taken from the Washington Pattern Instructions for Criminal cases. What the lawyers called 'the Whi-Picks.' They were the statements of the law that governed every type of case, from driving on a suspended license to murder in the first degree. The language had been proposed by a committee of prosecutors and defense attorneys and approved by the State Supreme Court. Judge Kirchner wouldn't deviate a single word from the pattern instructions.

But there were 34 of them that applied to Michael Jameson's case. It would take almost an hour for the judge to read them all out loud. The jurors would follow along, but the lawyers wouldn't. They would be going over their notes, readying themselves one last time before they stood up to speak to the jurors one last time. Talon was only half-aware of some of the more important phrases and sentences the judge was reading:

"A defendant is presumed innocent. This presumption continues throughout the entire trial unless, during your deliberations, you find it has been overcome beyond a reasonable doubt."

"A reasonable doubt may arise from the evidence or lack of evidence."

"The defendant is not required to testify. You may not use the fact that the defendant has not testified to infer guilt or to prejudice him in any way."

"You are the sole judges of the credibility of each witness."

"The law does not distinguish between direct and circumstantial evidence. One is not necessarily more or less valuable than the other."

"A person commits the crime of murder in the first degree when, with a premeditated intent to cause the death of another person, he or she causes the death of such person, or any third person."

"A person also commits the crime of murder in the first degree when, under circumstances manifesting an extreme indifference to human life, he or she engages in conduct which creates a grave risk of death to any person and thereby cause the death of any person."

"You have nothing whatever to do with any punishment that may be imposed in case of a violation of the law. You may not consider the fact that punishment may follow conviction, except insofar as it may tend to make you careful."

"As jurors, you are officers of the court. You must act impartially, with an earnest desire to reach a proper verdict."

"Because this is a criminal case, each of you must agree for you to return a verdict. When all of you have so agreed, fill in the verdict form to express your decision and notify the bailiff. The bailiff will bring you into court to declare your verdict."

Judge Kirchner paused upon completing the reading of the instructions. She set aside her copy of the instructions and took a sip of water. Then she looked up to address the jurors again.

"Ladies and Gentlemen, now please give your attention to Mr. Quinlan who will deliver the closing argument on behalf of the prosecution."

CHAPTER 43

"Justice delayed. Or justice denied." Quinlan began. "Those are your choices."

He stood directly in front of the jury box. His hands folded in front of him. Navy suit, white shirt, red tie. He looked every bit the part of dedicated District Attorney. People trusted their D.A. At least, they wanted to.

"Twenty-five years ago, the defendant," he turned and pointed, "Michael Jameson shot and killed Jordan McCabe. Did he do it intentionally, wanting to leave Jordy to bleed to death in the middle of Cushman Avenue? Or did he not care what happened, just firing into a crowd of kids standing there that night, indifferent—extremely indifferent—to whether he hit anyone? Actually, it doesn't matter. Either way he's guilty of murder in the first degree. Either way, he needs to be held responsible. He needs to be brought to justice."

Quinlan moved from his starting spot, centered before the jury, and began a slow, thoughtful pace.

"Let's go over what the witnesses said," he continued.

Talon breathed a little sigh of relief. His beginning had been strong. Catchy, direct, memorable. But now Quinlan was going to do what so many mediocre trial attorneys did: go over the evidence, witness by witness. As if the jurors hadn't been there, too, the whole trial.

"Remember what Joanne McCabe-Johnson told you," he began his summary. "Her son Jordy was a good kid, who liked computers and hanging out with his friends. And she identified his body the night he was murdered."

Quinlan reached the end of the jury box and turned back to pace in the other direction. "Remember what Detective Halcomb told you," he said. "They ran out of suspects and the case went cold."

Quinlan stopped again at his original starting point. "Remember what Detective Jefferson told you. Twenty-five years later, a handgun was recovered from the defendant's home."

Talon frowned slightly. That wasn't exactly accurate.

"And remember," Quinlan finished, "what Arnold Langston told you. The weapon from the defendant's home was the same one that killed Jordy McCabe."

Yep, Talon thought. That was the State's case in a nutshell. If the jury believed it, Michael was sunk. So the question wasn't whether the witnesses said that—they did. It was whether the witnesses were compelling. Whether the jury believed the witnesses. And whether they believed them *enough*.

So Quinlan, wisely, addressed the weaknesses in his case.

"Now, there may be some questions you still have," he said. "Most importantly, why did this happen? What was the motive?"

He nodded. "We always want to know the motive. Heck, that's one of the ways detectives identify suspects. Who had a motive? But the one thing we actually don't have to prove is motive.

We have to prove what happened, and who did it, but we don't have to prove why. Put another way, if you know what happened and who did it, you don't need to know why. You still vote guilty.

"Why was Jordy McCabe murdered that night so many years ago?" Quinlan shook his head. "We might never know. But we don't have to. Because we know who did it. The defendant, Michael Jameson."

Talon knew why it happened. But the jury didn't. Quinlan didn't want them to know his victim was a drug dealer. Fine with Talon. They didn't know Michael was either. He might not have to prove motive, but if the lack of motive left a reasonable doubt…

Quinlan continued. "There was also a disagreement between the experts in this case. But really it was only an apparent disagreement. When you really look at their testimony, they actually agreed where it really mattered."

Talon raised an eyebrow. *Oh, really?*

"Both of them agreed the defendant's weapon was exactly the type of weapon that shot the bullets that killed Jordy McCabe," Quinlan said. "The only difference was that Ms. St. Julian said she couldn't find enough evidence to link that particular gun to those particular ballistics. But Arnold Langston could. And that only makes sense. Ms. St. Julian retired several years ago. Science marches on and technologies improve. Of course, the person who's still doing this every day and who's completely up-to-date on all the latest advancements is going to be able to see more. And he told you, Michael Jameson's gun fired the shot that killed Jordy McCabe."

Talon had to hand it to Quinlan. That was about the best possible way to spin the experts' testimony. But prosecutors weren't really supposed to 'spin' evidence. She determined to make him pay for it when she got her chance to stand up.

"Finally, one thing you may struggle with," Quinlan said, "is the fact that you don't know exactly what happened out there that night. This is a very important decision. In fact, it's hard to imagine a more important decision than the one you're facing. It's only natural you would want to know every last answer to every last question. But you know what? You won't have that. And you don't need it."

He walked over and picked up his copy of the jury instructions. "The judge told you we have to prove every element of the crime beyond a reasonable doubt. And that's true. But you know what? If we do that, we don't have to prove anything else. If you're convinced beyond a reasonable doubt that Michael Jameson fired the shot that killed Jordy McCabe, then that's all that matters. You don't have to know anything else. You don't have to know what color shirt Jordy was wearing, or what model car Michael Jameson was driving, or anything else like that. Would you like to know that? Would we all like to know that? Of course. Do we all wish there was video of everything that happened so we wouldn't be left with those nagging questions that are inevitable in any case, let alone a twenty-five-year-old cold case? Of course. But do you need that video? Do you need answers to every last question? No."

He set the jury instruction packet on the bar, and turned back to the jurors to finish his summation.

"You need to be satisfied beyond a reasonable doubt that Michael Jameson committed the elements of murder in the first degree. That he killed Jordy McCabe and that he did it intentionally or with extreme indifference to human life. We have proven that. We have proven it beyond a reasonable doubt. Michael Jameson is guilty of murder in the first degree and we ask you to return that verdict. Thank you."

Quinlan walked back to the prosecution table and Talon

watched as he sat down and accepted congratulations from his partner. It was a good closing, Talon had to admit.

So it was time to give a great closing.

"Ladies and gentlemen," Judge Kirchner said, "now please give your attention to Ms. Winter who will deliver closing argument on behalf of the defendant."

CHAPTER 44

Talon didn't hurry as she took her place in front of the jury. It was the same exact spot where Quinlan had stood. In part, because that was the best place to stand when giving a closing, regardless of which side you were on. But also in part, to claim it. To take it away from Quinlan.

"Reasonable doubt," she started, "may arise from the evidence," then a pause, before finishing, "or the lack of evidence."

She nodded to the jurors, making eye contact with several of them in turn. "This case was all about lack of evidence."

She could point too. She pointed at Quinlan. "There's a reason the prosecutor told you not to worry about all the evidence they didn't present. It's because they barely presented any evidence. And they want you to overlook the huge, gaping holes in their case. They want you to forget your oath, ignore your instructions, and return a verdict of guilty on nothing more than a kiss and a promise. He did it. We promise. Trust us."

She shook her head. "No. Don't trust them. Don't ever trust them. Don't trust the government with all of its resources and advantages when they want to put a man away for murder. The judge said you can consider the fact that punishment may follow conviction insofar as it may tend to make you careful."

She pointed at the jurors and raised her voice. "Be careful."

It was aggressive, but she wasn't going to win being passive. Everything was in the State's favor. The jurors walked in wondering what the defendant had done. When the judge told them it was a murder case, they wondered how he did it. When the prosecutor told them it was a shooting, they were ready to convict. Or at least, that was the danger. And it was no time to be polite.

"Think back to what you thought when you walked into the courtroom the first time," she challenged. "You wondered what he'd done to end up in the defendant's chair. Because you don't want to live in a country where innocent people are prosecuted for crimes they didn't commit. You don't want to live in a country where mistakes are made and innocent men lose their lives for things someone else did.

"And good for you. None of us want to live in a country like that. But we know we do. We see the news reports. We watch the true crime shows. We know innocent people do get convicted. And we wonder, how did that happen? Well, I'll tell you. It happened because the jury wasn't careful. It happened because they trusted the government and the system and they didn't want to live in a country either where innocent people get prosecuted."

Another accusatory finger. She panned it across the jury box. "Don't be like those jurors. There's a reason the judge told you the defendant is presumed innocent." She looked over to her client. "Michael is presumed innocent. He is innocent. And the State, with all of its resources and advantages, didn't even come close to proving otherwise."

She took a step to her right, more to shift her weight than

anything else. She wasn't a pacer. Pacing was distracting. Quinlan did it; that was enough reason for her not to.

"Think about what Mr. Quinlan just told you. We didn't prove motive. We didn't prove what happened. We didn't prove who, what, where, or when. But we told you it was Michael Jameson because one person working in a crime lab thinks he can match a smashed bullet to a firearm twenty-five-years after the fact."

Another shake of her head. "Well, let's take a closer look at that, shall we? First of all, the State failed to actually link that particular firearm to Michael. You heard two different and distinct things. First, a firearm or firearms was stolen from Michael's home; and second, the firearm Arnold Langston claims was used to kill Jordan McCabe was pawned at the same time and by the same people who pawned Michael's stolen T.V. and laptop. But you know what you didn't hear? You didn't hear that Michael or his wife or anyone else actually identified that pawned gun as the one stolen from the Jameson home. Is it so unlikely that a burglar might pawn items from more than one burglary at the same time?"

She paused and let that sink in.

"Go ahead, check your notes when you get back in the deliberation room. No one ever linked them. You think they did. Some of you anyway. Some of you are sitting here right now, thinking, 'I'm pretty sure someone said that.' And you know what? You're wrong. I was listening for it. As much as anyone in this courtroom I was listening for it. That's my job. And I didn't hear it, because no one said it."

She raised a finger. "Now, this is a very important point. It might be the most important point in this entire trial. You swore an oath to follow the law. The law is, if they don't prove every element of the crime—*beyond a reasonable doubt*—then you *must* acquit. You have a duty to acquit. A duty.

"And even with that duty—that duty to acquit—some of you are still thinking, 'Well, it was implied. I mean, why would the prosecutor say it was the same gun if it wasn't the same gun? We're here for a reason, right?' And I am telling you right now, any of you who are thinking that—you are violating your oath. You are violating your duty. *You* are the reason innocent people go to prison."

She wasn't making any friends, Talon knew. But it wasn't about making friends. It was about making a point. Winning the argument. Winning the case.

The jurors were uncomfortable. But they were listening.

"And then the prosecutor, Mr. Quinlan, has the gall to stand in front of you and try to spin the ballistic testimony as if Anastasia St. Julian is some doddering old retiree who's fallen behind the times. How dare he? How dare he?"

It wasn't an unintentional pivot. Turn from whatever wrong thing her client might have done and let's talk about the wrong things the prosecution might have done.

"You heard her testimony. You heard how she explained it. Did Arnold Langston diagram anything for you? Did he try to educate you as to why he came to the conclusion he did? No. Because he came to the conclusion he did based, not on the evidence, not on the marking on the bullet, but based on the information on the lab request form. The defendant's name, the victim's name, the detective's name, and the crime. Murder. And not just a murder, a cold case murder. A chance to be the hero. He knew what the detectives wanted, so he gave it to them. A match. A perfect, exact, complete match. But one that couldn't withstand scrutiny.

"Ann St. Julian used to run that lab. She came in here and

she told you exactly why Arnold Langston was wrong. And he was wrong. But not as wrong as the prosecutor when he attacked Ms. St. Julian."

She took a step back to her left. "Do you remember what we talked about in jury selection? How the system hasn't always been fair to people of color, to Americans of color? But it's not just ethnicity. Do you remember retired Detective Halcomb? Do you remember how he didn't even bother to look at me when he answered my questions? And now Mr. Quinlan, in his perfect suit and red power tie, and alabaster skin and male anatomy, tells you to disregard the vastly more experienced and qualified woman because, hey, she's old, and Mr. Langston is, well, a mister. We can forgive an old woman her silly notions."

Again, not polite. Maybe not even fair. But effective. Or so she hoped.

"So when you go back there and deliberate the fate of Michael Jameson, don't just look at what little the State did prove. Look at all they didn't prove. They put on no evidence that Michael Jameson pulled the trigger. They put on no evidence that Michael Jameson was even there that night. The only evidence they put on was that a gun pawned by some thieves was the same type of gun that killed Jordy McCabe. That's not proof beyond a reasonable doubt. That's not proof at all."

She could have finished there. She'd made her points, and closing argument was about explaining how the evidence did, or didn't, prove the crime charged. But it wasn't enough. She had given them the reasons they could use to acquit Michael Jameson. But she had to make them want to.

She walked over to her client and stood behind him, placing her hands on his shoulders. They were going to look at her, so she made them look at him. "Michael Jameson is forty-three years old.

He's a husband, he's a father, and he's a good man. We don't know what happened that fateful night twenty-five years ago. The State hasn't been able to prove it. But we do know what's happening right here, right now. This man's fate is in your hands. Return a verdict that's consistent with your oath. Return a verdict that's consistent with your duty. Return a verdict of not guilty."

CHAPTER 45

Talon was pleased with her closing. Or at least satisfied. It would have been a good final word. And in a lot of states it would have been the final word. But not in Washington. In Washington, the prosecution got the last word. Ostensibly because they had the burden of proof. And to keep the defense attorney honest, knowing the state would be able to address whatever arguments the defense made. Amity McDaniels stood to deliver the states rebuttal argument

She took that same spot, centered before the jury, but only for a moment. "Pretty words," she started. "Pretty and powerful words from two lawyers. Professionals whose job it is to deliver pretty and powerful words."

She stepped over to where the exhibits sat on the bar in front of the bailiff. "But words are cheap," she said as she selected two pieces of paper and walked over to the projector. "It takes a thousand of them to equal one picture. So instead of more pretty words, let me show you two pictures."

She laid the exhibits on the glass and flipped the projector on. Two images filled the screen opposite the jurors: on the left, Jordy McCabe's yearbook photo; on the right, his lifeless, bloody body at the crime scene.

"This is what this case is really about. It's about Jordan McCabe and why he didn't get the chance to grow up to be a father and a husband and a neighbor and a coworker. And that reason is because the defendant murdered him. He shot him through the chest and left him to bleed to death on the cold asphalt of Cushman Avenue."

She clicked off the projector again. "And now he's gone. The defense is right about one thing. This is a circumstantial case, solved because the defendant held on to the murder weapon all these years. But the judge told you, circumstantial evidence is not necessarily worse than direct evidence. Especially where the reason we don't have that direct evidence is because of the actions of the defendant himself."

McDaniels didn't point at Michael. She didn't even look at him. Instead she returned to the jurors to deliver the case's final entreaty.

"Jordan McCabe can't tell you what happened that night because the defendant stole his voice from him. But you can be that voice. A quarter century later, you can speak for him. You can say what needs to be said. Say the word. Say justice. Say guilty to murder in the first degree."

McDaniels turned and returned to her seat. It was time for the judge to speak one last time.

"Ladies and gentlemen, that concludes the trial. You will now retire to the jury room to begin your deliberations."

The bailiff stood and led the jurors out. And it was finally over. The trial, the work, the preparation and the execution, and the daily grind of being 'on' every minute of every day for weeks on end. It was all over.

Almost.

Michael turned to Talon as the judge departed the courtroom and the bailiff began collecting the exhibits for the jury. "Now what do we do?"

"Now," Talon shrugged, "we wait."

CHAPTER 46

They would wait days, in fact. It had taken a month to put on the trial. They could hardly expect the jurors to return a verdict within just a few hours. That probably would have been bad news anyway. Juries were only supposed to convict if they were convinced beyond a reasonable doubt. If the jury was that convinced, they would probably know it right away. A quick verdict would mean a prosecution verdict. A guilty verdict.

Or maybe not. For every theory of what a jury might be doing and what it might mean, there was a competing theory that argued the opposite. The truth was, there was no way of knowing what they were doing or why or how long it would take. Hours dragged into days. A weekend interrupted the deliberations and it turned into weeks. Michael checked in at the end of every day, and he was always within thirty minutes of the courthouse, his cell phone fully charged and ringer volume up. The plan was clear: when the verdict came in, the bailiff would call Talon, and then Talon would call Michael. They would meet at the courthouse. Michael would walk into the courtroom not knowing whether he'd walk back out the same door he entered, with his wife and children, or exit through that secure back entrance, handcuffed and escorted by armed guards, never to live free again.

No pressure.

"He should go to Canada," Curt opined on the afternoon of Day 8. "If it's an acquittal, it won't matter if he's not there. If it's a guilty, well, it'd probably take a few years before they could get the extradition through. Vancouver's a pretty nice city."

Talon shook her head. Curt had brought coffee, so she could hardly turn him away when he sat down in her office. Besides, she didn't have any other cases, so it wasn't like she needed to be someplace else. "I'm not sure he'd want to sit in a Canadian jail for two years while the extradition played out."

"I dunno." Curt shrugged. "I bet Canadian jails are probably pretty nice. Polite. 'Excuse me, Mr. Inmate, sir, but would you mind turning your reading lamp off soon? It's about time for lights out.'"

Talon had to laugh at the dark humor. She was about to return with something about a prisoners' ice hockey league when the phone rang.

Her phone didn't ring much. Again, no cases, and no new business coming in either. She'd need to think about how to make it rain if she was going to grow her firm. But that was for later. For right then, every time the phone rang, her heart jumped. Was there a verdict? But until then, every phone call had been either a wrong number, a solicitor, or Curt asking if she wanted him to grab her a cup of coffee.

Until then.

"Ms. Winter?" Judge Kirchner's bailiff confirmed over the phone. "We have a verdict."

Holy crap, she thought to herself. Curt could read her expression.

"Verdict?" he whisper-asked.

She nodded to him. "Okay," she told the bailiff. "When does the judge want us there?"

"Judge Kirchner wants everyone convened in her courtroom in thirty minutes," the bailiff answered. "Please make sure Mr. Jameson is present."

"I will," Talon assured, although now that it was real, she thought maybe that Canada idea wasn't so bad after all. She hung up the phone.

"Shit," she breathed. "Here we go."

Curt reached out and patted her arm. "I'm sure it's a good verdict. You did great. Better than great."

But Talon shook her head, the rapidly growing knot in her stomach threatening to overcome her. "It doesn't matter how I did. It's over. One way or the other."

"That's good, right?' Curt asked.

Talon thought for a moment. "It depends on what the verdict is."

She picked up the phone again and dialed Michael's number.

"Verdict?" he answered the phone. Caller I.D., and no other reason for Talon to call.

"Yes," Talon confirmed. "The judge wants us all there in thirty minutes."

"Okay," Michael answered stoically. "We'll be there."

For a moment Talon considered mentioning the idea of Michael not showing up. But it wouldn't be ethical to tell a defendant to flee. And it wasn't Michael's style. He'd made it this far. He'd stare down the ultimate result, whatever it was. With Alicia at his side. Probably Kaylee too. Maybe Marcus.

But definitely Talon. And Curt.

She stood up. "Come on. Let's head over."

Curt stood up too. "Right. We don't want to be late for this."

Talon was about to try a snappy rejoinder, anything to take the edge off the sickening anticipation, when the phone rang again. She thought maybe it was the bailiff with a change in schedule, or even Quinlan for some reason. But it was neither of them.

"Talon? It's Sam. Sam Sullivan. Do you have a minute?"

Talon considered. "No, not really, Sam. I've got a verdict."

"A verdict?" Sullivan echoed. "Okay, I'll make this quick. I spoke with the managing partner at Gardelli, High and Steinmetz and I think—"

"I have a verdict, Sam," Talon interrupted. "I have to go."

"This'll just take a second," Sullivan assured. "I spoke with the partner and I got him to make a nuisance value offer of—"

"Does it pay your fee?" Talon interrupted again.

"Er, yes," Sullivan answered. "But just barely. And you wouldn't get your old job back."

"I don't want my old job back," Talon said. "So, you're paid off and the case is closed. I don't owe you anything any more?"

"Right, all my fees and expenses are covered, but there's really nothing left after that. I told him you'd reject it, but if we make a counter-offer, I think I can get you—"

"Accept the offer," Talon instructed. "No counter."

"But Talon," Sullivan tried.

"Accept the offer, Sam," Talon repeated. "Pay yourself, and send me whatever's left."

"It's not even worth printing the check," Sullivan responded. "Let's make a counter. That's how it works, Talon. You know that. You're a civil litigator."

Talon thought for a moment. She looked at her private investigator standing in her cramped office and let herself really feel the gnawing acid-pit of anxiety and fear and worry and hope in her stomach.

"No, Sam," she declared. "I'm a criminal defense attorney."

She hung up the phone then and grabbed her coat.

"Come on, Mr. Fairchild. Let's go take a verdict."

CHAPTER 47

Twenty minutes later and the courtroom was electric. Everyone who'd been there for the closings was there again, plus more. A few more junior prosecutors. A few more people from the public defender's office. Even a news camera. And Kaylee and Marcus Jameson.

Their father sat at the defendant's table, his expression hard, but his pulse visibly racing in his neck.

Talon put a hand on his arm. "I did everything I could," she said. "I hope it was enough."

Michael thought for a moment, then nodded. "I hope so too. Thank you."

After another moment, he asked, "What do you think the verdict will be?"

Talon frowned. "I don't know. I've tried a lot of civil cases, but this is my first criminal verdict. I don't think there's any way to know."

"Right. But what do you think?" he repeated. "What's your gut?"

Talon didn't answer immediately. She didn't know. That was what her gut told her. Or what was left of it after nearly thirty minutes of worry and panic. "I'd like to think the system works," she said finally.

Michael couldn't help but laugh slightly at that. Then he looked over his shoulder at his kids. "I'd like to think that too."

Talon took a moment to look around too. Alicia smiled at her—a frightened, hope-against-hope smile. Kaylee's face displayed her own terror at what might happen. Marcus was there, but he was staring at the floor.

A lot of the other lawyers and onlookers and gawkers had brought things to do to pass the minutes before the judge came out. Police reports on other cases to review, smartphones to play on, one even had a Kindle. For them, it was so much sport and they were just the spectators. With the media over their shoulder to record the victory. The only question left was, whose victory would it be?

She stole a glance at Quinlan and McDaniels. Quinlan had his hands folded on the tabletop in front of him and his eyes closed, as if he were meditating. Easier to disconnect from the moment if you don't have an actual client sitting next to you, Talon supposed. McDaniels was looking straight ahead, but seemed to notice Talon staring at her and turned. They met eyes for maybe the first time during the entire trial. McDaniels offered a slight nod.

And then the judge came out.

"All rise!" the bailiff called out, and the noise of dozens of people rising to their feet filled the courtroom. A few moments later, Judge Kirchner had ascended to the bench.

"Be seated," she instructed. She scanned the counsel tables. Everyone was there. No one was in Canada. "The jury has reached a verdict. Does either party wish to address any matters before we accept it?"

Quinlan's eyes were open again. He stood up, always the first to answer the judge's question. "Nothing from the State, Your Honor."

Talon followed suit. "Nothing from the defense."

"Bring in the jury," Kirchner ordered her bailiff. He rose from his station directly below her and crossed the courtroom to the jury room door. He knocked and entered. A few seconds later, he emerged again and the jury filed into the jury box. Talon knew the foreperson would be holding the verdict form. She hoped, as they walked into the courtroom, it would be Juror #29, the African-American woman. But it wasn't. It was Juror #9, a middle-aged White man. She wondered if that was good or bad. Also, as they walked in, they all kept their gazes down, not looking at either side. She also wondered if that was good or bad. And she wondered if she could stop guessing at the verdict and just know it already.

But there was still some formality left. She was dying inside. What must it be like for Michael?

"Will the presiding juror please stand?" Judge Kirchner said.

Juror #9 stood up.

"Has the jury reached a verdict?" she asked.

"Yes, Your Honor," the foreman answered, raising the verdict form slightly as an indication.

"Please hand the verdict form to the bailiff," Kirchner instructed. The juror complied and the bailiff walked the form to the judge.

Judge Kirchner took a moment to read the verdict. So now she knew the result. And so did the jurors. The bailiff had probably snuck a peek on his way to deliver it to the judge. Somehow that made the wait even worse.

"Will the defendant please stand," Judge Kirchner ordered.

Michael stood up. Talon did too.

They'd come this far together. She thought back to the moment Curt had brought him over to her office. *'This good man needs a lawyer.'* She thought about their late night strategy sessions, begging him to tell her what had really happened, driving all over the state with Curt, the advice from Olsen, the testimony from St. Julian, the backyard barbeque, and the visit with Ricky.

Talon grabbed Michael's hand just long enough to give it one last squeeze of encouragement. But he seized her hand and didn't let go.

"In the matter of The State of Washington versus Michael Jameson," Judge Kirchner read the verdict form into the record. "Case number CR8004127. We the jury…"

The judge paused, just the appropriate half-second pause required by the construction of the sentence, but an eternity for Talon, her hand shaking in her client's, "find the defendant…"

Another unending pause at the comma that separated off his name, "Michael Jameson…"

Talon's ears were ringing; she thought she might not be able to hear the judge's next words.

"…*not* guilty of the crime of murder in the first degree."

Talon dropped her head. Thank God.

She turned to shake Michael's hand but he embraced her in a bear hug. There was a lot of noise all of a sudden. Gasps of relief, cries of disbelief, her heart pounding in her ears. And Michael's voice.

"Thank you."

She pulled back and looked him in the eye. "My pleasure."

And that was the crazy part. All of it, everything, even the terror of a possible conviction—she'd loved it. All of it.

Quinlan and McDaniels were probably doing something, some sort of reaction. But she didn't look. She didn't care. It wasn't about beating them. Not exactly. It was about winning. They were just the obstacle. And anyway, Alicia and Kaylee and Marcus had spilled into the front of the courtroom to hug their husband and father. The man who would, after all, be going home with them that day.

Alicia hugged Talon, even tighter than Michael had, and she held on longer. She couldn't control her tears. "Thank you, Talon," she managed to squeak out between sobs. "Thank you so much."

Talon hugged her back. "Of course. You're welcome. Of course, of course."

The judge left the bench and retired to her chambers. The jurors were led back into the jury room by the bailiff; there were some administrative matters to attend to before they could be formally excused. The prosecutors made their way out of the courtroom. Mrs. McCabe-Johnson had come for the verdict, too, but Talon decided to avoid her gaze. It didn't matter. The courtroom cleared out and Curt finally made his way up to Talon.

He extended a hand. "Congratulations, counselor."

She cocked her head at him. A handshake? Really? She thought a hug was probably more in order. But she stopped herself, and reflected on their still ill-defined relationship. Maybe he was right. And maybe it was okay to meet him on his terms. She shook his hand. "I couldn't have done it without you, sir."

Curt laughed. "Don't lie to me, Talon. Do whatever else you want, but don't lie."

Talon liked the sound of that. She pumped the handshake one more time. "Deal."

The trial was over and the afterglow of the acquittal was already fading. The courtroom had cleared out, but Talon had one more thing she wanted to do.

"Alicia," she said. "Could I have a moment alone with

Michael. One last attorney-client thing I need to attend to."

She could have asked Alicia to do anything at that moment. "Of course, Talon. Of course. Come on kids, we'll wait for your dad in the hallway."

The hallway. Freedom.

Curt went with them and Talon and Michael found themselves alone in the courtroom.

"Okay," she said, looking him square in the eye. "The trial is over. You were acquitted. You can't be charged again. Double jeopardy. You could write a book about exactly how you did it, and you're glad you did it, and you'd do it again, and double jeopardy would still bar any retrial. So it's over. Now you can tell me."

She took his hand again. "Tell me, Michael. Did you do it?"

Michael smiled. He nodded lightly. He pulled his hand back.

"I already told you, Talon," he said. "It doesn't matter."

EPILOGUE

It doesn't matter.

Michael Jameson's words echoed in Talon's head as she drove through the rolling countryside southwest of Tacoma.

She was alone this time. It gave her time to think.

Did it matter whether Michael had shot Jordy? Did the intervening years of being a faithful husband, good father, and hard-working employee erase whatever eighteen-year-old Michael Jameson did?

If it didn't matter, what else didn't matter?

Did it matter that she got fired from Gardelli, High & Steinmetz?

Did it matter that she won the case?

Did it matter that she had sex with Curt?

And if none of that mattered, what did matter?

Alicia? Kaylee and Marcus?

Ricky?

Family?

Or nothing at all?

Or did she just like to pretend nothing mattered so she could stay aloof and aloft, above whatever might make her care, make her hurt?

Deep thoughts for a long drive, but eventually she arrived at her destination. Shelton, Washington. The Washington Corrections Center.

She drove past Grounds Zero and parked in the visitor lot. She locked her car—of course—and headed into the main entrance. At the reception desk she presented her bar card, proof she was an attorney and not restricted to the limited visiting hours of the general public. She provided the name of the inmate she wanted to meet with and took a seat in the waiting area. It was empty but for her. That was fine with her. Not that she was ashamed to be there. Why should she be? It didn't matter.

After about fifteen minutes, they called her name and escorted her to the meeting rooms. She took a seat in the small plastic chair on one side of the Formica table and waited for her counterpart.

Shelton was the processing facility. There were a few prisoners whose sentences were short enough that they served their few months right there, but mostly it was the prisoners who were just going in before serving a long sentence somewhere else. Or about to get out after that self-same type of sentence.

The secure door to the interior of the prison opened with a loud metallic clank. In walked a man. He was tall, with thick black hair and high cheekbones. He had a barrel chest and huge biceps, the product of years, and years, of lifting weights on the inside. He walked up to the table and looked down at her.

She returned his gaze, and forced a smile. "Hey, William."

William nodded at Talon. But he didn't smile. He just pulled out the plastic chair with a loud, long scuff and dropped his heavy build into the seat.

"Hey, sis."

END

ABOUT THE AUTHOR

Stephen Penner is an attorney, author, and artist from Seattle. In addition to the *Talon Winter* series, he pens the *David Brunelle* legal thriller series, starring homicide D.A. Dave Brunelle and a recurring cast of cops, lawyers, and murder.

For more information, please visit *www.stephenpenner.com*.

Made in the USA
Coppell, TX
19 January 2020